INTERSTELLAR ANGEL

An ASTRAL HEAT ROMANCE 1

LAURA NAVARRE

PROLOGUE
The Felon

He was sentenced to die in the fighting pit at dawn for butchering the Third Indomitable of the Mogadon Empire in his tyrannical and sociopathic sleep. But the Mogadon prison guards wanted to work Zorin over before he kicked the bucket. Same way they'd worked him over the last three nights running.

Well, that was A-okay with Zorin.

Matter of fact, he was counting on it.

While he stood waiting for the shindig to start, magnetoelectric cuffs shackled his muscled arms overhead, clamped his booted feet to the floor, and left his naked torso exposed to the biting temps in the Mogadon slammer. He definitely wouldn't have minded sporting more than leather pants and space boots on his ugly carcass while old Tiberius went to work with the boning knife.

But Zorin could roll with what he had going.

Sweating under the nuclear-powered fluorescents in the interrogation *cella*, Tiberius swaggered up to Zorin with a scowl on his fleshy mug. His two sidekicks skulked by the exit. True to habit, Boots and Pyro would only risk coming in close to get their jollies after the blood loss softened Zorin up.

Even chained to the wall, the deadly combo of his massive size and his brutal reputation still gave Zorin plenty of intimidation factor.

"Ready for a little fun, Theodophilus?" Tiberius slid his knife gently along Zorin's jaw. "You're gonna bite the big one in twelve clicks—just in time to make the interstellar broadcast. But we got plenty of time to play before Dex Draven meets you in the pit and puts you six cubits under."

While the lunker brandished his shank, Zorin snuck a peek at the timepiece strapped to the guy's wrist.

Two ticks to showtime.

Zorin hawked to clear out the blood still leaking down his throat from his nose. Which he hoped to hell wasn't busted again. "You wanna be careful with that one-armed scissor, Tibs. Pretty sure Dex's counting on killing me himself."

"You think I'm scared of that punk Draven?" Tiberius sneered, looking back at his buddies for validation. "That pretty-boy stunt pilot don't have his dad's moxie, even if you did just bump off his old man. Comets! Bet Dex'll thank me for softening you up."

Tick.

"One way to find out," Zorin said softly. A bear-baiting he'd probably regret, but he wanted the guy in close.

Tibs took the bait and closed on him with a snarl.

Attaboy, Tibs. Mosey on over.

The first cut burned through Zorin like a laser—a searing score carved down his naked side. He gasped as a line of white agony sizzled through his system. Liquid heat spilled down his skin and the meaty tang of fresh blood hit the back of his throat. The world blurred and darkened.

Tock.

The stone beneath his boots shuddered under the sonic *boom* of impact. That'd be the cyber bomb. Hitting the reactor bloc smack on schedule. Knocking out the defensive energon shield that bubbled the Mogadon capital. And plunging the whole city—including this funhouse down here—into blackness.

Knew I could count on my boys.

Tingling with an adrenaline rush of aggression, Zorin felt the metallic snick of the maglock release. The cuffs around his wrists and ankles sprang open and he got clear of the rack.

A tick later the backup generator lumbered to life. The ruddy wash of emergency lighting switched on. Giving him an up-close-and-personal of Tiberius's shocked and staring face. Their eyes met and locked.

One corner of Zorin's mouth lifted in a grin.

"Howdy, Tibs."

The guy's sweating face convulsed in sudden terror. "Look alive! He's *loose*—"

From barely a cubit away, the boning knife came at him. Then

Zorin's doubled fists, powered by the full force of his body and three days of pent-up rage, hammered down on the guy's noggin. The sharp *pop* of Tibs's neck cracked through the generator's asthmatic wheeze like a snapped wishbone. His torturer dropped at Zorin's feet.

Dead as a sack of moon rocks.

A primitive surge of bloodlust roared through Zorin's brain. The gamy musk of wolf and steel flooded the air, triggered by a heady spurt of Mogadon pheromones. Weakened by three days' torture with no grub to sustain him and blood still spilling down his side, Zorin's big body swayed on his feet. His adrenal glands were going haywire.

Jumpin' Jupiter. I'm weak as a pup—

A howl of rage brought Zorin's head snapping up. Just in time to see good old Pyro barreling at him with the flamethrower. A thermobaric weapon the Quorum had outlawed ages ago all across the galaxy, but Pyro kept the contraband relic squirreled away down here in the playroom.

And here comes the nozzle…

Zorin hunkered down and just charged the guy. He hit him at a dead run and knocked him sprawling. The nozzle of the flamethrower flew wide, spraying an inferno of blue fire across the *cella*. He landed on Pyro's sinewy frame like Vulcan's mythic hammer. Pyro writhed beneath him, ferret-sharp teeth bared and snapping in the bloody light.

Fighting like the dickens to bring that flamethrower around—still spewing fire—for another pass.

Zorin got both hands around Pyro's greasy head and slammed his skull into the floor with brutal force. The guy's weaselly face went blank and his eyes glassed over.

Permanently.

The flamethrower slipped from his grip and went dark.

Breathing heavily, Zorin rolled off him and wrestled the thermobaric out of the man's slack hand.

"Belay that, you space junk!" a shrill voice cried. "Or I'll put you down like a rabid dog. I swear to gods I will!"

Zorin's eyes flashed up to find his old pal Boots hunkered by the door with his shadow all distorted in the horror-flick half-light.

And his blaster leveled at Zorin's chest.

Zorin froze right where he crouched, one hand gripping the flamethrower, one knee braced against the floor. A steady drip from his gaping gash spattered Pyro's limp carcass.

Aw, shoot.

"Here's the deal," Zorin rasped, locked on the youngster's wild-eyed stare. "You can pull the trigger on that thing if you want. But you better make damn sure you take me down—cuz you're only gonna get one shot. You shoot and it's anything less than a kill shot? Then it's barbecue time. And once you're seared medium rare, if you ask me nicely? I'm gonna snap your neck like I did with Tibs and put you outta your misery."

"I got the drop on you." Holy helium, the kid's voice was shaking. "I got the drop on the First Indomitable! If I pull the trigger, I'll be First Indomitable myself."

Zorin kept his own voice nice and easy. "Pretty sure Dex wants that gig himself. Besides, you ain't exactly a crack shot, are ya, Boots? Or your centurion wouldn't have you pulling guard duty down here in the armpit of the Empire, would he? Keep your head screwed on straight and you can still walk away from this hootenanny."

Think it through, you big dummy. I can see your hands shake all the way over here.

Deaf and clueless to his silent urging, Boots straightened his scrawny shoulders and looked dazzled by the prospect. "I can be First Indomitable. Have the whole Mogadon army and the Mogadon fleet and the nukes and the novicide—the whole Empire at my command. Mine! I'll be the youngest First Indomitable in history."

Neptune's knickers, he's talking himself into it.

"Better be sure," Zorin said softly, his big body tensing to attack.

The silence was shattered by the soft *whomp* of an incoming missile. The slam of impact—no farther off than a Mogadon mile— made both of them stagger. A clamor of distant shouts echoed down the hall, thin and scattered under the whooping wail of the battle claxon.

Boots lowered his blaster in confusion. "What the seven bloody *hells*—?"

"That'll be the sound of Dex's dad getting the galactic war the old psycho was jonesing for when he kicked the bucket. The sound of the Valyrian fleet attacking this popsicle stand." Zorin clambered carefully to his feet and swallowed a groan as his side gave a wicked stab of protest. "Since my boys took out the main reactor, the dome's been down."

"The dome's *down*? But—we got the whole Valyrian fleet parked just off Parthon!"

"Yep." Zorin eased an arm against the oozing gash down his side in a bid to slow the bleeding. He needed a med kit like blazes. "And with the dome down, the Empire doesn't have squat to deflect those psi-powered weapons away from the city. Intel says the Precursor herself—strongest telepath in the whole damn galaxy—she's in orbit on the Valyrian flagship. And she's pretty ticked about that biowar Dex's dad just unleashed on her whole flipping race."

"The Precursor!" Boots gasped, in a tone usually reserved for Swarm cannibals or a spacepox outbreak.

Zorin tried to stay focused on the convo, but the blood loss was making him woozy. The blinking blaze of the hazard lights and the whooping wail of the battle siren weren't helping any.

Dimly he registered the heavy thud of running feet, the welcome sound of Boots losing his head and taking to his heels, clumsy in those titanium-toed clodhoppers of his. A factoid Zorin knew because he had the bruises on his aching ribs and back from those boots to prove it.

Hearing his footfalls fade, Zorin let the tension ease from his battered body.

Then he got his head together and staggered over to the guard cubby where his captors kept the med kit and the Mogadon whiskey. Squinting to focus his blurred vision, he slathered on a clotting agent and slapped the glossy square of a polymer bandage over the bloody gash.

Mars, he was gonna need nanostitches again, wasn't he? Old Doc Cicero was gonna chew him out bigtime—assuming they even made it to the *Relentless* like they'd all decided when they threw together this half-assed plan.

Grimacing, Zorin jabbed an antimicrobial booster into his deltoid.

Then he schlepped back to the *cella*, wrestled off Tibs's black uniform jacket with its double row of steel buttons, and eased his arms into the sleeves. Zorin's shoulders were too damn big and his chest way too wide for a standard jacket, so the thing gaped open all the way down his front. And he already knew there was no way he was getting his big feet into standard-issue army boots. His own clunky space boots would have to do the trick.

But maybe if he got lucky, with the reactor down and the

Valyrians attacking and this whole humdinger of a planet-wide crisis unfolding around him, he'd pass the once-over test.

Zorin tossed back a burning slug of Mogadon whiskey—a hit of thirty-curie fortitude that seared his sinuses and shot straight to his head—then made tracks for the rendezvous point. Where his boys and Julius, the cyber samurai behind the downed reactor, would hopefully still be waiting to rearm his sorry ass.

Cuz he might be out of the slammer, but he still needed to get the heck off Mogadon before the Precursor's attack mobilized the whole planet into furious retaliation.

And he needed to be a parsec away in deep space before Dex Draven figured out his dad's killer was MIA and had eluded the ruthless reckoning of Mogadon justice.

#

"Here's what I want." Dex Draven fired the staccato barrage of directives at a goggle-eyed prefect as he wrestled the fuel nozzle from the belly of his nuclear-armed Zephyr. "I want four wings of fighters under my command prepared to launch into exospheric orbit ASAP to protect the city. And I want every engineer in the Empire flown hotfoot to the power plant to bring that reactor back online. We *need* to get that dome up."

Around him, the cavernous expanse of the Mogadon capital's spaceport echoed with the drum of running feet on tarmac, curt voices shouting commands, the rumble of fuel trucks racing to feed Dex's wing of armed Zephyrs—flown by those men under his direct command he'd managed to mobilize since the first missile strike.

Beyond the immediate impact of his personal efforts, the claxon's wavering wail would muster every able-bodied soldier in the city to battle stations.

And if that prefect he was bossing like an illegal galley slave retained any wits at all amid the exigencies of the current crisis, he'd surely stop to question why newly minted Wing Commander Decimus Draven—who'd only just celebrated his twentieth birthday—was issuing orders that should rightfully be issued only by Second Indomitable Septimus, resident boozing blowhard and commander of the Mogadon civil defense force.

Or, failing that, by Dex's father.

If only Dex's father weren't already dead.

"B-but, Commander—" The youngster flinched as an incoming missile screamed past overhead. "Shouldn't I, uh—"

"Good lad." Dex forestalled the objection by thrusting the fuel hose into the prefect's unsteady hands and giving his adolescent shoulders a bracing shake. "I knew I could rely on you entirely. Make it happen."

Dex focused on unlocking the docking cable that tethered his fighter to the tarmac. But he was heartened to hear the prefect's booted feet beat a swift tattoo as he raced to carry out Dex's commands with gratifying alacrity.

No doubt his formidable father would've cuffed the poor kid to instill blind obedience. But Dex had opted early on not to emulate the extremes of his father's brutal command style.

Greatly to the old war dog's displeasure.

That displeasure had fueled their most bitter battles. Battles exceeded in intensity only by that final, furious, no-pulled-punches blowout the night Third Indomitable Maximus Draven accused his own son of craven cowardice.

The infamous night his father unleashed his genetically targeted bioweapon against the entire Valyrian race.

The high-pitched scream of dying thrusters dragged Dex's narrowed gaze from his preflight checklist to the crimson heavens, where the sleek silver ovule of a Valyrian cruiser spiraled across the sunset sky, the purple pulse of its psi-powered cannons pounding away pointlessly at empty air. A classic indication of his father's biological novicide—his *Valyrensis novicida*—eating away at the command crew's brains.

The streamlined spacecraft twisted into a death spiral that culminated in a holocaust of heliotrope fire in the Mogadon mountains, etched stark against the bloody sky. Dex's heart contracted with a wrenching spasm of grief.

Are you on that ship, Ben Nero? Or on the flagship, the Precursor's ship, the ship raining megaton warheads of psi-powered death on the southern cities, the ship I'll have to shoot out of the sky whether you're aboard or not?

His boyhood friend. His oathsworn brother. His closest ally in the youth ashram, where they'd been packed off in that laughably futile bid to build interracial tolerance.

Or did my father kill you weeks ago when he unleashed his novicide on the Valyrian homeworld?

Ben Nero with his psychic gifts and his flamboyant charm and his effortless ability to inspire indulgent affection in everyone he'd ever met. Ben Nero with his violet eyes and his silken hair and his secret smile that promised forbidden favors which Dex, with his emphatically masculine Mogadon DNA, had never known how to ask for.

Nor even how to name.

Between his bottled-up anguish over Ben Nero's unknown fate and his smothered guilt over the grief for his tyrannical father he should have felt but didn't, Dex's head was a space wreck.

He prayed it wouldn't fatally affect his judgment in battle.

Firmly banishing the past from the present, Dex slanted his head to fire his next barrage at the comm unit strapped to his wrist.

"Alpha wing, I want you in the air. Beta, Delta, be ready to launch on my command. Epsilon wing, I want you on standby in the stratosphere playing active defense against any Valyrian vessel that slips past our assault on the flagship. All wings, give me atomic torpedoes in the tubes with safety tethers engaged until we clear the thermosphere."

He'd just swung several rungs higher up the chain of command than his current rank merited. But he knew that Beta and Epsilon would follow him, with their own commanders offworld running scout patrols off Parthon. And the wing commander of Delta had always been diplomatically deferential to Max Draven's favorite son.

Planting a resolute boot on the Zephyr's boarding ladder while he assumed his flight helmet, Dex sliced an assessing glance across the tarmac to gauge his wing's readiness. Good pilots to a man, they'd be in orbit in less than ten ticks.

He was lowering the helmet over his head when a knot of activity surrounding a Sirocco scout shuttle caught his eye.

A knot of activity with a distinctly furtive air.

Suddenly Dex's battle sense was tingling.

By rights he ought to report the anomaly to spaceport security and get himself aloft. But someone had just cyber-bombed the main reactor and wiped out the dome. And intel whispered it was an inside job.

A Mogadon job.

For no logical reason, Dex found himself quietly lowering his helmet to the tarmac, checking the blaster holstered at his hip, and slipping across the flight deck toward the concealment of a blocky maintenance drone. Overhead, the first steely streaks of outbound Zephyrs, silent but for the hiss of displaced air, sliced across the darkening sky.

Dex himself needed badly to be among them. But there wasn't a pilot in the Empire he couldn't outfly. He'd catch up with his wing before they reached the exosphere.

The bulky concealment of the maintenance drone, tagged out and off grid for the night shift, rose before him. He eased his head cautiously around the battered neptunium casing to scope out the oddly furtive scene near the shuttle.

A scene that failed utterly to compute.

At a glance, the scrum of dreadlocked disreputables of all genders loitering about the Sirocco in their battle-scarred fighting leathers and space boots looked like dead ringers for Syndax pirates. Except for the irrefutable fact that the Syndax were emphatically outlaws—bloody nuisances to the Pax Mogadon—and expressly unwelcome on any civilized world.

But what truly confounded Dex were the three men in Mogadon uniforms racing the scout ship through its preflight checklist.

Men he knew.

Men he trusted.

Men who were, in fact, the First Indomitable's very own indispensable right-hand men.

Make that ex-First Indomitable, Dex corrected grimly. Fighting back the blistering surge of aching loss and furious incomprehension and anguished betrayal that short-circuited his system every blasted time he allowed himself to contemplate his father's friend. His father's murderer. Not to mention his own trusted mentor, his boyhood hero and the man Dex himself would be obliged to slaughter in the fighting pit come sunup.

And if these particular men with their particular loyalties were stealthily launching a getaway ship twelve clicks before the leader they revered was sentenced to meet Mogadon justice—just after some traitorous insider had sabotaged the reactor and torpedoed the dome—those factors could only possibly comprise one unavoidable truth.

Damnation.

Dex's battle sense was bloody *screaming*—

Even before he felt the unmistakable mass of a powerful body looming over him from behind. A cascade of warm breath spilled into his ear.

"Howdy, Dex," a familiar voice whispered. "Do me a solid and shimmy around real slow. I don't wanna have to hurt you."

Heart thudding like a Mogadon war drum, Dex eased into a slow pivot. Which indeed brought him eyeball to eyeball with his nemesis.

His teacher. His friend. His idol. His enemy.

"Zorin," he scraped out, feeling as though he were choking.

"Take it easy, kid." Looming larger than life a good cubit plus over Dex, the ex-First Indomitable of the Mogadon Empire stood deceptively at ease with booted legs spread.

Holding a blaster leveled squarely at Dex's chest.

Dex's eyes skated over the sinewed thighs encased in fighting leathers, the powerful abs and chest framed in an open uniform jacket that had to be at least three sizes too small, and finally the craggy features and square jaw and aqua-blue eyes of his father's killer. Crowned with an unruly thatch of sandy hair sprinkled with silver—hair the legendary First Indomitable had always worn a whisker too long and too unruly for regulation.

One corner of Zorin's full-lipped mouth lifted in a grin.

And Dex Draven, favorite son of the Third Indomitable, youngest wing commander in Empire history and relentlessly heterosexual Mogadon male to the last chromosome of his DNA, felt the same confused rush of tongue-tied, tingling heat he'd always felt every blooming time his boyhood idol smiled.

Blast. I thought I'd outgrown this dangerous nonsense. He's my father's killer, for Neptune's sake.

Dex dragged his wits together. "What the devil are you doing out of your cell?"

"Spoken like a true tyrant," Zorin said, blaster fixed firmly in place. "You're growing up to be more like Max every day. Just a chip off the old block."

"I suppose that means you'll want to butcher me in my bed as well. And I'm properly addressed as *commander*."

"Keep your voice down, *Commander*." Zorin's eyes flashed silver with caution as a phalanx of uniformed legions trotted past. He angled his big body so his blaster stayed hidden. "I don't wanna kill you—either in your bed or out of it. Which is why I'm splitting before our scheduled go-round in the fighting pit."

"You're escaping," Dex said bitterly. "And it's immaterial to you that you've exposed this planet to the full wrath of the Precursor and the vengeful Valyrian fleet."

"They're a dying race. Your dad saw to that." Zorin's massive chest heaved in a sigh. "I guess you'll finish the job he started. But I won't be hanging around to watch."

"Because you're a coward as well as a traitor?" Dex lashed out, voice dripping with contempt.

"Come on, kid. How many times have we fought together, back to back, hip-deep in the shit? I'm no coward and you know it."

A hundred memories seared through him. Memories of battles fought and triumphs shared. Under the weight of those treacherous memories, Dex's hard-won poise fractured like ice under a chainsaw.

His voice splintered, edges sharp enough to draw blood.

"Then why won't you face me in battle? Why won't you allow me at least the chance to—to avenge his honor and mine? Knowing if you win—knowing if you kill me—knowing it's over and done under Mogadon law and you'll keep your rank and your freedom. Even knowing you're my equal in combat."

"Wouldn't be a fair fight. Sure, you're smart and strong and fast on your feet in a fracas. I trained you myself, didn't I? Five years from now, maybe, when you got a little more meat on you? Then we'll be equals."

"Then you've no reason under the sun not to fight!" Dex pulled in a frustrated breath and, to his utter alarm, felt his eyes burn with thoroughly unmanly tears. "I simply can't—can't understand why…"

"Comets, Dex. Don't do that." Looking helpless, Zorin lowered the blaster and eased a step closer. "Don't cry, for the love of Juno. I can stand anything from you but tears."

Dex scowled fiercely to force back this unseemly weakness he flatly refused to tolerate. "Then you tell me *why*. I *deserve* to know why."

"Stars, kid. You don't wanna know why. You really, really don't." Zorin heaved a heavy sigh and braced one muscled arm against the drone beside Dex's head. His eyes darkened to navy and a shiver slid down Dex's spine. Suddenly, for no earthly reason, his heart was pounding and his entire body was tingling.

"Tell me why," Dex whispered stubbornly. His voice gone deep and husky for reasons he still couldn't fathom.

"You really want me to say it, do ya? After keeping my big mouth shut all this time? Well, hell with it," Zorin muttered. "Remember you asked for this."

And just leaned in and kissed him.

That singular moment was so extraordinary, so astonishing, so wildly unexpected that Dex stood as though frozen in carbonite and just let him do it. He gripped the man's waist to… push him away of course, that went without saying, and forcefully…

But the unprecedented feel of hot sleek skin rippling over miles of solid muscle right under his hands sucked every molecule of oxygen from his lungs.

Dex voiced a startled syllable of what was surely protest. Which gave the other man all the opportunity he needed to groan in response and deepen the kiss. One big hand engulfed the back of Dex's head to ease him closer. The slick heat of tongue meeting tongue shot through him like a stimulant, spiked with the peaty burn of Mogadon whiskey.

Filling the air between them, the predatory musk of Mogadon mating scent rose dark and potent.

Dex clutched him harder… in protest, this was *protest*… and their hips crashed together. Desire blasted through every determined barrier he'd built around his heart with the force of fifty Gs of thrust. Desire for *him*.

Zorin.

The hero he'd worshipped with a boy's innocence.

The soldier he'd craved with a man's passion.

An inferno of craving simultaneously stoked and smothered by years of desperate denial, suspended halfway between gratitude and despair when his shameful longing for what no red-blooded Mogadon male should ever want from another man stayed firmly unrequited. He'd finally managed to convince himself it was a boy's crush on a teacher he lionized.

A crush he'd outgrown years ago.

Until now.

Throbbing with passion and blind with need, Dex grappled to haul the man closer. Gods on the mountain, how he *needed*—

The *whoom* of a distant explosion jarred him to his senses. Dex summoned a superhuman effort and wrenched violently free, dragging the oxygen his lungs were starving to breathe past lips tingling with heat. Yet for some blasted reason, he still felt powerless to speak or move while Zorin leaned his forehead against Dex's and panted.

"Well, that's pretty much why," Zorin said wryly, shattering the spellbound silence. "Any questions?"

Far too late, Dex found his tongue. "What in the seven bloody *hells* was that? Are you trying to get us both *killed*?"

"It's okay, kid." Zorin heaved a sigh. "Your dad's not calling the shots on military morals around here anymore, is he?"

Rendered speechless with stupefaction, Dex could only stammer.

And pray with frantic fervor that no one had seen that catastrophe of a kiss.

He should be bloody outraged and offended as blazes. He *was* outraged and offended as blazes, damn it. In the army, male–male couplings were capital offenses. With his own late father the Empire's most rigorous enforcer.

Even a kiss like that could get them both crucified.

That bastard was mocking him, that's precisely what this was. His father's killer was eluding Mogadon justice. Now his father's killer was mocking him. Mocking this childish, unmanly, un-Mogadon infatuation it seemed Dex hadn't managed to hide and still hadn't— quite—outgrown.

Rage bloomed in his head. A rage born of withering shame. A rage directed equally against Zorin and himself.

"Zorin, dude, will you stop horsing around with that space cadet." Without warning, a dreadlocked head poked around the maintenance drone. "Precursor's entered orbit with guns blazing. And *Relentless*— she's all fired up in the troposphere and ready to rumble. Either your boyfriend's part of the package, or you gotta say sayonara."

Humiliation scorched the back of Dex's neck. His scandalized outrage at being called any man's *boyfriend*, as though he were some bloody catamite, was eclipsed only by the shock of sudden comprehension as the full brazen outline of his former hero's escape plan zoomed into focus.

"You're stealing the *Relentless*?" Dex's appalled gaze swung from the tattooed Syndax back to Zorin. "She's a damn retired Tornado-class battleship. She'll never clear orbit. She's scheduled for the scrap heap!"

Zorin waved off the Syndax and lifted one shoulder in a rueful shrug. "Yeah, well, so am I. Listen, Dex—I gotta skedaddle."

"Like bloody hell you are," Dex said furiously. "I'm taking you to spaceport security straightaway—"

The blow he never saw coming, a crisp clip from the butt of Zorin's blaster, collided with his temple and knocked him sprawling. He fought to get his wobbly legs under him, the spaceport swirling with light and sound. Zorin's powerful arms eased him gently to the tarmac.

"Sorry about that, Dex. Afraid you're gonna have a real thumper of a headache. Try to forgive me for all this someday, will ya?" Dimly, the wretch's voice reached him through a telescoping tunnel of darkness.

Dex struggled to articulate the merest whisper of the incandescent fury that consumed him. "Never forgive... *never*..."

"Yeah, I pretty much figured." Zorin's resigned sigh chased him down into blackness. "See you around, kid."

As Zorin's big-shouldered frame receded in his kaleidoscoped vision, Dex wrestled desperately to hold the swirling oblivion at bay.

#

Zorin was hauling tail up the Sirocco's boarding ramp, while wings of Zephyrs streaked past overhead and psi-powered missiles rained down around him like parade confetti, when the shrill whine of a blaster made him duck and curse.

A blue burst of laser fire ripped over his head to burn a hole in the shuttle's blast shields.

He hunkered down and powered up the ramp, sneaking a peek over his shoulder as he bolted. He caught a single skewed glimpse of a formidable figure in uniform black, blazing with tawny hair and rows of gleaming buttons, clutching the maintenance drone for balance and unsteadily raising a blaster.

Zorin was two ticks from shelter when the next burst caught his shoulder and spun him around, gasping under the searing burn of impact.

By sheer stubborn luck he managed to fall into the cockpit rather than off the ramp onto the tarmac. While the world went blurry and soft around him, friendly arms hauled him to safety and retracted the ramp. The engine throbbed beneath him and the floor tilted gently as the Sirocco lifted off.

And for the next eight years, while the ex-First Indomitable of the Mogadon Empire achieved lasting notoriety in the outer colonies as the scourge of the galaxy, head honcho of that galactic menace, the Syndax horde, Zorin would wonder if his former student—a crack marksman and compulsive perfectionist at every pastime to which he ever applied himself—had been trying not to kill him.

Or if he'd really meant to see Zorin dead.

CHAPTER ONE
The Fugitive
Eight Years Later

Kaia launched into the cyberverse from underneath—the way she always liked for a covert entry. Crouched in her sleek black cybersuit on the glowing insertion disc, utility belt loaded with custom exploits riding her hips, she caught her breath in awe.

Around her, the star-studded expanse of the cyberverse flared to life and became her universe, streaked with silent lasers that pulsed with lethal menace.

Deep in the Alpha Sector, the warlike Mogadon had engineered their cyberverse to commemorate the deep space skirmish that annihilated their rival Valyria.

For Kaia, an outlawed half-Valyrian hybrid, the unsubtle artwork screamed a warning.

Heart hammering with adrenaline and skin sizzling with nerves, she leaped from the insertion disc to the neon platform of the entry node and landed in a tense crouch. One quick pivot and she'd cleared her six.

No macrodroids.

The humming tension in her channels ratcheted back a notch. Her breath slipped out in a whisper that *shussed* in the tense silence.

Against the digital backdrop, where planets revolved in majestic arcs around the crimson Mogadon sun, no digital army hovered in the crisp dry cool of cyberspace, warned and waiting to arrest her.

Best of all, no sign of the dreaded killer droids that incinerated intruders on sight.

She hated those killer droids with a passion born of terror. Because when you died in the cyberverse, your physical body died back home.

But Kaia had picked up the habit of not dying. She'd had plenty of practice staying alive since she'd slipped the leash of her tyrannical father.

The father her whole race worshipped as a god.

Snap out of it, samurai. Dreaming on your feet won't get you past the Mogadon perimeter to tag the First Indomitable. And dreaming won't get you those ten thousand creds you need to fix the antimatter drive on the Angel *and get the hell off this rock before the war starts.*

Dreaming will only get you killed.

Swiftly she tapped out a command on the keypad strapped to her wrist. The insertion disc shot off with a *shoom*, leaving her stranded in cyberspace. From her utility belt, she palmed the glowing pyramid she'd won from a Mogadon cyberspy over a high-stakes game of cosmic poker. She slid the key into the console.

An ultraviolet beam shot silently from the console to arc across the sky. A superhighway through cyberspace, ready to carry her right where she needed to go.

Her synapses hummed with a jolt of exhilaration, potent as a contraband biodrug.

Angels and asteroids!

Her physical body, wired into a rented cyberport under a borrowed identity deep in the Mogadon homeworld, whispered the words.

She hadn't been sure the nav key would work. The Mogadon really should've changed their locks, the way their ruthlessly effective security protocol demanded, before the First Indomitable rallied the Empire with his formal declaration of war against the Syndax. A declaration scheduled to be broadcast through the cyberverse on all nine billion nodes in less than a click.

Maybe her luck was finally turning. Because for once, it seemed the militant Mogadon were complacent. Maybe they didn't expect a threat right in their own backyard. Maybe the galaxy's ruling race had gotten lazy.

Maybe it's about time you caught a break.

Grinning, Kaia tucked the key in her belt and pivoted toward the highway.

From the infinite depths of cyberspace, a streak of silver flashed toward her.

Instantly she dropped to a crouch, one hand splayed against the platform for balance. Back on Mogadon, her physical body crouched in the cyberport. In a microsecond of reaction time, she ID'ed the spiked sphere shooting toward her. A blaster bolt of recognition nailed her square in the heart.

Dendroid.

Before she could trigger a defense, her digital eyes were blinded by a silent strobe of light. In a nanoflash, the dendroid processed the intel from its data scan and beamed its forensics on the intruder—Kaia—back to a mother node.

Blast. I'm punked.

Knowing she had heartbeats to disappear before the node dispatched something nasty, Kaia shook the stars from her eyes and exploded into motion. Springing forward and up, she tucked into a tight double somersault that vaulted her over the dendroid.

Back in the Mogadon cyberport, her physical body tucked into a double flip and landed upright on her cyberpad.

All those years hiding as an anonymous acrobat with the solar circus were sure coming in handy. Because the skills of your physical body dictated what your avatar could do in the cyberverse.

Beneath her, the dendroid whirred. A slice of blue light speared through space—so close it singed her booted heels. But Kaia stuck the landing, light as breath, feet first on the ultraviolet highway. Stars streaked and planets blurred around her as the neural node propelled her electrons across the cyberverse.

Leaving the droid behind in an eyeblink.

Kaia expelled her breath with a shudder of relief. She definitely hadn't expected that dendroid to appear so flipping fast. Was it just another run of rotten luck for a fugitive samurai who lived on luck like oxygen? Or was Mogadon security on the eve of the next apocalypse torqued a whole lot tighter than she'd hoped?

If it is, you're punked. You don't have time to abort and try again later. Not with the Mogadon going to war.

You need to get off this rock before the Syndax attack.

Fighting through her jittery nerves, she tapped out a quick command. A glowing string of coordinates floated before her as she shot through cyberspace. A gust of digital wind, sharp and metallic as tin on her tongue, lifted her heavy rope of burgundy hair and sent it streaming in her wake.

Against the electric backdrop, the stylized holograms of Mogadon battleships silently blasted a scatter of doomed Valyrian cruisers to subatomic smithereens. The infamous slaughter played out with majestic slowness, nuclear explosions flaring white and cobalt around the planet with its violet rings.

Not exactly a fair fight, since her Valyrian kin had already been fatally infected by the bioweapon that all but exterminated their race.

Even now, years after the genocide, a fist of grief twisted her heart. She'd lost her lifemate in that biowar.

But she'd lost Ben Nero way before that, hadn't she? Lost him the day he rolled over for the Quorum of Four and just sashayed away from their forbidden lifebond.

Leaving her alone to face her royal father's wrath.

Her microcomputer chirped out a warning. Amber digits flashed and pulsed. Her destination loomed over her—the formidable coliseum of the Council of Indomitables.

Or at least its digital construct.

A noose of nerves throttled her throat and dried her mouth to space dust. With a practiced sweep, she freed the cybersword strapped to her back.

Back at the port, her physical body unsheathed her cyber saber, threaded with digital sensors.

A precision leap propelled her from the highway. She landed on her feet, saber whirling in a glittering arc. The blade deflected a beam of neon light from the coliseum that nearly sliced off her arm.

Angels of Anaxos! Those are killer droids. They have farking killer droids up there.

Then the ultra-high frequency of the shock beam attack tripped her defensive exploit. Twin torques of platinum circled her wrists. She dropped to one knee, arms crossed in a defensive X.

A fury of cobalt beams crisscrossed the starry sky and ricocheted from her crossed arms. Desperately she scanned the battlements, searching for a weak spot, as a dozen portals yawned wide.

And a dozen macrodroids rolled out.

Kaia was both relieved and offended.

Relieved because the Mogadon hadn't rolled out the big guns to finish her off. Macrodroids were the beat cops of the cyberverse, programmed to detain rather than destroy.

And offended because whoever was running this circus apparently thought a few fat macros could detain a Prime Class samurai like Kaia.

The macros rolled swiftly toward her, glowing green spheres that stood hip high. Just big enough to engulf an offending intruder and transport her to cyber security's tender mercies. She deflected the first with a scything sweep, the second with a spinning kick that sent the thing sailing through cyberspace.

With the next wave of macros closing in, she sheathed her sword and activated an exploit from her utility belt. Twin jets fired a propulsive burst that launched her soundlessly into space.

She tucked and tumbled in a triple somersault. Then landed, still rolling, on the battlement.

Stars and comets! I really dig that propulsion exploit. Too bad it can only be triggered once a run. Gotta find me some way to boost that battery—

As she rolled to her feet, the high-frequency *choom-choom* of shock beams kept her moving, shifting smoothly to a run. A beam sliced the air—so close it singed her eyebrows. She dove underneath, her silk-sheathed hip skidding across the floor, into the protective cover of a pedestrian tunnel. Panting, she scrambled to her feet and tapped out another command.

Her cloaking app was her best and baddest exploit. As in, her very best. Like all her best exploits, she'd programmed that code herself.

Lying in wait all around her, unseen but deadly in their dens, a lethal army of killer droids chittered and clacked, their orbital sensors blinded—for now. The crablike droids with their armored pincers and protruding eyes would cycle at hyperspeed through all nine billion nodes until they found her.

And fried her.

Unless she tagged her target and claimed her prize before she got tagged herself.

First law of the cyberverse. If I tag the First Indomitable, that law's in play.

Silently she ghosted down a slanting tunnel. A humming force field enclosed the arena, but her Mogadon nav key bought her the electronic blip in the current she needed to slip past.

A vast echoing space opened before her. The coliseum of the Council of Indomitables, the elite military command of the Mogadon

Empire. Dominated by the podium at its heart, ringed with tiers of empty wings, this digital construct mirrored the physical structure where the First Indomitable would broadcast his declaration of war.

Until the broadcast—utterly empty.

Except for the slender black-clad shadow who stood quietly behind the podium, limned in the console's amber light.

Her fingertips tingled with the lighting charge of triumph.

Almost close enough to taste.

Damn, but she knew her target. She'd timed her moment like magic. And her fickle samurai's luck was holding. Barely half a click before showtime, the First Indomitable of the Mogadon Empire had slipped into the cyberverse to test his defenses.

That last Indomitable, the fat guy, he would've been too arrogant to bother. But this one…

Dex Draven.

The youngest First Indomitable in galactic history. The one who'd slaughtered the fat guy in formal combat. This one was wary.

Methodical.

Meticulous.

They said he left absolutely nothing to chance.

Which meant Dex Draven would be checking his six in the cyberverse.

Which meant he was *hers*.

Running swift and silent as spilled ink, shrouded in the shadowy folds of her cloaking app, Kaia launched over the balustrade to land lightly on the arena floor. She'd calculated her entry angle when she planned her run. Now the Indomitable's avatar stood squarely with his back to her.

Just like she'd planned.

Every sense alert and tingling, she raced across the arena. Wired into the cyberport, her physical skin sweated and her physical heart pounded and a treadmill of cyber turf unspooled under her physical feet as adrenaline jacked her performance sky high.

Sly and insidious as a whispered rumor, suspicion stole through her. This run was unfolding *way* too smoothly.

Enough with the paranoia, angel. The Mogadon Empire hasn't faced mortal danger in years. Pretty soon they'll mop the floor with the Syndax—who may be space pirates, but they're mighty fine hackers. The Mogadon are overconfident, and you are paranoid.

But paranoia was what kept her alive instead of dead in the Mogadon biowar and free instead of chained in the Patriarch's harem.

Instincts screaming in warning, she pelted past the empty tiers toward the stairs that soared to the podium. As the battery in her belt started to drain, the shadowy folds of her cloaking app flickered out. She closed in a silent rush.

A blink before contact, she vaulted over the first three steps without touching them, planted a handspring on the fourth, and cartwheeled through space to land silently on the platform.

The First Indomitable stood close enough to touch. Back imposing in Mogadon black, shoulders straight under the platinum bars of his imperial rank, edged in amber light. He studied the console before him, powerful sun-bronzed hands resting quietly on the panel. The heavy epaulets he wore so easily, the contained force that inhabited his still frame, the distinctive hammered gold of his close-cropped hair…

Everything checked out.

It was *him*.

Kaia crossed her fingers for luck and leaned in to whisper a single word in Dex Draven's ear.

"Tag."

The guy didn't even flinch.

Which made him a mighty cool customer, in supreme command of every reflex. But what the flip did she expect from a guy who'd kept his iron grip on the Mogadon high command by killing every man who challenged him?

Quickly, before he triggered a few defensive exploits of his own, she got out the rest.

"Don't worry—I'm not the Syndax. But if I can breach your perimeter, you better believe so can they. Ten thousand creds and I'll cover your six while you're on the air. So you can declare war in, uh, peace."

Still he said nothing. But the humming aura of danger that emanated from his focused form, like an anvil of crushing force suspended over her by a thread, was definitely making her jumpy.

"You're done with your broadcast in a click and you'll never see me again—that's a promise. One and done and I'm off this rock." She paused for a response that still wasn't coming, then finished a tad lamely. "First rule of cyberspace. If I can tag you, I've earned the right to defend you, true? And I *really* need the money to get off this hunk of junk. Preferably before the Syndax attack."

Finally, before this endless convo drained her battery for real and she died of old age in her cyberport, the First Indomitable stirred.

Just barely.

A voice like amber silk, smooth with amusement, slid straight through her senses.

"Whatever desperately misguided notion led you to believe I obey anyone's rules? I compel the entire galaxy to obey *mine*."

His gleaming golden head snapped toward her. And eyes like pinwheels of cobalt fire blazed straight through her. She felt his impact like a laser blast. A sonic explosion of sound drove her back, falling, barely catching herself with an outflung palm before she sprawled on her ass.

She lost precious ticks while her befuddled senses struggled to make sense of him, this black-clad titan who towered over her, crowned in gold with eyes streaming fire.

While back in the physical world, a real-life *kaboom* blew the locked and trip-wired door of her cyberport clear from its hinges.

For an endless jangling instant she reeled between two worlds— the cyber and the physical—as a swarm of armored figures in the black fighting leathers of the Mogadon Empire poured through the charred and burning portal of her rented cyberport.

Her physical body floundered in a tangle of singed wires and smoking sensors.

Six cubits away in her cyberport, an intruder sporting a centurion's titanium bars lifted a wrist unit to his mouth and spoke curtly. "First Indomitable? We have the maharani in custody."

A vise of terror—as wild and unreasoning as her mother's madness—snapped shut like a bear trap around her frantic heart.

In the cyberverse, the blinding visage of Dex Draven's avatar spared her a smile of quiet satisfaction. "Well done, centurion. Well done."

A trap! Stars and comets, it's a trap. And somehow—gods!—he knows who I am. He knows I'm the Patriarch's daughter.

Torn between reality and cyberspace, consumed by an animal's instinct to fight to the death or burrow deep in her den, Kaia unsheathed her saber and shot to her feet with a snarl. "You'll never live to collect your bounty! I'll kill you before I go back to Kryll and that farking harem, you hear me? I'll kill you or I swear I'll die trying, I *swear*—"

Calmly the First Indomitable clipped out a single word.

"Execute."

The shrill whine of a blaster pierced her physical ears. Then the cyberverse, her cyberport and everything she'd ever been vanished in a wall of hot white light.

CHAPTER TWO
The Indomitable

A deafening roar dragged her back to life. The roar of ten thousand throats voicing a collective howl for someone's blood. As Kaia's eyes flashed open, she devoutly hoped it wasn't hers.

Angels and asteroids.

I am punked.

Senses racing on hyperdrive, she slitted her eyes. She lay crumpled on the floor of an unfamiliar room, barely lit by a wash of ruddy light seeping from solar-powered ceiling panels. Her head throbbed, her bones ached, and the tinny tang of the cyberverse tasted like scorched metal in her mouth.

Gods of her father. Someone had nailed her with a blaster set on stun. Because if they hadn't exercised that modicum of restraint, she'd definitely be dead.

Which would be vastly preferable to her current state.

Not to mention her current fate.

Panic plucked at her nerves, but she forced it back. She was alive. She was *alive*. And that howling mob, whoever they were, had to be half a Mogadon mile off, muffled if not muted by walls. Even if they were screaming with a raw animal hunger that would only be sated when that savage horde saw blood spilled and flesh torn.

She closed her eyes against her hammering head and groaned.

The First Indomitable. The war. He's launching it right now. Which means the Syndax are coming. And I'm still on Mogadon.

Not to mention her captor—because she had definitely been captured—knew precisely who and what she was.

The *Angel*'s disabled drive.

That oh-so-serendipitous cosmic poker victory.

Her apparent ease in eluding the amassed might of the Mogadon Empire…

Dex Draven had designed the perfect trap.

And, like a Prime Class fool, she'd ambled right into it.

Fear scrabbled at the edges of her mind. They knew who she was. Which could only mean the Patriarch had sent them.

Her father.

Sudden and sharp as a heart attack, panic exploded.

Gods no never go back chains prison chains—

For a breath she lay perfectly still, eyes squeezed shut against the cresting tide of terror. Then she crammed the swell of panic into the box in her brain where it lived and forced down the lid.

Easy, angel. You're still in the Alpha Sector. Dear old Dad's back in Gamma. Which means you can still escape.

And you will escape.

She dragged in a shuddering breath, all the way down to her diaphragm, that fed the slow burn of resolve. Her heart slowed and her pulse steadied.

Kaia opened her eyes and took stock.

Instantly the circus performer in her pegged the scene. A dressing room enclosed in rolling racks of opulent threads, ruby and jet and tourmaline, heavy and gleaming with a dazzle of gold and silver. An overloaded table looming before a mirror. A scatter of perfume flasks strangled in ropes of jewels.

Nothing she recognized. Except her cyber saber propped neatly beside the closed door, and her utility belt coiled on the chair.

They left me my weapons?

Incredulous, she sat up, bones stiff and aching from prolonged contact with the floor, body shivering through the thin silk of her cybersuit. Her stomach heaved and the room revolved. Flogged by the scourge of urgency, she wobbled to her feet.

Step by step by step, she made her way to the sword and slung it over her shoulder. An anemic trickle of courage seeped through her cold limbs, but didn't do squat to warm her. Shivering, she buckled on her utility belt.

Bizarrely, they'd left her everything. Everything but access to a cyberport.

Which only meant they weren't stupid.

Of course she checked the door. Which of course was locked.

When a fresh howl from that ravening mob iced her blood, she clenched her teeth around a shudder. The Mogadon on their mountainous megaplanet liked it colder than her countrymen on the hot desert world of Kryll, where she'd been raised in the Patriarch's harem. She was hurt and cold and hungry, and she'd need every brain cell she owned firing at full thrust to get out of this mess.

Shaking hard enough to rattle her bones, she beelined for the nearest rack. Looking for a cowl, a cloak, a jacket, anything.

She fingered a gown of heavy crimson silk—and the electric shock of recognition made her gasp. In mounting dread, she pawed through the rest.

Already knowing what she'd find.

A fortune in fabrics worth a small planet. All cut to the same design for the same despicable purpose—the distinctive Kryll corset left the wearer's breasts naked, offering them like canapés on a cocktail tray for public enjoyment.

These were Tombola gowns.

Numbly she groped for the chair and sank into it. She was going to be sick, right here on the floor of this silken prison. The Tombola was the prison sentence she'd defied her fate and her father to escape. The ceremonial auction for her hand and her bed, dictated by holy ritual but driven by mortal greed.

The fate she'd spent half her life fleeing.

"Damn you to hell, Father," she whispered, for the benefit of any hidden sensors. This was one message she flipping well *meant* to be heard. "I swear by all Ninety-Nine of your Kryllian Gods I'll slit my wrists with my own saber before I let you auction me off the way you did Kira."

Gritting her teeth, she lifted her head and met her own gaze in the mirror. Her hybrid features stared grimly back. Eyes wide with alarm instead of mischief, mouth set in a fierce line instead of her usual daredevil grin, golden skin kissed by desert sun but pale with resolve. Tendrils slipping free from her braid—singed all to hell by that blaster. The platinum lightning bolt of Valyrian psi tech flashing at her ear. Her samurai's cyberjack an icy glitter at her temple.

Yep, she looked terrified. But she also looked determined.

Gods help the misguided man who thinks he's going to buy his way into this woman's bed—

The soft click of the opening door lodged her heart in her throat. She sprang to her feet and spun with a hiss, saber flying from her sheath with a *shing* that promised violence.

Two troopers tromped in, sinister in the black fighting leathers of the Mogadon Empire, faceless behind lowered visors.

Blasters holstered at their hips in casual menace.

Kaia wasn't afraid of them—she *wasn't*—despite the Mogadon reputation for brutality. Logically she knew no one went to this kind of trouble to capture a Prime Class samurai alive, only to execute their captive. Besides, the Patriarch needed her whole and undamaged… at least physically… for his farking Tombola.

In a show of bravado she was light-years away from feeling, she lowered her cyber saber and planted a hand on her hip.

"High time someone shows up around here. Even if it's just Faceless One and Faceless Two." She went for indignation rather than babbling terror, which wasn't a good look for her. "It's cold as Chiron in here. *And* I'm starving. I'm a galactic citizen, you know? I have rights."

"The First Indomitable is ready for you now," Faceless One intoned. All too clearly unimpressed.

Probably because he knew she was unsanctioned by the Quorum and her citizenship papers were fake.

Which meant she *had* no galactic rights.

"Oh, is he?" She cocked a hip and gave her best attitude. "Well, you can bet your blaster I'm more than ready for his indomitable ass. Bring him on."

Yet even as she sheathed her blade and sashayed past the goon squad, cool as Kryll's renegade comet, she had the proverbial bad feeling.

Whatever the First Indomitable has in the hopper is something I'm not going to like.

#

That Mogadon mob was going wild.

Kaia stared at the dark tunnel that burrowed through half a mile of Mogadon granite into the belly of the beast—the real-world coliseum—and knew one fact to a mathematical certainty.

I am well and truly punked.

Because the Mogadon weren't only notorious for their cutting-edge arsenal and ruthlessness in battle. They were notorious for their brutal gladiatorial games, inspired by some barbaric custom from their Terran past.

They were notorious because they baptized their military ventures in blood.

Her helmeted goon squad—multiplied now to a scary six—marched her like some kind of felon through the echoing tunnel. With every step, a little more of her bravado trickled away. The animal roar of the mob swelled to an earsplitting howl.

Punctuated by the crisp diction of an amplified voice that could only belong to the First Indomitable.

"… require no reminder of what happened to Valyria the last time our adversaries incurred Mogadon wrath. This particular Syndax warlord, of all men living… perfectly placed to comprehend… *Valyrensis novicida*… far from the only bioweapon in the Mogadon arsenal."

The sick feeling in her stomach pushed into her throat. Calm as a scientist describing a lab experiment, the guy was threatening to launch another biowar like the one that killed her lifemate, maddened and murdered her mother, and eradicated half her bloodline. True, the motley crew of outcasts and outlaws who flocked to the Syndax horde might not share the genetic homogeneity that rendered the Valyrian novicide so relentlessly effective.

But apparently the Empire scientists had overcome that technical hurdle.

"… seems our exiled Indomitable, this man the Syndax call the Voortrekker… reprehensible traitor to his bloodline, his oath, his men, his people… forgotten the Empire's military and technical prowess. However, countrymen, we have not forgotten him."

Now, without adding even a decibel of volume, that cultured voice dripped contempt. The screaming mob echoed him with a vitriol she found terrifying.

"Traitor! Murderer! Crucify him!"

The floor beneath her feet trembled under the thunder of twenty thousand angry boots. The air hung heavy with the reek of blood and vengeance. Over the bedlam, that perfectly controlled voice flogged the mob to a frothing frenzy.

"And our exiled commander would betray his own kind twice over by joining those cannibalistic parasites—"

Whoa now… cannibals?

"—those deep-space demons—those flesh-rotting monstrosities with their shape-shifting god who threaten the Pax Mogadon and all order in the galaxy. The Swarm."

And now the farking Swarm are coming?

Kaia had as much moxie as the next samurai, but she suddenly found she couldn't move. Thirty cubits from the strobe-lit arena, her booted feet felt hammered to the floor.

Rough hands closed around her elbows to shove her forward.

"What's the problem, samurai?" Faceless One jeered behind his visor. "Thought you wanted to 'bring him on'?"

I might've made a tactical error. Just a teeny one.

Well, she'd never been one to run from a fight. With a rush of adrenaline that nearly blew her head off, she embraced the inevitability of this one.

Resisting the harsh hands that narrowed her options to one, she sucked air deep into her lungs. Then she pivoted on one heel and sent a knife-edge kick hammering into an armored chest.

The blow connected with a satisfying *thwomp*.

Someone yelled, hands fell, goons dove for their blasters.

And for one electrifying instant she was free.

Kaia ducked and spun, one leg sweeping out to knock a goon off his feet. Still moving, braid flying, she freed her saber with a steely *shiss* and sent the blade skidding down the sloping floor toward the arena, metal striking sparks from stone.

An eyeblink later she was pelting after it, scattered shouts chasing her down the tunnel. Expecting every tick to feel the deadly heat of a blaster burning a hole in her back. Senses firing on overdrive, she cartwheeled into a handspring and sailed into the arena with a triple somersault to launch her over the head of anything human.

She landed in a crouch, scooped up the saber as it slid past, and whirled in a scything defense to clear her six of every opponent.

Except there *was* no opponent.

Because the tunnel led not to the arena floor and death by combat, but merely to a private viewing box perched high above the fray.

A box that stood empty.

Poised for ambush, adrenaline flooding every synapse, Kaia spun toward the tunnel. But the goon squad seemed satisfied they had her where they wanted. Leisurely they spread across the exit, blocking her escape.

But giving her the space she needed to clear her head.

She whirled toward the arena and gaped. Tier upon tier of stadium seats packed with thousands upon thousands of Mogadon troops, hellishly lit by the epileptic flash of strobes in freeze-frame images of raised fists and twisted faces. The stadium floor stained and splotched with drying blood under booted feet.

An ocean of men gleaming with titanium and seething with rage.

Apparently she'd missed the violent gladiatorial games. Now the Empire's elite battalions were massed and armored for war.

All of them deadly, all of them fierce, all of them poised on the razor's edge of violence. All held effortlessly in check by the slim erect figure standing at the podium, clad in jet and crowned in gold.

He doesn't even need a vid screen to hold them, she marveled, spellbound by him like all the rest. *Just his voice and his presence and all that perfectly contained power.*

I'm in this so far over my head I can't even remember what it feels like to breathe.

And in that moment of perfect despair, when she acknowledged what he was across the coliseum's vast length, that distant figure turned his head and saw her.

Even though he stood hundreds of cubits away and couldn't *possibly* see her—a single spark of defiance in the tundra whose cold sun rose and sank at his command—she felt he spoke to her alone.

"Be of good cheer, countrymen." Dex Draven's murmur echoed from the vaulted ceiling. "The Swarm and the Syndax are worthy adversaries. As worthy an adversary as the Voortrekker himself. Their extermination will be glorious. But we shall defend the Pax Mogadon, which has delivered justice and order to a grateful galaxy for a millennium. For today, we claim a new ally of our own."

In a flash of sinking dread, she understood.

Finally, she got him.

Why the First Indomitable of the Mogadon Empire—first among independent equals on the Council, closest in rank to the Imperator himself—would stoop to bother with a stray hybrid like Kaia.

By capturing the Patriarch's fugitive daughter and easing that thorn from his mighty paw, Dex Draven had just secured the alliance he needed with the lion of Kryll to wage his precious war.

Speechless, she stared at that formidable figure, saber hanging limp from her grip. Until, inevitably, she heard him confirm it.

"Today I swore alliance against the Syndax with the Patriarch of Kryll. Together, countrymen, we will bury that traitor Zorin."

All around her, the Mogadon were losing their collective minds.

Gods of the nine unknown realms. I'm his purchase price. I'm what he's trading for all Kryll's gold to bankroll his armageddon.

Before the magnitude of his vision, the prospect of her certain enslavement and sexual degradation dwindled to a footnote. Between them, Dex Draven and the piratical Syndax would tear the galaxy apart. Murder millions. Unleash another biowar on children and innocents.

Somehow, gods help her, she had to escape him.

And then she had to stop him.

CHAPTER THREE
The Orgy

"I'll need twenty more executions for the fighting pit at dawn." Dex Draven strode swiftly down the tunnel from the coliseum and fired off commands to the prefect trotting breathlessly alongside. "Today's attrition rate was steeper than expected."

A ripple of anticipation rustled through the quartet of troopers marching at his heels. All handpicked men he'd trained himself, all blooded and battle-hardened, his elite praetorian guard. In point of fact, his bodyguard.

And he trusted none of them at his back with a blaster.

Because the only way to become First Indomitable of the Mogadon Empire was to kill the current incumbent.

Just as Dex himself had recently done.

The prefect shot him a cautious look. "After today's bloodbath, the civil prisons are empty."

"What, we're all out of pedophiles and rapists?" Dex scrolled through dossiers on his digital tablet, tapping through child molesters, serial killers, a man who'd raped his daughter and killed her to hide the crime. All of them destined for the fighting pit. "Then open the brig. I want soldiers convicted of treason, dereliction of duty, felony insubordination and criminal integrity violations."

Another mutter from the troops at his heels, this time displeasure for the fate of their disgraced brethren. Only his battle sense—that infallible sixth sense he'd actively cultivated and learned to trust—told him no one was drawing his weapon.

At least not yet.

"Ah, well, a thousand pardons, Indomitable. The thing is, those are uniformed men," the prefect pointed out. "Once their appeals are exhausted, they're entitled to death by combat."

This prefect was gutsier than most. Dex admired that kind of spirit. The lad was undoubtedly wasted in admin.

"And that's precisely what they'll get. In the fighting pit." Dex placed his palm against the screen to add his biometric signature to the execution orders he'd just authorized. "Twenty men, prefect. Make it happen."

"Right away, Indomitable."

The prefect trotted off, to be replaced instantly by Dex's reliable right-hand man, a war-hardened older officer with humble antecedents and a harried look. Dex tamped down a flicker of irritation—he'd retained the tablet for a reason and his attention tonight was decidedly elsewhere—and flicked him a narrowed glance.

"Well, *Optio*? A trifle late for another crisis, isn't it?"

"Never too late for one more, is it?" Undaunted by brusqueness or anything else Dex ever threw at him, the *optio* hoisted his shaggy brows. "Valyrian envoy's waiting in your quarters."

Dex stared blankly for a heartbeat, then uttered a soft curse. He'd forgotten the farking envoy who'd flown so many parsecs to meet him, and Jupiter knew he'd no time for the man now. Not with the Kryll maharani in his grasp, an exceedingly complex ritual to master, and a war he'd been waiting eight years to wage.

"Send him to the saturnalia," Dex said shortly. "I'll meet the bloke there. And if the impact of twelve hundred drunken Mogadon at an orgy is too much for his telepathic sensibilities to tolerate, he can bloody well wait until I've won this war."

Behind him, one of his guard guffawed. Diplomatically the *optio* studied the ruddy light of the solar panels overhead and chewed his mustache.

"Well?" Dex prompted, tapping a command on his tablet to call up the vid feed he'd ordered on the maharani. He'd expected a weepy Kryll sex slave, sulky but ultimately docile from a lifetime chained in the Patriarch's harem. Turned out that wasn't what he'd gotten. Instead, his incandescent encounter with that furious girl in the cyberverse had rather piqued his interest—

"Valyrian's not gonna like that, boss, is he?" his *optio* muttered. "He's not some mewling clerk. He's the Senate of Psychics' new Precursor."

"Is he indeed?" Reluctantly Dex shifted his attention from the tablet. The Precursor was tantamount to a war minister—or he would be, if Maximus Draven's biowar had left the telepathic race any semblance of a fighting force. "All the better. The fellow ought to be able to stomach an orgy or two. Who knows? If he's soldier enough, he might even enjoy it. Make it happen."

With the familiarity born of long and distinguished service to the Empire, the *optio* rolled his eyes toward one of the flanking guards, who smothered a grin—apparently envisioning the new Precursor's response to this edict. But the *optio*, a solidly trained plebeian grimly accustomed to humoring the whims of patrician elites like Dex, muttered a resigned affirmative and shifted doggedly to the next topic.

"You ordered a sit rep every hour on the Syndax?"

"So I did." Dex swallowed a sigh and lowered the tablet. At this rate, the maharani would be dead of old age by the time he retrieved his vid feed. Which would be rather a pity if the real-life princess looked anything at all like her avatar. "Report quickly."

"Well, since you don't want a magnum opus," his *optio* said wryly. "Sad to say, no change. Syndax fleet's still scattered to the far corners of the Omega Sector. No effort at all to muster for battle, far's our scout ships can see. Pretty handy at evading combat, and that's a fact."

"Of course they are." Absently Dex nodded as a passing centurion snapped him an Empire salute. "Zorin trained and taught at the Empire Academy and commanded the imperial legions. He knows our battle tactics as well as his consort's own body. Except the intel says he doesn't have a current consort."

As always when the exiled Indomitable came to mind, the slow burn of rage—old but still potent—swelled his chest to bursting. Dex had done his level best to forget he'd ever lionized his old mentor. But he'd never forget—or forgive—the reprehensible method of the wretch's escape from Mogadon. That infamous night Zorin betrayed everything the Mogadon stood for, merely to save his own skin. The capital city had nearly fallen.

Certainly would have fallen, if not for Dex.

Even if the reprobate *had* done them all the favor of killing Dex's rabid father. He'd needed killing—Dex could admit that now. At least, he could admit it privately to himself after a stiff whiskey. But no man deserved to die the way Zorin had killed him.

Killed his own best friend.

Maximus Draven had died disarmed and dishonored in his bed. For a Mogadon male of the ruling class, there was no greater disgrace. As his son and heir, Dex had inherited the stigma.

Barely survived it, in fact.

And for that, he blamed Zorin.

Not to mention his father's killer—now the Syndax Voortrekker—had been poking Dex in the eye with lightning skirmishes and pirate raids on the outer colonies ever since Dex ascended.

Rumor had it Zorin intended to reclaim everything he'd lost in his exile. Including his former command as First Indomitable.

Too bad that command was currently occupied.

By Dex.

The distant throb of asteroid punk made the silica floor vibrate beneath his boots. Ahead, dim figures milled in the flashing lights and smoky haze that swirled around the open doors.

The distinctive sounds and scents of a Mogadon saturnalia.

Dex reined in the familiar pulse of anger and pitched his voice to carry.

"Tell your scouts to probe him, *Optio*. Bloody force an engagement. I want a Syndax battleship blown to bits. Then I want to know precisely how their precious Voortrekker reacts."

During the next few ticks, while his guard cleared a path to the doors, Dex divided his attention between the milling crowd—cheering him at the moment, but that could change in a heartbeat, as seven hundred and nine assassinated ex-First Indomitables could vividly attest—and his vid screen.

The coliseum feed from the rally was wretched, but he saw enough of the maharani's explosive entrance to make him smile. That tumbling run of hers would make any circus-master proud. And the soldier in him thoroughly approved of the way the girl handled that saber.

Even if her skills as a Prime Class samurai did make the next few days a bit more complicated.

And at a time he could ill afford distraction.

She'd warrant careful handling, the Patriarch's daughter. She'd been running wild through the galaxy for years, thumbing her nose at her royal father and getting mixed up in all manner of unsavory trouble.

Not to mention getting sanctioned by the Quorum of Four for that adolescent fling with her Valyrian—

Abruptly he was engulfed in the sensory overload of an Empire saturnalia.

The sweet smoke of hallucinogenic mercury billowed from the hookahs in one corner, punctuated by meaty thumps and groans from another where two naked brutes, oiled and straining, grappled in the sand of the wrestling pit. All underscored by the flash and chink of creds changing hands as excited spectators laid their wagers under the band's aggressive grind.

Directly before him, a vast sheet of polyglass framed a glittering expanse of starlit sky. Two of Mogadon's moons were full tonight, and four others were visible. The ringed planet of indigo Parthon—the gas giant—dominated the heavens with its secretive silhouette.

Beneath the glass sprawled the spacious couches on their viewing platforms, cushioned in silk and ready for play. Mostly empty this early in the night, except for a lusty quartet already in medias res on one couch and a burly centurion pistoning his male consort on another. Beyond the centurion's thrusting buttocks, Dex glimpsed the consort's face pressed into the cushions, mouth open and gasping in pleasure beneath a black silk mask.

Hastily Dex averted his gaze, a hint of warmth climbing his neck. The crushing weight of two millennia of Mogadon tradition would accommodate—barely—the sexual catharsis of these unconventional male–male couplings within the anything-goes context of an all-night saturnalia. The entire purpose of a public orgy like this one was to let the troops blow off steam on the jittery eve of battle. His own father's draconian interdict against male–male couplings in the army, with convicted offenders crucified for their sins, had not survived Maximus Draven's death.

Still, across the Empire, the stigma lingered.

Any man willing to be at the receiving end of another man's passion earned every soldier's contempt. Those willing... even eager... to tolerate the subordinate placement typically wore a mask during the act to shield themselves and their families from public disgrace.

Someone thrust a cup in his hand—a cup whose contents he wouldn't touch, since he hadn't seen where it came from—and a pair of magistrates clamored for his attention. Wanting to bend his ear about the war tax, of all the infernal topics. While he fended them off, still calculating how much trouble he was likely to get from the maharani—what was her name again?—his eyes slid indifferently past the writhing sea of the dance floor.

Instinct plucked at his nerves, and slowly he turned back. Just in time to watch that tide of bodies part and a woman emerge from an ocean of clutching limbs.

Her name whispered through his brain.

Kaia.

After his strategic display of authority in the coliseum, he'd ordered his captive princess given a loose rein, within the confines of the Council's fortified compound and under extremely rigorous guard, as a gambit to soften her resistance. Indeed, he was prepared to be positively indulgent—for him—once the girl submitted to her fate.

Until this very moment, she'd seemed anything but submissive. Yet here she was, this alien woman whose thwarted rebellion would finance his war, gliding confidently through the midst of a Mogadon saturnalia.

And, as luck would have it, she was the perfect twin of that insolent avatar he'd encountered in the cyberverse.

Lean and sleek as a whippet in her cybersuit, lithe and supple with strength, taut curves sheathed in black silk. A cloud of hair swirling loose around her shoulders and halfway to her hips, wine-red and gold and burgundy in the moonlight. Silver flashing like a star in one ear and glittering at her temple. Utility belt riding her sinuous hips, saber jutting over one proud shoulder—all the flawless mirror of her alarmingly effective avatar.

Kaia.

As though he'd spoken her name across the crowded floor, her head turned slowly, inevitably, and found him. Her eyes widened—lilac eyes, Valyrian eyes, which happened to be one of his secret kinks.

Her confident frame rippled with a visible shiver of recognition.

Because Dex too resembled his avatar. In a room packed to the air vents with twelve hundred senior Mogadon officers, half of them still uniformed and half heading rapidly toward naked, she knew him without question. A savage sense of satisfaction whipped through him.

No need for introductions. Not between the two of us.

And if she was bold enough to show up alone at a Mogadon saturnalia, that suited him to perfection. He'd inform her precisely how matters were destined to play out between them. Then they could commence the infernal ritual, get the maharani auctioned off to the highest bidder among her traditional five hundred suitors, and Dex could get on with his war.

Without breaking her gaze, he beckoned. A prefect appeared at his side.

"Indomitable?"

"Bring me the Kryll maharani."

Her perceptive gaze flickered from Dex to the prefect arrowing toward her. Her shapely head tilted, that mane of fiery hair falling over one shoulder. He caught the fleeting sense of a far-too-clever brain calculating a lightning-swift strategy behind those electric eyes. Then she pivoted away and touched the sleeve of the man beside her. Who happened to be one of his fellow Indomitables.

Belatedly, Dex realized she had *three* of them trailing her.

Three of the most powerful men on Mogadon.

And they were more than trailing her. Hanging on her every word and gesture, in fact. Besotted with her, every one of them, the fools— and the girl herself doing nothing at all to discourage them.

Abruptly it dawned on Dex that the first of her five hundred suitors would likely be making their bids for her bed right here at the saturnalia. And why in Ceres that should annoy him, when he had every incentive in the world to see her whisked promptly from the market and out of his keeping, Dex could barely begin to fathom.

And why is she suddenly so bloody compliant?

Eyes narrowed, he studied her delicate profile as she pointedly ignored him. Recalling her colorful history and the fiery declaration she'd made in the cyberverse, he was nothing but suspicious of her apparent submission.

Besides, if she were really submitting, she'd be wearing a Tombola gown.

"… of the war tax? I say, are you even listening to me, Indomitable?"

"I'm afraid not," Dex admitted. "Magistrate, you're wasting your breath. Our Imperator, like the good citizen he is, fully supports the war effort. Which means he's rather enthusiastic about financing it."

In fact, the Imperator was far more eager to see Syndax blood spilled than Dex was himself. If Claudius were First Indomitable instead of civilian head of state, they'd be locked in perpetual war. The entire galaxy was fortunate he and Dex had a gentlemen's agreement to keep the worst of the Imperator's bloodthirsty tendencies in check.

"Well, his enthusiasm threatens to beggar us! Can't you at least advocate for—?"

"You know the Imperator makes the laws," Dex said brusquely. "I merely enforce them. I'm the Empire's sword, not its pocketbook— yes, Marcus? What is it?"

His *optio* was back, saying something about the Precursor that was obscured by the grinding music and a hoarse shout of triumph from the orgy couches. The vigorous sexual climax of the burly centurion and his anonymous male consort inspired a round of raucous cheers.

"*Veni, vidi, vici,*" Dex murmured, sedulously careful to keep his eyes from lingering on the naked centurion or his all-too-willing paramour. *I came. I saw. I conquered.* He wondered what his reluctant Kryll houseguest thought of all this debauchery.

"… Syndax courier ship."

"What now?" Sharply Dex refocused on his *optio.*

And hoped like hell he wasn't blushing.

"Sorry to barge in," muttered his long-suffering lieutenant, doggedly ignoring the distraction of the orgy couch. "But you're gonna want to hear this. We got a Syndax ship asking permission to enter the Alpha Sector. Says they're sending someone to, uh, negotiate."

"To negotiate *what*? A surrender?" Dex was flatly incredulous. "Zorin will surrender when his fleet's blown to bits, his men are in open mutiny, and I'm pointing a blaster at the bastard's chest from six cubits away—and not a tick sooner."

"They haven't said surrender. Only parley. Wanna let 'em in?"

"Parley." Dex pondered. This was unexpected. Mogadon Indomitables rarely parleyed, and Zorin had been one of the best until his exile. "Who's he sending?"

"That's the funny bit. The only ID they'll broadcast is *candidate eighty-nine.*"

Dex hadn't the first damn notion what that meant, but he arched a brow at his *optio*'s knowing look. "Well, man, out with it."

"It's all over the betting pool, ain't it? It'll make interstellar news by midnight. Bidding opened for the maharani's bed six clicks ago. So far, eighty-eight candidates have paid the whatchamacallit... the munificence... and bought into the auction."

"Pluto's coldest *hell*." Dex scowled.

Damn that woman and her fortune and her notoriety and her allure. She couldn't just be another Kryll sex slave. She has to be a bloody galactic sensation! I'm going to have five hundred men at each other's throats down here.

"And the Syndax are sending some damn tattooed space pirate into *my* sector to bid for her?" Dex snorted. "His High Holiness the Patriarch will never approve."

"Well, the thing is, boss, apparently the Patriarch *has*. Ritual neutrality and all that. His transmission beamed in right before the Syndax. Old lion says let him bid—"

"A Syndax pirate and one of Zorin's rabid dogs? The devil I will."

"Something about the sanctity of the Kryllian gods and their sacred ritual and you swearing an oath to honor it?" The *optio* eyed him. "Assuming you still want his treasury at your disposal for your war?"

Dex rarely allowed himself the luxury of losing his temper, but he felt perilously close to losing it now. Between them, Zorin and the old lion had him laid crosswise over a barrel with his trousers around his ankles, and he knew it. Frustration swelling in his throat—that familiar sense of being thwarted and fuming that only Zorin could invoke— Dex clenched his fists and snapped out a single blistering curse. "Let him in then, this *candidate*. I want a full-fleet escort. And you warn him, Marcus—you warn him for me. If that bastard so much as twitches, I'll blow him straight back to the Beta Sector, and to the seven hells with the Patriarch—"

"Poor Indomitable. It seems I'm causing you a bit of trouble," a woman's throaty voice murmured in his ear. "Maybe you should have accepted my original offer, paid me my ten thousand creds, and let me sashay away." A soft laugh brushed the back of his neck. "That offer still stands, in case you're wondering."

#

Maybe walking into the middle of a Mogadon orgy wasn't your best maneuver, angel.

Kaia had just watched her Mogadon suitors scatter like space mice before the First Indomitable's summons. As she trailed the politely insistent prefect past a row of orgy couches, she wasn't above admitting privately she'd made a serious mistake. She'd planned—to the extent she *had* a plan—to take advantage of the inexplicable freedom of movement Dex Draven seemed willing to allow her to scope out the lay of the land. To escape from the Mogadon compound, she needed to know its terrain, its defenses, its vulnerabilities.

And she needed allies.

Which meant she needed a charm offensive.

What she hadn't anticipated was the overwhelming physiological and biological impact of twelve hundred rutting Mogadon. Under cover of the pounding music and a veil of hallucinogenic smoke, she skirted a massive couch with her eyes mostly elsewhere, but couldn't resist sneaking a little peek.

A voluptuous woman lay naked on her back, breathless and moaning under the muscled trooper who thrust between her thighs, fighting leathers around his ankles. Another naked man stood over her, eyes glazed with passion as he fisted his swollen length.

Impatiently waiting for his turn.

Kaia tore her fascinated gaze away, heat climbing in her cheeks as the woman moaned with mounting urgency. Under the intoxicating smoke, the dark musk of arousal filled her head and swamped her senses in pulsing waves that matched the rhythm of the writhing bodies.

It was spaceport gossip that Mogadon males exuded pheromones when aroused. Biochemicals that served the sexual function of marking their consorts—sort of the chemical equivalent of a "No Trespassing" sign to warn off the competition. But the dark spicy scent served also to stimulate their lovers. She'd heard it was an involuntary reflex, those pheromones, an animal instinct beyond conscious control.

When they were hard, they scented.

Which made Mogadon males little better than beasts, to her way of thinking, despite the lofty trappings of their galactic civilization.

Now the collective impact of several hundred rutting males was spurring them all on.

And, notwithstanding a lifetime of evidence to the contrary, Kaia herself seemed far from immune.

She'd felt the first salvo on the dance floor, rubbing elbows with a hundred sweating Mogadon, the very moment she discovered Dex Draven on the distant viewing deck looking down on her. Even cast in silhouette by the pulsing lights, epaulets flashing on his shoulders, that sense of watchful stillness and contained power that inhabited his quiet frame was as unique as a biometric signature.

And the powerful surge of physical yearning that rolled through her, leaving her weak and aching, was more than a little inconvenient.

Even when she knew it was attributable solely to the pheromones filling the air and decidedly *not* to the First Indomitable's personal appeal.

Directly before her, a petite woman knelt over a naked man, his big hands kneading her full breasts as she rode him. A second male stood behind her, fitting his swollen length to her rear channel. Kaia gasped aloud as he eased his way in and the woman flung back her head in ecstasy.

Two on one? I didn't even know that was anatomically possible. Although, admittedly, I'm running a smidge short on direct experience.

Losing your lifemate at age sixteen would do that to a girl. Because Valyrians—even half-Valyrian hybrids like Kaia—were prey to their own involuntary instincts. Foremost among them the biochemical generation of unbreakable sexual and romantic lifebonds.

The bottom line was brutal. The only guy who'd ever flipped her switch was Ben Nero. Even though he'd abandoned her to her father's dubious mercies when the Quorum of Four banned their union. In the end, he'd left her with nothing. Just a good-bye gift of heartbreak, galactic notoriety, and the term of endearment he used to whisper in her ear when they were intimate.

Love you so much, angel.

Despite a few dutiful experiments on her part over the years, no other guy had ever revved her engine.

Until tonight.

Feeling breathless, flustered, and way too warm, she hurried past the couch and followed the prefect to the viewing deck. Absorbed in murmured counsel with an older officer, Dex Draven stood facing away. An oasis of fully clad propriety as his entire senior command dissolved into debauchery around them.

Seeing the First Indomitable up close and personal—the most

powerful guy in the galaxy, not to mention the youngest ever to hold that honor—was more than enough to give any girl the jitters. Her heart was pounding so hard she could practically hear it thunder against her eardrums over the band's thrashing tempo. Her face felt flushed and her tummy felt fluttery.

Steady on, samurai. He's just a man.

Not even a particularly large one, she was surprised to see. Slim and fighting fit under tailored black jacket, shoulders straight under platinum epaulets, hips lean and legs muscled under trousers and high boots. The crown of her head would easily graze his chin. She studied the back of his neck, a handspan of suntanned skin under impeccably cropped hair of burnished gold, and clasped her hands behind her back before she did something completely disastrous.

Like touching him.

It's the pheromones. He's a monster.

Yet even knowing what he was, she found herself compelled to steal closer, ignoring the prefect's startled attempt to wave her off.

"—let him in then, this *candidate*. I want a full-fleet escort—"

Crackling with fury and crisp with command, the timbre of his voice made her shiver. Like he'd slid a finger under her cybersuit to trace her naked spine.

And she couldn't seem to stop herself from leaning in close to the First Indomitable of the Mogadon Empire and whispering in Dex Draven's ear.

"Poor Indomitable. It seems I'm causing you a bit of trouble."

If Kaia's life until that night had been a planet spinning blindly around the sun she called freedom, he was the flaming comet hurtling through the heavens that smashed through her determined orbit and knocked her irrevocably off course.

He's so young.

Barely older than she. Which surprised her all over again. What imperatives had his harsh upbringing imposed to propel him to rise so early and so high? His personal hardships, whatever they were, had chiseled all softness from strong cheekbones and square jaw. His eyes were cobalt suns that blazed with the cold fire of an intellect as piercing and unsoftened by sentiment as arctic ice. She wondered what the hard slant of his mouth would look like when he smiled.

If he ever smiled.

Snap out of it, samurai. He's a killer with zero remorse. And half your race is on his hit list.

"Maharani." His golden head inclined in a carefully correct courtesy she hadn't expected. "I'll confess I'm rather surprised to find you enjoying my saturnalia rather than plotting your escape. I'm told you haven't yet made the obligatory attempt. Is that because you'd rather simply kill me?"

His tone was impeccable inquiry, as though he merely asked whether she'd prefer sugar or milk in her *chaco*. But his alert gaze was sharp with interest as he took her measure.

Damn if he didn't rouse the very devil in her.

Casually she shook back her loose hair. "I'm not really the killing type. Except in self-defense. Although I have to admit… in your case? I'm tempted. Especially once you announced your intent to exterminate the Syndax in another of your biowars. No civilization deserves that, not even a horde of pirates."

"If you'd witnessed the atrocities they inflict upon innocent civilians in the outer colonies, perhaps you would change your mind."

She tilted her head to study him in honest curiosity. "I'm pretty sure you know I'm a Prime Class samurai. Why'd you let me keep my weapons?"

He blinked as though she'd surprised him. "Because you haven't done anything to dishonor them. For a Mogadon, to disarm a man—or a woman for that matter, although typically ours don't fight—is the ultimate disgrace."

For a breath, his eyes went distant and his jaw clenched.

"So by keeping my weapons, I've kept my honor?" Now it was her turn to be surprised. Considering the fate her father had planned for her, and this man's role in delivering her to it like a parcel he'd purchased, the last thing she'd expected was consideration for her honor.

"Until you violate your prisoner's parole… which of course you will." His neon eyes narrowed and one corner of his mouth quirked up. "Allow me to offer you a bit of unsolicited advice."

Without waiting for her acquiescence, he closed the distance between them and lifted her face. Holding her immobile with a single light touch beneath her jaw—a fleeting contact that paralyzed her. His eyes were ice.

Yet his skin was anything but.

Hyperaware of him the way she was, flames seemed to spark where they touched. Tendrils of heat raced along her body, licking at the handspan of open air between them.

Blast these pheromones. He's a killer. Even if he's standing close enough to kiss.

Meeting him breath for breath, she held his gaze, every sense violently alive and tingling with danger.

"Our paths run in parallel orbits, Kaia of Kryll. At least for the present time. Until you enter another man's keeping, you're far too valuable to release from mine. Until then, my advice is to accustom yourself to it." His voice roughened. "And to me."

"I don't think that's possible," she heard herself whisper, stripped of every artifice, speaking nothing but truth. She squared her shoulders and faced him down. "I won't just surrender my freedom and my future without one hell of a struggle, Dex Draven. And that's my honor talking."

"Thanks for the warning."

This time he actually smiled, which complicated the hell out of her breathing. Especially when his hand curved under her chin, hardened fingers sliding lightly along her jaw in an unmistakable caress before his hand dropped.

Kaia was working to reorder her shattered senses when violence erupted from the orgy couches. Two naked men reeled toward them, locked in savage hand-to-hand combat.

Running on instinct, she pivoted away and reached for her saber.

But Dex Draven was already in the thick of it, deflecting the brawling pair with a sharp word and a powerful shove that sent them both sprawling. The two hit the floor and came up snarling, spoiling for blood.

One look at the straight black figure looming over them, perfectly still with eyes blazing like lasers, drained the rage from their faces. Shoulders slumping, they muttered apologies and shuffled off.

Eyeing the slender man who'd made them back down without so much as drawing his blaster, notwithstanding their superior size, Kaia was reminded of a pack of Kryllian sand wolves. Savage beasts all, but reduced to belly-crawling servitude before their leader.

These Mogadon are wolves, all right.

And Dex Draven is their undisputed alpha.

Standing for the moment outside his compelling orbit, she realized the saturnalia had taken a savage turn. Piles of bodies writhed on the big orgy couches, while smaller knots of tangled limbs filled the private couches along the walls. Scattered fistfights were breaking out along the periphery. Some bloodied and battered bruiser was being beaten half to death in the wrestling pit.

And almost without exception, the Mogadon males in her vicinity who weren't already occupied either fighting or fucking were eyeing her—the only unclaimed female in their midst. All knowledge of her role and status forgotten as powerful pheromones flooded their senses and biological imperatives kicked in, their predators' eyes were wolves' eyes.

And she was the prey.

Casually she circled to put the wall at her back and drew her cyber saber.

Abruptly Dex Draven towered before her, those incandescent eyes still blazing.

"Put that blasted weapon away, damn it!" he snapped. "Do you want to start a bloodbath in here? Drawing a weapon at a saturnalia is one of our most powerful taboos."

Adrenaline and pheromones flooding her system, she struggled to rein in her own battle instincts. But the Mogadon wolves were backing off, clearly deterred by their alpha. Much as it stuck in her craw to rely on Dex Draven for protection, she reluctantly swallowed the indignity and sheathed her sword.

"I think I've had enough Mogadon hospitality for one night. It's certainly been, ah, memorable." She cleared her throat. "My ship's disabled in your hangar bay, as I'm pretty sure you know, since you're probably the one responsible for my being stranded on this rock in the first place. Any objection if I sleep there tonight?"

"At the height of an orgy, Mogadon males are notoriously difficult to control. Even for me." Deftly ignoring her query, he fell in beside her. "Tonight you require my protection, Maharani, whether you fancy it or not."

Instead of being shepherded toward the exit, a thoroughly alarmed Kaia found herself drawn deeper into the belly of the beast.

Despite being not much taller than she was, he managed to project the impression of looming protectively over her. Which she found pretty flipping ironic, considering *he* was the primary threat she needed protection from.

His hand grazed her lower back, urging her unwillingly before him from the viewing deck to the main floor.

Which at least had the advantage of easing them away from the orgy couches.

"Seriously," she pressed, "I'd rather sleep in my own berth. And it's no risk to you, because my cruiser's not spaceworthy with her antimatter drive disabled. You can check that with your people at the bay. She's call sign ANGL-X-43. The *Interstellar Angel*."

"I'm fully aware." Another light touch directed her toward the flashing pulse of the dance floor, lit from beneath in crimson and cobalt. "I'm rather afraid I *am* the culprit responsible for your unfortunate engine troubles."

Beyond, another span of polyglass opened on star-filled heavens edged with the jagged silhouette of the Mogadon mountains. Above, the flaming comet whose elliptical orbit swung periodically through the Alpha Sector seared a smoldering score through the heavens.

Hearing Dex Draven confirm his role in the *Angel*'s disablement was pretty much what she'd figured.

But it still flipped her off.

"Afraid I'd outrun you?" She quickened her pace to stay ahead of the light touch grazing the small of her back. "Or maybe outgun you?"

"You do enjoy a certain reputation, samurai," he murmured at her ear. "You're unpredictable. Resourceful. Reckless. And you seem to possess the devil's own luck."

"A samurai makes her own luck," she countered.

Even if mine's been lousy of late.

"Then we have that in common." His voice hardened. "In short, I fear you're far too important to the course of this war for me to allow you to risk your pretty neck in another of your daredevil exploits."

Angels of Anaxos, he's arrogant.

Kaia had tolerated more than enough of this high-handed treatment. He planned to deliver her to a life of slavery and degradation. That didn't give him the right to boss her around like one of his hapless prefects.

On the edge of the dance floor, she planted both hands on her hips and balked.

"Believe it or not, Indomitable, you may run half the galaxy, but you don't make decisions for me. And, as you've just admitted, I'm entirely capable of my own protection." Fuming at her lack of agency, she tossed back her hair. "If you're so flipping afraid of what I'll do overnight in my own berth on a cruiser you've personally ensured is disabled, where do you want me tonight?"

His electric eyes threw sparks and his tone roughened. "Right here."

Deftly he spun her toward him. His hands settled at her hips. Suddenly, shockingly, she was in his arms.

With nothing between them but breath.

Her entire traitorous body flared to life, flaming like the comet that seared the Mogadon skies. His hips and thighs, solid with muscle under all that tailored civility, fit against hers like she'd been made for him.

Which alarmed her far worse than anything else he'd done.

Even declaring interstellar war.

"Whoa there, space cadet! Hold on a tick. I'm… not the dancing type." Sounding far too breathless, she gripped his shoulders to impose some distance. Their gazes locked, and that dangerous current of electricity crackled between them.

"Neither am I, normally." Holding her as easily as if he did it every night, he eased her into a rhythm that matched the music's slow throb. "Bear with me. This display serves a useful function."

"You don't need to display me." Even to herself, she sounded bitter. "Thanks to my father, the entire galaxy knows I'm for sale."

"This display is necessary for your protection, not your purchase price." His voice vibrated against her open palms, and she couldn't contain a shiver. He eased her closer—a seemingly unconscious adjustment that only unsettled her more. "I'm telling every man here you're firmly under my protection."

"You're not listening. I just told you I don't *need* your protection—"

"Kaia." The sigh of her name on his lips sent contrails of heat shooting through her like a meteor shower. "A notable number of your declared suitors are Mogadon. It's fear of me that will make them toe the line."

A dark bracing scent rose from his skin that made her tingle. For a monster, he smelled kind of amazing. She could hardly help but notice.

The better to lure you in, angel.

"That could be risky for you, though, couldn't it?" she pointed out, voice husky.

He shrugged as though a little mortal danger were a trifling thing. "The suitors you're drawing are powerful men, some of the biggest names in the Empire. If one of them is powerful enough and wants you badly enough, he'll challenge me for you. And any challenge rendered to a First Indomitable is by combat to the death. The clearer I make my claim, the longer they'll hesitate before they attack."

"And you think one dance will deter them all?" Incredulous, she pulled in a long breath, head swimming with his scent.

Then, suddenly, she got it.

"Wait a sec. It isn't the dance at all, is it? You're Mogadon. That thing with the pheromones. Are you… *scenting* me?"

"I am the dominant male of my race. Every Mogadon in the Alpha Sector knows my scent. So, yes, this is how I'm claiming you."

His cool confirmation flipped all her switches. Didn't he get that she'd spent half her life ensuring over and over again that no man could ever *claim* her?

Even if her headstrong libido had chosen tonight, of all possible nights, to put Ben Nero in her rearview mirror.

Had to be the pheromones he was kicking out. He was the blood-sworn enemy of her mother's people. He would cheerfully consign her to a fate she'd kill to avoid. But damn if the slow sway of his powerful frame against hers didn't short-circuit every synapse in her body.

Afire with agitated energy, she shifted against his contained strength. "It's barbaric. There has to be another way."

"Oh, I assure you there is." His gaslight gaze seared through her. "All Indomitables have private couches. A little time together on one of those, and you'll smell like me for a month."

A blazing image of the two of them, tangled naked on an orgy couch, burrowed through her brain. She shuddered under the impact. An impact that wrung from her lungs a soft sound—almost a whimper.

His hands tightened at her hips and pulled her close.

And that combustible spark of contact with the hardened length of fully aroused Mogadon male nearly made her knees buckle.

"I won't pretend I'm not tempted, Kaia of Kryll," he growled. A tendril of golden hair fell into his eyes, doing nothing at all to blunt his appeal. "You're the most desirable woman in the galaxy tonight. Your father and his infamous ritual saw to that. And I'm a Mogadon male at an orgy without a current consort."

Nothing like a reference to the gods-cursed Tombola to get a girl's head screwed on straight.

"That sounds inconvenient for you, Indomitable." She eased back from his dangerous orbit and put a handspan of open air between them. "I'm sure we can both agree, the sooner I'm out of your hair, the better. When do you deliver me to the Patriarch?"

Because she refused to call him her father.

"I don't." Seeing her confusion, he smiled faintly. "Your father anointed me Tombola master in his place. Starting tomorrow, I'll accept bids for your bed on his behalf and commend the best for his decision."

Kaia stumbled in her cyber boots and probably would have fallen on her derrière—if not for his firm hands at her waist holding her up. Inside the shell of her body, everything that made her Kaia was spiraling in a nosedive.

The bidding starts tomorrow? I thought I'd have more time. More time to escape. Great Ninety-Nine Gods, I need more time.

From an unbridgeable distance, Dex Draven calmly laid down the law. As if he hadn't just threatened her whole damn universe.

"Here's how this Tombola's going to proceed. We'll ascend at oh-six-hundred clicks to my flagship, which currently resides in orbit around this planet—in other words, a locale whose security lies under my complete control. There we'll assemble your five hundred suitors and commence the ritual at high noon with your first public viewing."

Her gut churned with dread. She thrashed through the nausea and fired the words at him like supersonic missiles. "My first public viewing? Do you have the first farking clue what that means?"

Because if you did, space cadet, and if you had the first farking clue about me, you'd know there isn't going to be a public viewing. Before I wear one of those bare-breasted Tombola gowns in public, I'll cyber-bomb your battleship and your whole flipping fleet.

And if that doesn't stop you, I'll walk out an airlock without a spacesuit.

Well, the man wasn't unobservant. She'd give him that much. Whatever he saw in her face or felt in her body gave him a flicker of pause.

"Don't despair." He spared her a brief smile that conveyed nothing at all of reassurance. "Given the level of interest you're generating, we may not require a display of that nature to achieve the desired objective. With even a little luck, we'll have you auctioned off in no time."

CHAPTER FOUR
The Precursor

Barely one excruciating click into the peak of a Mogadon orgy, Dex was compelled to acknowledge the unavoidable.

He needed a woman in the worst way.

And not just any woman.

Months after he'd severed ties with the latest of his infrequent and typically unsatisfying carnal conquests, it was his own damn misfortune that the only woman on the planet he wanted to tumble onto an orgy couch tonight was Kaia.

Who also happened to be the only woman on the planet he couldn't have.

And not only because he'd sworn that infernal oath to her father, or because he was fairly certain his role as honest broker of a sacred ritual precluded his sampling the wares. Now that she'd discerned his role as master of ceremonies in her impending degradation, the Kryll maharani herself would rather make love to a Solarian sea snake than entertain sexual overtures from Dex.

All of which unfortunately meant that while Dex left his mating scent all over Kaia and fantasized about unzipping her sleek black cybersuit with his teeth, the maharani watched him like a cockroach that had fallen in her *chaco*.

Correction, he noted glumly. *At this point in the proceedings, she isn't watching me at all.*

Instead her inscrutable eyes, narrowed in unhappy thought, were fixed at some point beyond his right shoulder. Beneath the shimmer of tawny skin, her delicate jaw was clenched and her lush mouth tight. He hadn't the first notion what she was thinking.

Which left him feeling distinctly uneasy.

This wasn't a woman he could afford to underestimate.

As though she were reading his mind—and with her Valyrian blood, she very well could be—her perceptive gaze veered to his.

"So you're the emcee who'll wield the gavel and auction me off like a pedigreed sand-runner to the highest bidder," she said, tone brittle. A statement of fact he could scarcely dispute, even if he took offense at the visual. "Have any idea how a Kryll Tombola actually works?"

He had to appreciate her ability to pinpoint unerringly his grand bargain's principal weakness. She might be reckless, this rebel maharani, but she was far from foolish.

"I signed a binding contract with your father—"

"But you haven't read the Apocrypha, have you? Certainly not all twelve volumes." Accurately deciphering his expression, she flashed him a smile bitter as quinine. "To answer your question, it's the Kryll scripture. The sacred text. And the first thing to understand about the Tombola is that it's much more than an interplanetary business transaction. Or even the biggest interstellar entertainment since my twin sister Kira's auction six years ago—a blockbuster broadcast live on every network."

That ill-timed reference to her far more compliant twin sister reminded Dex of something else about this entire affair that now left him distinctly uneasy. But he'd agreed to those terms when he signed the contract. When the war was all that mattered.

"You can safely assume I haven't read the Apocrypha. Perhaps you'll indulge me?"

Her jaw tightened. "It describes the Tombola as a sacred ritual in nauseating detail. Performed properly, it honors all Ninety-Nine Gods in the Kryll pantheon. Performed poorly, it blasphemes them. And you'd better believe my father is the faith's most fanatical disciple. So if you screw this up, space cadet, he'll have your head served on a platter with a garnish of candied figs for his midsummer banquet."

"He actually warned me to that effect." Dex shrugged. "If the Patriarch of Kryll decides to wield his ceremonial scimitar and make me a ritual sacrifice, he'll have to stand in line. But don't expect me to be losing sleep over the prospect of your father's wrath. I parry assassination attempts the way other men swat sand flies."

"Men." She sighed. "Don't flatter yourself. On Kryll, the Patriarch's considered to *be* the Ninety-Ninth God—and he's worshipped as such. To his way of thinking, he's unselfish. Omnipotent. The ender of all wars. The suppressor of all heresies. If you slip up in this Tombola gig and he declares you apostate, he won't dirty his hands wielding the blade himself." Her face tightened with old pain, smooth skin creasing between copper brows. "He'll declare a kill edict against you for dishonoring his gods. And let his faithful legions compete for the honor of bringing him your head."

Dex had lost any fear of violent death ages ago. As the Empire's seven-hundred-and-tenth First Indomitable, he was all but guaranteed one.

Men of his rank never died peacefully in their beds.

But it occurred to him now that, perhaps, a religious edict that inspired hordes of fanatical worshipers to compete for the honor of beheading him was a risk he should have considered before he signed the contract.

"Want to keep your head?" Her harsh tone spared him nothing. "The Kryll's most sacred value is neutrality. The Patriarch's divine duty, the way he sees it, is to maintain balance in the galaxy. And it's a duty he'll kill to fulfill. As his surrogate, he'll expect you to observe meticulous objectivity. Favor none of my five hundred suitors, including your Mogadon war buddies. Give everyone the same chance—including that Syndax pirate you're fuming over."

Dex clenched his teeth over an irritable retort. Before he let one of Zorin's tattooed underlings go slouching off with the gleaming circlet of the Kryll Corona in his pocket and the Kryll maharani in his bed, Dex would damn well claim her himself.

Faced with his obdurate silence, she arched a skeptical brow. "That going to be a problem for you, space cadet?"

He unclenched his jaw and clipped out, "I'll get you bedded and bred to the best bidder in seven days, never fear, precisely as I swore. If your Kryllian fanatics decide they'd fancy my head to grace your father's serving platter, I wish them joy in the attempt."

That reminder of her inexorable timeline—seven days until she submitted to the very real shackles of a Kryllian mating ritual and went in chains to a stranger's bed—stripped away her protective armor. Beneath his hands, still curved possessively around the erotic swell of her hips, her wire-thin frame vibrated with the electric charge of desperation.

Dex felt his own skin tingle in response.

"Bedded and bred." A husky quiver ran through her voice. "He hasn't told you anything, has he?"

A prickle of instinct shot up Dex's spine and tightened his arms around her. By sheer force of will, he kept his tone casual. "Some bit of fine print I missed in your Tombola contract?"

"Try an entire flipping appendix." Color rode high on her sculpted cheekbones. "I'm half Valyrian, Commander. Unlike the Kryll—or the Mogadon, apparently—for whom procreation is a mere biological impulse, any man with any woman, rutting like beasts in a field when the moons are full—it's different for Valyrians. We mate by genetic conjugation with precisely the right lover. Who's typically a lifemate, but not always. What is invariably true is that, for Valyrian women, impregnation is an act of will."

At his look of incomprehension, she pushed out an impatient breath. "A royal Tombola is only blessed as sacred—*and* permanent— once the bride gives birth to an heir to the Kryll Corona. A divine heir to wear my father's crown. It's *all* about perpetuating the royal line. My dutiful twin—a half-Kryll hybrid like me, of course—is a true believer. Just like my father. Kira's gone through four would-be consorts in six years patiently looking for her genetic match. And still no luck. So in order to *breed*, as you so gracefully put it—in order to conceive—I'd have to will it to happen.

"Which means I'd have to desire my lover."

He must've been still looking blank, because she rolled her eloquent eyes skyward for patience. "Which *means*, unless you want to void the Tombola and trigger the aforementioned kill edict, you need my consent to whomever you choose for my bed. And guess how likely I am to give it?"

"Can you possibly be trying to tell me… ?"

Dex found he couldn't bring himself to complete the sentence. The preposterous notion that the viability of his hard-won military alliance rested upon the rickety bulwark of a rebel maharani's sexual whims was too appalling.

"I'm trying to tell you negotiating the big bids is only part of your problem. Because so far, the only guy who's ever done it for me was my lifemate." An acrid smile curved her lips. "You'd better hope one of those five hundred suitors revs my engine, space cadet. Or get ready for your kill edict."

He didn't know whether he wanted to swear or shake some sense into her. If the singular way she'd just responded to his own impulsive and ill-considered advances was any indication, he would have zero difficulty igniting a sexual response from Kaia of Kryll.

Or at least, he would if she didn't despise him. And if he hadn't idiotically eliminated himself from the bidding—

"Sorry to bust in, boss."

Hearing an unapologetic mutter at his shoulder, he bristled. "Damn it to hell, Marcus! Not now."

"Afraid you'll have to tell him that yourself."

"Who?" he demanded irritably without turning.

"The Valyrian Precursor."

In his arms, Kaia went rigid. The most extraordinary farrago of emotions flitted across her expressive face. Shock, astonishment, incredulity, anger—all eclipsed by a flash of the most incandescent joy he'd ever witnessed. Beneath his hands she was quicksilver mercury. For one exceptional instant, she clung to his shoulders as though she'd collapse without his support. Dex found himself holding her up.

Holding her like he'd never let her go.

"Ben?" she breathed, a whisper of breath against his cheek.

"Hello, Kaia." The serene tenor at his shoulder plunged the jagged knife of memory right through Dex's heart and twisted. "And you as well, Dex. It's been a long time."

#

Two achingly familiar faces stared up at him—Kaia utterly transcendent, and Dex utterly appalled. If not for the gravity of this desperately unwanted mission weighing him down like a pair of maglock space boots, Valyrian Precursor Ben Nero would have laughed.

He truly hadn't known what to expect when he saw these two. The two he'd loved in his distant youth, back when he was capable of love. The two he'd left—one from duty, the other from fear. The woman he yearned always to remember—

And the man he kept trying to forget.

True to character, Dex pulled himself together with the electric swiftness of a lightning strike. Following that atomic flash of horrified recognition, the coldly correct mask of the First Indomitable shuttered his handsome face. He offered a crisp nod. "Welcome to Mogadon, Precursor. My apologies for any misunderstanding. We'd been expecting… someone else."

So that's how he wants to play this. We were more than friends that summer. We were oathsworn brothers. Until everything changed. And now we're nothing.

Except enemies.

"Entirely understandable," Nero said smoothly, sweeping his cloak aside with an ironic bow. The bow he'd give a perfect stranger. "My predecessor's barely been dead a month."

Besides which, he hadn't wanted Dex to know he was coming.

And damn if his boyhood buddy hadn't grown into one good-looking devil. Dex would be breaking hearts across the Five Sectors if he made half an effort. Except that of course, being Dex, he didn't make the effort. Because Dex made no effort that didn't advance his paramount ambition.

To command the whole galaxy.

Instead of only half of it.

"Ben?" Kaia's voice was husky with shock, but she too had snapped back, always quick-footed as a moorcat in a crisis.

She released Dex—and if Nero hadn't battened down his heart for this encounter like a cruiser caught crosswise in a sun storm, seeing the two of them wrapped in each other's arms would've given him one hell of a jolt.

Wary, she stepped forward, her beautiful face guarded and locked. And, gods of Solaris, she *was* beautiful. And strong and sleek and savvy. For half a lifetime he'd watched her grow into her exquisite appeal—but always from a distance.

Because, being half Valyrian, she'd know if he ever got close.

"How?" she breathed, wasting no words. "Ben, I thought you *died*. In the biowar."

"They missed me." Nero smoothed back a long swath of raven hair and slanted a sardonic look at Dex. "Although not for lack of trying, eh, Dex? Despite his best effort, your father missed a good twelve percent of the Valyrian population. We wanted to give Zorin a medal for killing him."

"You'd honor a man who gutted his rival like a fish in his bed?" Dex sneered. "How Valyrian."

Normally Nero would be using all his advantages to control this volatile situation. The formidable telepathic gifts he'd honed and sacrificed everything he loved to advance. The exceptional abilities that earned him his envied place in the Senate of Psychics, Valyria's ruling body. But for this encounter, he'd ensured his mental barriers were airtight. Nothing came in, and nothing went out. Otherwise they'd both be picking up thoughts he wanted kept strictly secret.

Because Kaia was his lifemate. His involuntary, irrevocable, once-in-a-lifetime psychic mate.

And Dex was Dex.

"For gods' sake, never mind about Zorin!" Kaia shook back her hair, the flashing lights of the dance floor edging her lithe frame.

He'd left her. He'd *had* to leave her.

But she was his lifemate.

Barrier or no barrier, Quorum or no Quorum, he was burning for her. It was all Nero could manage not to tumble her into his arms.

And history or no history, he still wanted to kiss the hell out of Dex. Just to prove he could. And to prove that Dex would like it. If he'd followed his instincts and kissed Dex senseless years ago, before the biowar, Nero would've been long over him by now.

Instead, Dex was the one who got away.

And Nero would always wonder if the blame for the biowar was his own.

"Gods of my father, Ben, don't just stand there like some brooding enigma!" Kaia planted hands on hips and scowled. "Talk! What in the nine unknown realms are you doing here?"

Now comes the fun part.

Grounding his barriers firmly in place with all the psychic strength at his command, Nero clasped leather-gloved hands behind his back and held her impatient gaze.

"Kaia," he said gently. Because he'd rather tear out his own heart than hurt her any more than he'd already hurt her. "My deepest condolences for the death of your sister."

And in that instant, while she stared at him blankly, he understood all over again what an utter and complete bastard Dex had become. Because he'd had Kaia in his keeping for clicks now and somehow, clearly, he still hadn't told her.

"W-what?" She fell back a step and held out a hand.

Like she could fend off the grief that was coming.

Dex shot Nero a narrow look and slid a cautious arm around Kaia's waist to brace her. And, despite the pending crisis, seeing him loom possessively over her in his trademark Mogadon manner—already claiming her every way he could, short of bidding for her in the auction himself, damn him—threatened to make Nero's cock explode.

Because watching Dex with his hands all over Kaia turned out to be one hell of a turn-on.

Gods and demons, they'd be combustible in bed. He could come just watching them.

"D-did something happen… to Kylie?" she asked in a tiny voice.

Seeing the blood drain from her face, Nero pulled his brain out of his breeches and told her quickly, "Your kid sister's fine, Kaia."

"Then… ?" She swallowed hard. *"Kira?"*

Silently Nero cursed Dex for making him the one to tell her. She idolized her twin—all the more so because Kira had made Kaia's survival a condition of her own compliance.

Kira had sacrificed her own freedom not only because she was a true fanatic who worshipped her father as a god. She'd sacrificed her freedom to secure her twin's.

And Kaia had never forgotten.

"Her cruiser was shot down three weeks ago—by Swarm spacebots," Nero said gently, meeting the mute and uncomprehending misery in her gaze. "Total disintegration, with no survivors. Your father embargoed the news to prevent political unrest."

"Kira," she whispered in a shred of her vibrant voice. Shaking hands rose to cover her shell-shocked face. "No. I don't believe it."

Even when dealt a mortal blow, she kept her weight on her feet and her head on her shoulders. He knew the instant his lifemate pulled her head together, the instant she realized Dex was holding her up—

And the instant she realized he'd known.

With excruciating care, she detached herself from Dex's touch and put several cubits of open space between them. "So *that's* why he needs me to make the Tombola. Suddenly this all makes a lot more sense."

Undoubtedly she was going to fall apart. She was going to shatter into a trillion pieces. But not anywhere her enemies could see.

"You." Her accusing gaze swung toward Dex. And even with his barriers still firmly soldered in place, the raw fury in her incendiary eyes scorched through Nero like a sulfur fire. "What possible reason could you have had for not telling me?"

Clearly resolved to salvage what little he could from this fiasco, Dex faced down her fury. "Your father felt you'd be easier to control if you thought your sister's comfort depended on your own compliance."

Despite feeling zero sympathy for the mess Dex had gotten himself into, Nero couldn't contain a wince.

"'Easier to control'?" She tilted her head to study Dex. "Is that what you're looking for?"

Before her withering stare, Dex raised a placating hand. "I realize this comes as a blow."

"You think?" Kaia swung toward him and cocked a hip. "Actually, Indomitable, *this* comes as a blow."

Out of nowhere, her furious fist shot forward and connected with his jaw.

Dex staggered back and barely kept his feet. For the second time that night, the look of stunned disbelief on his face left Nero fighting an utterly inappropriate impulse to laugh.

"You unmitigated *ass*!" she shouted. "You'd better be flipping thankful for your gods-damned taboo against weapons at an orgy. Or I would have used the sword!"

Then she was racing for the exit, fast and fleet as the Prime Class samurai she was, flinging herself into a perfect triple flip to evade the startled and utterly ineffective attempts of Dex's army of prefects to contain her.

"Go!" Dex roared at them, hair falling into his blazing eyes. "Stay with her. And don't you dare let her escape! If she ventures a single step from this compound, I'll execute every mother-loving one of you for dereliction of duty myself."

Seeing crisply contained Dex Draven so utterly undone was a sight Nero would savor in his secret soul. But Kaia desperately needed solace, and she wasn't going to accept it from Dex.

In fact, he'd be exceedingly lucky if she'd deign to accept it from Nero.

"I can't believe you didn't tell her." Nero shook his head and uttered a short laugh. "Same old Dex."

Pivoting on his booted heel, Nero launched himself in pursuit of her swiftly fleeing form.

#

Left behind by both of them, Dex stood alone on the dance floor. Master of half the known galaxy.

But, in that moment, he felt like an utter dick.

CHAPTER FIVE
The Diversion

Kaia hunched over her shot glass of Kryllian firewater at the Mogadon spaceport bar. Beyond the curving steel counter, a broad expanse of polyglass framed a rough-and-tumble view of the hangar bay, still bustling with industry well after midnight. Tucked discreetly to one side under heavy guard, her disabled cruiser stood tethered to a docking cable.

In her earlobe, the platinum lightning bolt hummed. The bolt was Valyrian tech—psi-powered—her remote link to the *Interstellar Angel*.

And she'd activated it when she gave her call sign to Dex Draven.

Overlooked in the hurly-burly as deckhands unloaded a Solarian ore freighter, the *Angel* gently drew power through the docking cable to recharge her solar generator. She'd never achieve orbit with her primary drive disabled, but the backup generator would be plenty to charge her defensive shields.

After the staggering blows she'd suffered tonight, Kaia fully intended to spend the night in her own berth on her own cruiser. Licking her wounds in private. If a single living soul on this pug-faced planet tried to stop her, they'd be sorry.

And if Dex Draven didn't like it? He could kiss her acrobatic Prime Class samurai ass.

Kira.

Numb with shock, Kaia's brain veered away from the smoking crater in her torpedoed heart. Rigid with resolve, she glared down the bar, grimy from a thousand alien hands.

And grimaced at the conspicuous circle of empty space around her.

It could be the twenty-four/seven press coverage of the auction with her image plastered all over it flashing on the midnight broadcast, under the melancholic warble of the sad-faced soprano crooning over her keyboard in the corner about lost love and last chances. It could be the uniformed goon squad with their blank-faced helmets, dispatched by her captor and stationed around her perimeter to keep her from bolting.

But she'd bet her nonexistent next paycheck it was really Dex Draven's mating scent all over her that kept the huddled masses at bay.

Just the way he wanted.

Meteors, she wasn't even Mogadon and she could smell his dark spice rising from her skin, crisp and bracing as an autumn rain.

Which, given the spectacular mood she was sporting, made her just flipping furious.

She tossed back her firewater and gasped when it seared her sinuses like magma. When her eyes stopped watering, Ben Nero was draping his tall frame gracefully over the barstool beside her.

Despite every single thing between them—the way she'd loved him, the way he'd left her, the way he'd kept his distance for nine *years* and let her believe he was dead—despite the minefield of soul-deep anger that simmered in her gut, she was glad he'd survived.

And now, despite everything, her thirsty eyes drank him in. Because ten thousand years of meticulously programmed Valyrian genetics had fashioned a thing of beauty when they fashioned him.

At seventeen he'd been tall and lanky and graceful as a girl. But nine years doing gods knew what to survive had broadened his supple shoulders under the sable cloak, stretched the tunic of deep claret across his powerful chest, and lined the long booted legs straddling his barstool with sinuous muscle. Now his sleek mane fell well past his shoulders, framing a sculpted face that would still make angels weep.

And the violet eyes, high cheekbones and succulent mouth that had driven her wild at innocent sixteen still had the same lethal impact.

She guessed he'd added the black leather gauntlets for protection, because he was a manual telepath who channeled his formidable psychic power through touch. A fist-sized amethyst pinned the cloak at his shoulder—the biggest focusing stone she'd ever seen, one only a Precursor would ever dare to wield. Hardship and grief for his dying race had etched fine brackets around his mouth that were new.

But the brooding beauty of his indolent frame was classic Nero.

Eyeing her empty glass, he caught the barkeep's eye and held up two gloved fingers. As a torrent of crystal-clear firewater arced into her glass, he murmured, "I'm sorry about Kira. Dex really should have told you."

She stiffened in her seat. Her soul hardened to stone. She still couldn't bring herself to believe her twin was truly… gone. She'd always believed if anything ever happened to Kira, she'd know. That she'd sense it. She still couldn't believe she hadn't.

But she wasn't going to talk about Kira.

Just.

Not.

Happening.

And if he didn't have his psychic and physical barriers jacked so high she'd need a catapult to get over them, he'd farking well know how she felt. The way he always used to.

"Well, *you* should have told me you weren't dead. Along with eighty-eight percent of Valyrian civilization." She didn't bother to hide her disgust. "Gods, Ben. Would it have killed you to beam me a message?"

"It was supposed to be easier," he said softly into his glass. "For both of us."

Actually, Ben, it was only easier for you.

Years of bitter recriminations burned to be spoken. But what was the point? He'd emphatically left her a year before the biowar. Just tamely accepted the Quorum of Four's unyielding judgment against their mating and walked away.

Maybe he felt he owed her nothing.

She tipped her glass and bolted the contents. She was losing track of how many she'd had, but a samurai knew how to hold her liquor.

Through the burn in her throat, she said, "Why are you here?"

A mordant smile twisted his mouth. "Believe it or not—your father sent me."

"My father?" She recoiled, then slammed down her empty glass. "For punk's sake, why? Does he expect you to bid for me yourself? That ship sailed years ago."

"Not exactly." Nero caught the barkeep's eye in a silent command to keep the firewater coming. Serene and untroubled, his liquid tenor rolled over her. "Let's just say the Patriarch's learned a few things from your twin's failed matings. And he's even learned a few things from you. He knows the only way this Tombola works is if you walk into it willingly."

"If he knew me the way you say, he'd know that's impossible," she fired back. "And if you're not here to bid, what does he want from you?"

"A counterweight," he said simply. "To Dex."

For a heartbeat, his words meant nothing. Then realization pinged through her, followed by a sickening lurch of betrayal.

"A neutral second," she whispered through lips numb with denial. "He wants you to monitor the auction."

He wants you to sell me willingly to some man I'll despise. And betray me all over again.

Apparently oblivious to her mounting fury, he kept right on talking. "Your father doesn't trust the Empire, and who could blame him? I swore to protect his interests—"

"When we bonded, you swore to protect *mine*." Beneath the unbearable strain of the past few clicks, her self-control finally shattered. Kaia snatched up her brimming glass and—

Quick as a pouncing panther, his gloved hand engulfed her wrist and pinned it to the bar. Icy liquor splashed over the rim and stung her hand. His fingers were steel, but the leather encasing them was soft as silk against her rioting pulse. The husky croon from the keyboard receded to a whisper. Her furious eyes flashed to his. That mesmerizing gaze she'd fought so hard not to meet.

Because one look into Ben Nero's fathomless amethyst eyes… and she was utterly lost.

Same as always.

Suddenly she was terrified she'd weep.

Before her desperate face, his hard grip softened. His lids dropped before she could read him. His head bowed, a sleek curtain of midnight hair slipping forward to conceal him.

And if the Valyrian Precursor didn't want to be read, a half-Kryll hybrid like Kaia wasn't reading him. Sure, she'd picked up a few parlor tricks—intermittent telepathy, crude telekinetic manipulation, an erratic and unreliable splash of foresight—during her year at the Psi Academy on Hegemon. That sun-dazzled world of silver oceans and balmy beaches where they'd met in the lagoon at moonrise.

But in this, he had no equal.

He was the pinnacle of their race.

Which would be why they'd made him Precursor. Just the way he'd always wanted.

With a sigh, he lifted her hand to his lips. The shocking heat of his mouth seared through her. The sizzling spark of contact wrung from her soul a desperate gasp of protest.

But she didn't pull free—because she couldn't. Deep down where it mattered, she'd never be free of him.

No matter how he'd betrayed her.

"You smell like Dex," he murmured, breathing her in. "His mating scent's all over you. You need to be careful with him, Kaia."

It was impossible to think with Ben Nero's mouth on her skin. That had been her whole problem before, and it hadn't gotten any easier.

She struggled to clear the firewater fumes from her head. "That sounds like a warning."

He turned her hand and nuzzled her palm.

Which made it *really* hard to focus.

"The drive to possess is a powerful genetic instinct in the Mogadon male." His warm breath licked her skin. Her nerves hummed with an electric current of raw pleasure. "Dex Draven is the supreme example. He may claim it's his duty to protect you for whoever places the winning bid. He may even believe it's true. But it's plain as an orbiting planet you've caught his eye. Watching him with his hands all over you…"

His voice went deep and his breath went ragged. "Unless you want him to void the Tombola and claim you himself, angel, you need to stop encouraging him."

"Encouraging him?" Aching over the term of endearment she'd cherished a lifetime ago—the only shred of comfort he'd left her to claim for herself when he walked—her heart exploded with outrage. "I'm *not*! He's a monster—"

"Kaia." A long slow sigh slipped through him. "If I hadn't interrupted when I did, that so-called monster would have been kissing you. And you would have been letting him. Believe me. I know how… appealing he can be."

His voice was unruffled as a monk at morning devotions. But Kaia knew him. And she knew his secrets.

Secrets he'd told only her.

"Wait a tick." Her eyes flew wide. "Is *he* the one you told me about? From the ashram?"

Against her skin, he made a dismissive noise. A never-mind noise. A classic I-don't-want-to-discuss-it noise.

A Nero noise.

Completely intrigued—and, she had to admit, titillated—she scooted her stool closer. "What did he say when you—?"

"We never discussed it."

That was Nero at his most uncommunicative, his barriers absolutely airtight. But Kaia was nowhere near dissuaded.

"You mean you just left?" She snorted. "After *that*? How typical."

He shot her a brooding look. "Dex and I are ancient history."

"How nice to be you," she said pointedly, snatching her hand free. "The one who's always leaving."

Instead of the one who gets left.

"Suffice it to say, I realize perfectly well he's damn near irresistible," Nero muttered. "But you know Valyrian genetic law as well as I do. Your mother saw to that."

No telepath could mate without the Senate's sanction, to strengthen the bloodlines and concentrate the psychic traits. Unconventional pairings did nothing for the breeding program, which was precisely why they were forbidden among the aristocracy.

Long lashes fell over his sullen gaze. "Besides which, Dex has his own hang-ups. Believe me, he was nothing but relieved when I left."

Exerting a monumental effort of will, Kaia shut down the inflammatory stream of images scrolling through her superheated brain. Images of Dex Draven and Ben Nero. Doing to each other all the things she'd seen men doing to men at the orgy. The thought of Nero, with his silken mane and sinuous grace, slithering naked to his knees before Dex...

Blast, it's getting hot in here.

She loosened her collar and cleared her throat. "I hope your seat on the Senate of Psychics was worth it."

"It was!" he fired back. "I don't regret my choices, Kaia. Not a single solitary one."

Gods save her from ambitious men.

"Look." She sighed. A crushing fatigue seeped through her like a sedative. "I've had a doozy of a day. I'm done in. If you're here about the Tombola, we can talk more tomorrow—"

"It's better if we talk now." He leaned in close, chiseled face blazing with resolve. "I have a message for you. From your father."

Her stomach lurched in a parabola of dread. Because she knew whatever the Patriarch had to tell her was nothing she wanted to hear.

But she also knew Ben Nero wouldn't give her any choice.

"This ought to be fun. What is it?"

His shuttered eyes locked on hers. "Your father fully intends to celebrate a Tombola, whether you're compliant or not. With no heir to the Kryll Corona from Kira, the survival of his dynasty requires it. He's the Ninety-Ninth God in an unbroken chain. And if you're not up for perpetuating the theocracy—he'll auction Kylie."

"Kylie?" She'd thought she was ready for anything, but her kid sister's name nearly knocked her off her barstool. "Ben, she's only *twelve*!"

"Exactly. Far too young to cause problems the way you did, running away after Hegemon and joining the damn circus."

"I ran away because he left me no other choice!" Kaia flared. *And because you'd already betrayed me.* "Besides, my sister… she can't even… she can't…"

"Breed?" Nero arched a wry brow. "He's talking injections to accelerate puberty. If she mates this season while she's too young to have a preference, he'll probably get what he wants. She'll be pregnant."

"But she'll still be *twelve*! There's no injection in the galaxy to fix that." Kaia found she was on her feet and shouting, to the considerable interest of her Mogadon goon squad. She was way past caring. "He can't possibly be serious. It's obscene!"

"You know he's serious." He too was on his feet, one hand outstretched in a futile plea for calm. "And the entire tradition's obscene. But with Kira gone, you're the prime maharani."

Her gut heaved and roiled with revulsion. Kaia felt like screaming aloud to purge it.

"I don't want the title. I've never wanted the title! Comets! You know I hate that flipping title."

"But it gives you the power to save her." Intent, he loomed over her. "Make the Tombola yourself, and Kylie's free to enjoy her own childhood and choose her own mate in her own time. That's the bargain he's offering."

Caught in the crushing vise of an ultimatum she could never escape—not if she wanted to live with herself—her overloaded circuits shut down. The bone-deep ache that lingered in her joints, a hangover from being hit with a blaster set on stun, started her head throbbing. Her legs all but buckled with exhaustion.

Turning away from her treacherous lifemate and his all-too-perceptive gaze, she staggered to the viewport and stared blindly at her tethered cruiser. Tucked neatly in a service bay with her boarding ramp lowered for inspection, the sleek silver *Angel* looked ready to fly.

Right now, she'd give ten years of her life for the freedom to board her and streak away.

Ben Nero materialized in the polyglass like the tempting demon of the Kryll Apocrypha. His sweeping cloak brushed her back and his exotic incense filled her senses, familiar as her own heartbeat. Then he was pressing something smooth and cool into her hand.

Dull with fatigue, she glanced down without comprehension at the neon blue glow leaking through her fingers.

"It's a converter for the hyperdrive on the *Angel*," he murmured, silken lips brushing her ear. A reflexive shiver skidded through her. "I think that's what's wrong with your primary propulsion. At least according to that blockhead guarding her. I can read a mind like his a hundred parsecs away."

"A bad converter, huh?" she said slowly. *Maybe and maybe not.* "And you… want me to use this? If you swore to my father, in exchange for whatever he's giving you, then why would you help me escape?"

"Pay attention, angel. I've already told you." He nuzzled her neck, and she barely swallowed a moan. His voice thickened in response. "Gods, Kaia. The only way this Tombola works is if you consent. Otherwise you'll hurl yourself against the bars of your prison—either until they break, or until you do. Your father doesn't get that, and neither does Dex. But I know you. *I know you.* With Kylie's whole future and the Kryll Corona in play, all you need is breathing room to make the right choice."

"But the guards," she said, stupid as a stump with weariness.

"All they need is a diversion." With a final searing kiss, he stepped back. "Ready?"

"Wait—"

Calmly his floating reflection peeled off a glove. A psychic wind rippled Ben Nero's black cloak and stirred the ends of his long hair. A purple glow spilled from his eyes, shifting the shadows around them to lavender.

"I said *wait* a tick, will you? Meteors, you're not even using your focusing object."

"I don't need a focusing object. Not anymore. Don't you get it?" He smiled with terrifying gentleness. "I *am* a focusing object."

Spellbound, all she could do was watch.

He opened his bare hand, palm facing up. A magenta aurora of psychic energy pulsed around his splayed fingers. Idly he turned his hand and pointed. A wall of psychic force surged from his silent form. She staggered as it rippled over her.

The Solarian freighter exploded in a roar of white heat.

All through the spaceport bar, men shot to their feet, shouting. Claxons shrieked and a mushroom cloud of flame billowed toward the hangar bay ceiling. Boots rang on steel as men scattered in every direction, yelling curses and commands.

"There's the hatch to the hangar bay." Nero spun her away from the pyrotechnic display and gave her a gentle shove. "Run."

Electrified, she stared up at his glowing eyes and the savage joy that animated his chiseled face. He was unearthly. He was more than human. He was mortal blood and mortal bone burning with all the fiery beauty of a wrathful angel.

Years ago, when he used his power he'd been frightening.

Now he was a god.

"Ben," she whispered, throat aching with unshed tears.

"*Go*, Kaia!" Voice thundering like bronze bells, he propelled her hard through the hatch that tunneled to the hangar bay, then slammed the door between them.

Kaia dragged her wits together, unsheathed her cyber saber, and ran.

CHAPTER SIX
The Prophecy

"Damage report," Dex said tersely.

"You got eighteen men and women in the stevedores' union laid up in the infirmary with burns and blunt force trauma. Four of 'em critical. Plus nine troopers sliced to ribbons by that samurai's sword. But, by some bloomin' miracle, no fatalities. *Yet.*" His *optio* hustled after Dex through the hangar bay's smoldering wreckage. "Freighter's a total loss, of course. Solarians want compensation. Lucky for us no one's dead."

"Lucky." Keeping his voice and bearing under rigid control, Dex bent to inspect a shorn docking cable. Sliced neatly in half like a knife through new moon cheese. "The maharani clearly meant to disable, not kill, and that's precisely what she achieved. Pity the bloody Precursor—" he bared his teeth "—showed no such restraint."

The charred stench of burnt flesh and the chemical tang of extinguishing agent coated his tongue with bitterness. Nearby, the fire brigade sprayed down the smoking ruins of an overturned ore cart. If that freighter had been carrying any cargo more radioactive than industrial-grade neptunium—like, say, plutonium for the smelting reactors at the planet's core—they'd need ten years and a full-time decon squad to contain the fallout.

His blood burned with a killing rage. The killing rage he'd always reserved exclusively for that traitor Zorin.

Until tonight.

Now his head throbbed with the need to enact Mogadon vengeance. But he was scrupulously careful to betray not one inkling of the erupting volcano in his head. Because they were all watching— all those would-be First Indomitables waiting in the wings. Watching to gauge his response and weighing how much it weakened him.

That infallible sixth sense—the battle sense that never failed him—was tingling.

With icy control, he praised the soot-grimed members of the fire brigade and dispatched a prefect to the barracks for a relief crew. All the while never once turning his back on the elite escort of praetorian guards who flanked him.

The ones he kept close.

But never made the mistake of trusting.

Across the hangar bay, Kaia's cruiser was long gone. Along with Kaia herself. A loss that hollowed his gut. One whose disastrous consequences he was still fighting to wrap his head around.

Unless he recovered the rebel maharani in the next few clicks, his indispensable alliance with His Holiness the Patriarch was space dust.

And there went his splendid little war. To be followed in rapid succession by his prestige, his position, and his life.

I'll be the jesting-stock of the galaxy. The running joke of the Five Sectors. Zorin will laugh himself sick.

At least until the Patriarch issues an edict for my head. Then Zorin can command his victory parade.

He felt like he'd swallowed a bowl of ground glass. Which was actually how one of his predecessors had met his agonizing end. At the hand of a vengeful consort, if memory served.

If Dex hadn't quarantined the combustible news of the maharani's flight by the simple expedient of throwing the entire Mogadon press corps into the brig, over their collective howl of protest about this gross violation of their galactic rights, they'd already be beaming out the broadcast.

He'd even unplugged the planet from the cyberverse under the flimsy guise of a security drill—a ruse he couldn't maintain for long.

Thanks to that bit of nimble thinking, Kaia wouldn't be conducting any of her daredevil exploits in the cyberverse until she cleared Mogadon airspace.

Where in the nine unknown realms is she?

"Keep scanning for the *Interstellar Angel*," he said curtly. "She can't outgun a Typhoon-class battleship, and she can't outrun a sun clipper. All we need to do is find her. Make it happen." He made a deliberate effort to unclench his fists. "And you bring Ben Nero to my ready room. You bring him right now."

His *optio* shot him a dubious look, clearly questioning the wisdom of the fight Dex was spoiling for. But Marcus finally grunted, wordless but eloquent, and trudged off to execute his orders. Flanked by his elite guard, Dex strode from the smoking wreckage of his hangar bay. Still watching the eyes and hands and blasters of his allegedly loyal men.

If he was challenged—*when* he was challenged—they'd be the likely source. He himself had risen to his current station directly from a rotation in the praetorian guard when he challenged and killed his predecessor in formal combat.

Although his fellow Indomitables on the Council would also bear watching.

Particularly the three Indomitables who'd already paid the munificence to bid for Kaia's bed.

None of them deserved her. They'd bore her to bedlam in a week. Despite his contractual commitment to neutrality, he had no intention of letting the three of them anywhere near her.

But until he recovered the runaway maharani—which he *would*— the entire explosive issue of who placed the winning bid for her bed was utterly moot.

Alone at last in the solid comfort of his ready room, a bastion of patrician order with its subdued amber lighting and dark-paneled walls, beneath the mounted head of a Mogadon cave bear snarling over the vast expanse of his well-worn desk, Dex sank into his command chair with a sigh. Weariness pulled at him like quicksand. Swinging his feet up to the desktop and crossing his booted ankles, he powered on his vid screen and called up the feed from the spaceport bar.

Although the dive-bar diva's throaty warble blotted out the audio, the visual alone told him plenty.

It told him Kaia still loved the former flame with whom she'd ignited a galactic scandal nine years ago, barely a year after he'd last seen Ben Nero himself. It told him his boyhood best friend might have abandoned her—just hightailed it for the hills when his Senate snapped its autocratic fingers—but clearly he hadn't forgotten her. It told him they'd been more than childhood sweethearts.

The powerful sexual tension that crackled between them like an electrical force field told him they'd been one hell of a pair of lovers.

Juno, he could just imagine the two of them going at it. Both so beautiful it hurt to look at them. Naked in bed together, Kaia's feline grace nibbling her way down Nero's sinuous body, her curtain of wine-red hair trailing over his sleek skin. That thermonuclear image alone, a mere figment mined from the depths of his apparently fertile imagination, was sufficient to leave him breathless and aching.

Not to mention hard as Mogadon steel.

Which was going to be a problem, wasn't it?

Staring through the vid screen at Ben Nero's sculpted beauty, all silken hair and sulky mouth and those deep purple eyes, Dex allowed himself a singular moment of one particular weakness he almost never indulged.

He let himself remember what happened that summer.

Ten years past, it felt like a lifetime. Yet he remembered the ruin of their friendship like it was yesterday. By then they'd been inseparable for three summers running, the most improbable alliance at the interracial youth ashram where senior leaders dispatched their heirs to grease the gears of galactic relations. Nero was two years younger, which should have been an eternity to boys their age. But somehow it never seemed to matter. They'd sworn to be brothers and best friends forever.

Until that summer.

It would be Dex's last at the ashram before he gained his majority and went on to grander things. He was more than ready—already a man. By then he'd killed his first man, and he was eager to bed his first woman. He'd shown up at the ashram determined to make it happen.

But then he'd seen Nero.

Valyrians matured early, both legally and physically, and his best friend had suddenly become a man himself. His voice deeper, his face harder, his lanky frame all sinewy muscle and lethal grace. They'd embraced like brothers, same as always. That hair like ebony silk caressing Dex's cheek, that scent of exotic sandalwood filling his head, the pyrophoric spark of that lean supple length grazing his violently startled body.

"Look at you, all grown up," Nero murmured, lips brushing his ear like the devil's own kiss. "Miss me?"

And from that moment, the only living soul in that ashram Dex dreamed about bedding was Nero.

He'd made damn bloody certain never to show it. The man was his oathsworn brother. Even beyond the army where his father's interdict against such liaisons reigned supreme, any Mogadon male–

male union lowered the prestige of the dominant partner, and obliterated the subordinate's status. He respected Nero too much to insult him like that.

Not to mention Dex's own father held all such unions in sneering contempt. He was crucifying soldiers who pursued them. And at that age, Dex had still been desperate to please the rabid dog.

So the sudden onset of this torrid fantasy about bedding his male best friend was more than a trifle inconvenient. He'd done his best not to think about it, not talk about it, certainly not act upon it.

Although he couldn't help dreaming about it.

Every blessed night that summer he'd woken with his cock in his hand and his best friend's name on his lips. Sticky with his own release.

While all that summer, Nero was Nero. Reckless, rakehell, scornful of the rules, everyone's favorite, far too alluring not to love. All the things Dex—the perfectionist, the introvert, the overachiever, fiercely competitive and jealous as hell—wasn't and could never be.

And all that summer, tempting as a demon and knowing it, Nero turned into an impossible tease with everyone.

Especially Dex.

And it nearly drove him mad.

He could just manage to keep his hands to himself and his mouth closed about how he felt. But Nero's careless hugs, his secret smiles, his midnight visits, his roughhouse wrestling and tickling and just general *touching* were slowly driving Dex to despair.

It was almost like he *wanted* Dex to insult him with some off-color proposition. Like he was daring Dex to do it.

They never discussed it. But hells, Nero was a telepath, wasn't he? He had to sense the explosive tension building between them.

Until that unforgettable night when Dex, restless and wakeful after his latest wet dream, snuck off to the bathhouse for another late-night cold shower. He was already inside before he realized someone else had beaten him to it.

Gods knew he'd been in no mood for company. Which meant the hiss of water on tile and the billow of steam over the shower wall would normally have driven him right back out again. Even before he heard the rhythmic gasp and slap of flesh on flesh. More than familiar, after the summer he was having, with the sound of a sexually frustrated male getting himself off, he backed silently toward the exit—

Only to hear his best friend groan Dex's name.

And then no force in the Five Sectors could have stopped him from creeping forward, mouth dry and heart pounding, to peek around the wall.

He'd been scrupulously careful all summer never to see Nero naked. Now, for all that was good and holy in the universe, he couldn't stop looking.

Slick with steamy water and ropes of sudsy soap, Nero stood braced with one hand against the wall and his dark head bent. Sinew flexing under smooth tanned skin as he stroked well over a handspan of swollen cock. Gasping, trembling, jerky with need as he neared his climax.

"Dex," he moaned. "Need you inside me so bad—oh gods—oh please—*Dex*."

Well, Dex was only human.

Feet bolted to the floor, hard enough to explode and just about having a damn heart attack, Dex heard a noise slip out of himself that sounded pretty close to a whimper of sheer yearning.

Quick as a moorcat, Nero twisted toward him, hand frozen on all that taut hard length. Through ribbons of soaked black hair, his purple eyes were startled—then smoking with sudden heat.

Dex stared into that incendiary gaze, pretty sure his mouth was hanging open, but lacking the wherewithal to do anything but gape.

"Well?" Nero's voice was husky with need and just about the sexiest sound Dex had ever heard. "Are you just going to stand there and watch?"

In that moment, Dex knew he'd lost not only the battle, but the entire infernal war. Because no power in the galaxy was going to stop him from shucking every stitch of clothing right there and—

The sudden slam of a door flying open must have made him jump three cubits in the air. Laughing and jostling, a pair of roughhousing juniors tumbled into the shower house. Dex lit out of there like a scalded sand-runner and didn't stop running until he reached his dorm.

And the next day Nero was gone.

Offworld.

Called home, someone claimed.

Apparently Dex wasn't the only one who'd embarrassed the hell out of himself that night.

Dex never saw his best friend again, and he did his damnedest never to think of him. Especially not two years later once Maximus Draven unleashed his *Valyrensis novicida*. A biological weapon insidiously engineered to target the genetically homogenous Valyrian DNA.

A weapon launched after Dex argued himself black in the face to stop it.

He'd always believed Ben Nero, his oathsworn brother, died in the biowar. Killed, in essence, by Dex's own father. And Dex had spent the past eight years obliterated by guilt, wondering what more he could possibly have done to save him—

The chime of the entry portal jerked him back to the here and now. He lowered the hand that covered his eyes and checked the monitor. Beyond the perimeter shield that warded his ready room, Ben Nero stood waiting.

Dex dragged in a ragged breath and ran a hand over his hair. After the rally, the orgy, the maharani, the explosion, and now this combustible memory, he wasn't in the mood for Ben Nero.

The Valyrian Precursor had better watch his telepathic ass with me tonight.

He punched the command to disengage the lock and growled, "Get in here."

#

"Eighteen civilians in the infirmary and my hangar bay's a bloody war zone," Dex snapped out without preamble, eyes flashing with cobalt lightning. "Give me one damn reason why I shouldn't revoke your diplomatic immunity and throw you in the brig right now."

As the door whooshed shut behind him, Nero glanced over the gleaming wood and solid comfort around him—the purely masculine den of an upper-class Mogadon male—to confirm what his senses already told him. That Dex was here alone. His eyes lingered on the oversized leather couch. Big enough for an orgy couch, and he wondered if that was how Dex used it.

Normally any fantasy that conflated the concepts of *Dex Draven* and *orgy couch* would have been one wallop of a distraction.

Tonight, being alone in a room with the real deal for the first time since that disastrous shower scene commanded his full attention.

Despite the abysmally late hour, Dex still managed to look impeccable in his tailored black jacket, jaw chiseled granite, platinum bars flashing on broad shoulders—every atom the First Indomitable. Except he'd propped his booted legs on his desk and his burnished hair was tousled.

And despite everything that stood between them now—like the small matter of the biowar and the virtual extermination of his race—Nero still ached to run his hands through that gleaming hair the way he'd always wanted.

"Well?" Dex barked. "Can't think of a reason?"

Nero pulled his head together, strolled casually to the couch, and sank into it. A placement designed to ease the tension he didn't need telepathy to feel sizzling between them.

I can think of six billion reasons. One for every Valyrian who died in the Draven biowar.

But vengeance wasn't the reason he was here. Little as he liked admitting it, another war with the Mogadon would only finish the job Dex and his dad had started.

The final extermination of his failing race.

"I'll give you three reasons," Nero murmured, voice pitched to soothe the savage Mogadon. "First, you agreed to a neutral second when you signed the Patriarch's contract. And I'm the one he sent."

"So he tells me," Dex said irritably. "I had a transmission from him before you blew up my hangar bay."

"In that case, you know throwing me into… your brig, was it?… would violate the agreement and bring down a death warrant on your indomitable head."

"I'm well aware." Dex sliced him a sharp look. "And don't try any of your telepathic flimflam with me. Perhaps you'll allow the precise terms of the Patriarch's contract seem to be somewhat irrelevant with the Patriarch's daughter *missing*? Due directly to your interference, I might add."

"Which brings me to reason number two. She's going to come back." Deliberately Nero stretched his arms across the back of the couch in a posture that projected ease.

Behind all his pomp and circumstance, Dex looked tired to the bone. Nero could sympathize, having a fairly intense longing for his own berth on the envoy ship at this hour.

"Oh, will she?" Dex arched a skeptical golden brow. "Perhaps you'll condescend to share the logic by which you leaped to that conclusion?"

"Dex." He sighed. "She's willing. Her father made sure she would be, believe me. All you need to do is wait."

"For how long?" Dex swung his feet to the floor and strode to the well-stocked liquor cabinet. "This Tombola starts in ten bloody clicks! At last tally, I have two hundred and twenty-nine suitors already on my flagship and more on the way, all panting to see her in one of those provocative gowns. And she's just put men in the infirmary breaking out of custody precisely to avoid that fate. Yet you suggest I should simply twiddle my thumbs and wait?"

"She knows the timeline as well as you do," Nero said, far more patiently than he felt. "She'll be back as soon as she wraps her head around what she needs to do. And the reason her father wanted me here is because I know her."

"Extremely well, apparently." As he splashed amber liquor into two crystal tumblers, Dex shot him a shuttered look Nero couldn't read.

Was he jealous of Nero and Kaia's shared history? Or was it only that genetic Mogadon possessiveness?

Because if it was any more than that, if Dex wanted Kaia for himself, they were going to have real trouble.

"That's why the Patriarch chose me," Nero reminded him, accepting the glass Dex managed to hand over without touching him. The peaty burn of Mogadon whiskey singed his nostrils.

Silently Nero warned himself not to touch the stuff.

A few hits of that potent brew on an empty stomach, and he'd be pouring out for his boyhood best friend any number of bitter grievances and inflammatory truths that were far better left unsaid.

Dex leaned against the desk and swirled his whiskey. With the width of the room and the whole world between them.

Nero hunkered forward, elbows on knees, glass dangling from gloved fingers. "You agreed to a neutral second—"

"I never agreed to *you*!" Dex slammed his glass on the desk so hard Nero expected the crystal to shatter. "Pluto's coldest *hell*, Ben. What in blazes did you—?"

By sheer force of will, Dex cut off the rest, but Nero heard the thought as if he'd shouted.

What in blazes did you think I was going to do? Welcome you with open arms the way I used to? After the way we—

"And stay out of my head." Curtly Dex tossed back a swallow of liquid gold. "What's the third reason?"

Nero needed a tick to remember what third reason he was supposed to be citing. Because, dogged by bone-deep exhaustion himself, Dex's high-handed rudeness was finally starting to flip him off.

Possessed by the imp of annoyance, he said coolly, "The third reason you're not going to throw me in the brig is because you couldn't hold me."

Dex uttered a short laugh. "Couldn't I?"

Their gazes locked and clashed—Dex utterly confident here on the Mogadon homeworld where he ruled like a tyrant, nominally subordinate only to the Imperator himself. Who happened to be an invalid who rarely left his *domus* at Quorum Central Starbase.

But Nero was the Precursor.

"No," Nero said softly. "You couldn't. I'm not that boy you used to wrestle anymore. But you're welcome to come over here and try if you like."

Come over here and finish what we started all those years ago. So I can finally get you out of my head.

He hadn't meant to project the thought. But he saw by the sudden flush rising on Dex's cheekbones and the hot glitter in his ice-blue eyes that he'd heard every word.

In fact, he looked remarkably like the boy he'd been years ago, the unforgettable night he stood and watched Nero get off moaning his name. And just knowing he was watching had nearly been enough to make Nero climax on the spot.

"Enough." Dex pivoted away and circled the desk. Imposing a physical barrier between them. When he sank back in his chair to confront him, the coldly correct Indomitable was back. "Why did you come here to Mogadon, Precursor? What did the Patriarch promise you that was so bloody irresistible?"

"Nothing," Nero said softly.

"Are you trying to tell me you came for Kaia? The woman you abandoned to her father's brutal mercies?" Dex's voice had roughened to a decidedly aggressive pitch. There it was again, that flash of dominance and possession.

He can't stand the thought of another man touching her, Nero realized grimly. *Which is one more way we're alike. He's all but claimed her himself—except, being Dex, he doesn't even know it.*

And he's just ensured he's the one man in the universe she can't mate.

Along with myself, of course.

Somewhere, the gods must be laughing.

"Yes, I came for Kaia. But not in the way you're thinking." Mouth twisting, Nero hunched over his glass and peered into its tawny depths. "You know prescience—foresight—is one of the Valyrian gifts. I don't have it, but others of my kin do. Thanks to them, there's a brand-new prophecy in the Senate of Psychics. A prophecy about Kaia."

Dex snorted. "Is the prophecy that she'll escape? And make me a running joke among the Syndax?"

"Gods of Solaris, I told you she's coming back." Nero tossed back his whiskey and welcomed the swirling burn in his gut. *Consequence be damned.* "The prophecy concerns her firstborn child, who will be male. Whoever she mates, whoever wins the Tombola—their son's going to rule the whole galaxy."

Dex blinked. "No one rules the whole galaxy. Except the Quorum—or so they allege. Besides which, I don't believe in prophecies, but of course you Valyrians do. And you intend to ensure that man isn't Mogadon?"

"I intend to ensure that man is a friend to Valyria." Nero leaned back and closed his eyes. "And because you're Mogadon, and I'm Valyrian, and the Patriarch fancies himself the arbiter of ultimate balance in the galaxy, he's happy to have me do it."

Gods and demons, he was exhausted. And if Dex wasn't going to allow him the basic courtesy of retiring to his own berth before dawn, he didn't mind crashing right here in the First Indomitable's ready room. Damn if there wasn't something electric about being with Dex again, despite every blasted thing between them, that made Nero feel like smiling…

"Ben, wake up. You can't sleep here."

He must have drifted off, because Dex was actually touching him. Even if only to give his shoulder a brisk shake.

Without opening his eyes, he reached up and closed his gloved hand over Dex's. Just to stop the shaking, of course.

"Where do you want me to sleep?" he murmured.

"Not. Here." *Or anywhere else I sleep.*

That was only a thought, but Nero heard it.

"Should try it," he mumbled without opening his eyes. "You might like it."

Dex laughed uncomfortably and slid his hand free. "Get up. You know I don't possess those particular proclivities."

I know nothing of the kind—

The shrill *blip* of an alarm brought Nero upright on the couch. With a short curse, Dex lifted the comm unit strapped to his wrist.

"What is it, Marcus?"

"Boss, we found the maharani. She's on her way in."

Dex clenched his fists and drilled Nero with a look of triumph. Clearly attributing Kaia's resurfacing to all that imperial effort rather than her own deliberate choice. While Nero strove mightily not to say *I told you so.*

"Where is she, *Optio?*"

"Up to her eyeballs in trouble. She's being pursued."

The news lifted Nero all the way to his feet, mind reaching by instinct for his lifemate. Almost at once he sensed her unmistakable presence. Along with an echo of panic overlaid by grim determination.

Kaia.

Ben? I, um, think I'm pretty punked.

Dex gripped the edge of his desk and scowled. "By whom? Jupiter, if this is some overeager suitor—"

"Looks like Swarm spacebots. She's losing ground pretty fast, boss."

The same way her sister died.

Nero swore and bolted for the door.

Dex was right behind him, firing orders into his wrist unit. "Send a battleship to intercept and scramble the fighters. All men to battle stations."

CHAPTER SEVEN
The Spy

Kaia gripped the yoke of her cruiser and dove straight down in a spiral that threw her back in her pilot's harness and made the *Angel*'s engine scream. Stars blurred as her twisting dive plunged through the Swarm of silver spacebots speeding toward her from every conceivable quadrant.

On every side, tiny autopiloted bots streaked by, lasers firing as she plummeted past. Her proximity sensors shrilled a constant warning of disaster she definitely didn't need. Against her starboard hull, the sickening thud of impact threw her sideways in her harness.

All along her command console, a row of crimson lights bloomed. *Hull damage.*

"Blast!" Her fingers danced across the array, shunting auxiliary power to bolster her faltering shields.

That was the problem with Swarm spacebots. A single bot was a flea bite. But a full Swarm numbered hundreds, even thousands—far too many for any cruiser to outmaneuver, especially with her hyperdrive still hinky. Even a cruiser as souped-up as the *Angel.*

Which was precisely how her sister died.

"*Interstellar Angel* to Mogadon base. I say again—does anyone copy? Because you're going to have a voided Tombola and one flipped-off First Indomitable on your hands if I don't get some quality backup here PDQ."

"This is Mogadon One. Steady on, *Angel*, we have you." Crisp and cool as a man ordering toast with his morning *chaco*, Dex Draven's commanding voice on the comm channel sent a powerful surge of relief shooting through every synapse.

Although she would've swallowed her tongue rather than admit it.

"I'm, ah, taking a little heat." *Not to mention losing both weapons and thrust.* Which led her to wonder if, in addition to peppering her with starfire, those spacebots weren't screwing with her cyber. "What've you got for me?"

"I trust a Typhoon-class battleship equipped with a full fighting wing and a sun clipper escort meets with your approval?"

The man might be permanently on her not-so-nice list for holding her hostage like some sort of felon, but she had to admit he knew how to steady a girl in a crisis. Even his bone-dry sarcasm was bracing.

"Yeah, that'll work." She pulled in a careful breath. *Gotta love a guy you can count on in a dogfight.*

"You're welcome."

"How long till your boys get here?"

"Maintain your present speed and bearing. Four ticks to intercept."

Her prox sensors blasted the alarm a breath before the next battalion of spacebots streaked into view. Acting on instinct and adrenaline, she twisted the yoke and dove hard to port, harness digging into her shoulders. The *Angel* pitched into a barrel roll that left her inverted, dizzy and breathless.

Despite every lightning reflex in the samurai playbook, an orange line of laser fire seared across her nose cone. The cruiser shuddered like a wounded falcon and her interior lights went black.

Flying in Stygian darkness, Kaia muttered, "Not good."

"What's not good?" Dex demanded. "Give me a proper status."

"Hold on a sec."

After a worrisome wait, her amber auxiliary lights flickered on. But none of the data streaming across her console was even remotely reassuring.

"Samurai." Now the First Indomitable's voice crackled with annoyance. *"Report."*

What was he going to do? Write her up for insubordination?

"They're hacking my cyber," she muttered, one hand typing out a diagnostic command. "Slowing my responses. Draining my shields. Life support's hanging by a thread. I have propulsion, but my hyperdrive's still on the fritz. And I can't jack into the cyberverse *and* keep these bots from smashing me into space dust. You want my bottom line? I'm not gonna last another four ticks."

She'd scraped through plenty of tight spots in her short but colorful life. Yet despite the benefit of all that valuable life experience, a swell of panic was drying her mouth and closing her throat.

This must have been how Kira felt with the Swarm closing in. Oh gods... Kira...

Ben Nero's smooth tenor slid through the comm link. "Sounds like you could use a copilot."

"Yeah. Remind me to hire one. With my nonexistent next paycheck."

Spotting the telltale glitter of spacebots arrowing up from below, she pulled the yoke straight back and the *Angel* shot up. The ringed indigo planet that was Mogadon's nearest neighbor swung into view, studded with still more of the flashing silver bots.

Where in the seven hells are they all coming from? How does the Swarm even get into Mogadon airspace with the whole blasted sector on battle alert without—

"Listen to me, Kaia," Nero said calmly. They were all calm as mendicant monks down there while she sweated through her cybersuit. "Jack in and fix your cyber. Dex will cover your six. And I'll fly the *Angel*."

"You?" She blurted a startled laugh. "Yeah, you're one hell of a telekinetic, but I'm halfway to Parthon right now."

"I'm not using telekinesis—just simple telepathy. I'm the Senate's strongest telepath, and you're my lifemate."

Like she could ever forget. "Meaning?"

A low chuckle rolled through the cockpit. "Meaning while you're in the cyberverse, angel, I'll be in your head."

As if the prospect of Ben Nero in her head could ever be anything but dangerous.

She hadn't even started to sort out her feelings about finding him alive and kicking instead of long dead in the biowar. He'd been silent for eight years. Left her grieving for eight years. The very least of what she felt toward him now was incinerating anger.

Until she sorted out the wreckage in her head, the last thing she needed to give Ben Nero was a front-row seat to view the damage.

"Ever flown a K-class cruiser?" she demanded.

"No, but you have. It'll be your body flying the ship—your training, your instinct. I'm just the animating intelligence while you're away."

She gaped at the comm unit. "Blast it, Ben. You're asking for one hell of a leap of faith!"

And the last time I trusted you, you walked away and left me.

Which, being her lifemate and already half inside her head, he picked up with perfect clarity.

I know I let you down before. But that's not what I'm going to do now. You can trust me. His voice in her head turned bitter. *At least, you can trust me this time.*

She'd trust him the day Kryllian sand-runners grew wings.

But she was running pretty low on options.

"Okay," she said curtly, letting him know she didn't like it. "I'm jacking in."

"You can't possibly be serious." That was Dex. Sounding skeptical, as any reasonable person would be. "Damnation, the *Inevitable* will be there in three ticks."

But she didn't have three ticks. Those bots were closing way too fast. Without her cyber or her weapons, she'd be dead. "No time to put this to a planetary vote. The *Angel*'s bleeding velocity and I'm running out of magic rabbits. It's my ship and my neck. We're doing this."

The channel between them sizzled with a frisson of blistering silence.

"After this little adventure, expect a clarifying discussion about who gives the orders in this sector," Dex growled.

Her heart was slamming against her ribs and her palms were sweating. But her skin was ice. Moving on autopilot, she caught the dangling cable swinging from her console and plugged it into the cyberjack at her temple.

Her K-class cruiser was a custom-built starship with a full-body cyberport. But without a copilot she couldn't slide out of the pilot's chair to port into the cyberverse. Which meant she'd be going in a literal ghost, a force of will without an avatar, without her full arsenal of exploits. Without being wired into a full-body cyberport the way she'd been when she first met Dex, a Prime Class samurai wasn't much more than a glorified hacker.

And any power she routed manually to triage her bleeding ship would only siphon more power from the only auxiliary systems she still had—barely—running. Including her life support.

Let's hope you can hold your breath long enough, samurai.

Because she needed to get those spacebots out of her cyber.

No matter the risk.

In the background Dex was grimly firing orders. Clearly not happy, but already assuming command of the suboptimal situation she'd given him.

Nero was in her head, a tangible presence in the cockpit, the powerful sense of his supple hands closing warmly over hers on the yoke. The ends of her hair stirred with the psychic wind of his nearness. Between her and the viewport, filled with the icy glitter of spacebots and crisscrossed with lines of laser fire, hovered the shadowy image of his uncanny beauty, hair floating around sculpted features, light spilling from ultraviolet eyes.

Go, Kaia. I've got you.

She didn't trust him. She *couldn't* trust him. Not after the way he'd walked. But right now, she had to trust him.

And hope like hell trusting him wasn't about to get her killed.

She swallowed hard. "The *Angel*'s yours. Try not to break her."

Then she closed her eyes against the starfire streaking straight toward her and dropped like a falling meteor.

Straight into cyberspace.

#

The consciousness that was Kaia shot through half a Mogadon mile of fiber optic cable in a flash. Streaks of neon light streamed past her dazzled eyes and the metallic tang of the cyberverse tingled on her bone-dry tongue.

Swimming in the *Angel*'s digital architecture, she thought, *Weapons bay.*

In an eyeblink she hovered in its shadowy confines, the whole ship transparent in her bodiless state. She saw what the *Angel* saw; her eyes were the ship's sensors. Through her shimmering hull, wings of silver spacebots zipped past in uncanny silence, lethal starfire streaming from their nozzles. The *Angel* swerved and flipped and spiraled to avoid the deadly barrage.

A nifty piece of piloting.

Even if it was her hand at the helm.

Beyond the indigo orb of the floating gas giant Parthon loomed the massive titanium bulk of a Mogadon battleship. A real monster, one of their Typhoons just like Dex had promised, deftly flanked by the billowing solar sails of two agile sun clippers. Even now, a glittering line of Zephyr-class fighters—tiny and purposeful as flying hornets—streamed from the battleship's belly.

Another few ticks and they'd be close enough to cover her six. The trick was to stay alive until they closed the distance.

Without oxygen.

"Gotta love a guy who keeps his promises," her physical body whispered on a scrap of precious breath. "I could almost start to like you, Dex Draven."

"Kaia." Nero's voice in her head made her jump. "Stop thinking about Dex and give me weapons."

"Right. Uh, sorry."

Immersed in cyberspace, she zipped for the torpedo bay. Her digital eyes absorbed the unnerving sight of the mass of glowing green cobwebs plastered over the muzzle of her psi-powered cannon.

Sealing it shut.

"Angels and asteroids," she gasped. Her chest ached for oxygen. "It's cyber, all right. I'm punked."

Around her, the ship shuddered and pitched. Her digital world plunged into impenetrable night.

"Um, Kaia," Nero said softly. "Not to rush you or anything, but it's pretty much now or never."

Floating in darkness, she triggered a system debug and whispered, "Ignite."

A flamethrower streaming with silver flame illuminated the darkness with icy light. Kaia trained her nozzle on the sickly green glow and incinerated the cobwebs to ash.

"Weapons… online," she panted, a verbal instruction to the *Angel* from the cockpit. "Release authorization… KLX-Delta."

Her psi-powered cannon hummed to life.

"That should help," Nero muttered. "But you *really* need oxygen, angel. You're drowning in carbon dioxide. If you black out, I'll lose the link."

Drowning. Not good. Kaia doused the flames and thought, *Life support.*

Light blurred around her as she streaked through the cyberverse. While Nero did his damage at the helm, the distant boom of detonations echoed through her hull.

By the time her life support materialized, the Swarm cyber had already adapted. And the vital circuits that regulated oxygen and pressurized her cockpit were crawling with chittering metal spiders.

Each hyper-aggressive arachnid the size of her head. Covered in wiry black bristles.

And they jumped.

The moment she materialized, they swarmed over the web and skittered hungrily toward her.

"Shit!"

With a yell she was back in the cockpit, anchored in her shuddering body, chills of visceral loathing crawling over clammy skin. Meanwhile her physical hands flew across the console of their own volition, arming psi-powered payloads and firing at Nero's command. All around her, bots exploded in showers of emerald sparks.

Ice rimed her windows and frost puffed from her mouth. Her chest was burning with a crushing need for air. Cabin pressure was plunging, her eardrums screaming, eyes bugging from her head. And she could barely feel her fingers.

Apparently they'd killed her climate control *and* nixed her oxygen.

"You're in the way," Nero gritted through the comm link. "I've got this. You need that life support. And you *need* to trust me."

Which, given their mutual history, was a real pisser, wasn't it?

Desperately she dove back into cyberspace and triggered the debug to spray the cobwebs with cyber fire. The critters emitted ear-piercing shrieks at deafening decibels that shot through her skull like a shower of spikes. Under her desperate barrage, the loathsome things finally curled into smoking balls and chittered into ash.

Hastily she swept charred wreckage from her circuits and toggled a set of switches. Far away, a feeble trickle of lifesaving air dribbled into the cockpit with a serpentine *siss*. Which meant she still had cyber critters somewhere, shunting most of her precious power from where she needed it most.

Her starved lungs heaved, dragging in a few molecules of precious oxygen, frantic to ease the burning ache in her chest. Cabin pressure was still plummeting. Her eyes were practically exploding in her skull.

Damn it, Dex Draven. Where's that flashy rescue?

Still linked with shipboard sensors, she peered desperately through the transparent hull into the deep space battle raging all around the *Angel*.

The Mogadon battleship *Inevitable* filled the skies like a calamity, all armored bulk and militant might, pulses of red fire streaming from a hundred ports and searing through a flying carpet of bots. Sleek gold Zephyrs sliced through the heavens in choreographed array, mowing through clusters of spacebots that managed to evade the battleship's arsenal like scythes through wheat.

Directly below her feet, the full-bellied sails of the sun clippers darted through the debris, sweeping wreckage and rogue spacebots away from the *Angel*'s exposed underbelly.

Watching the vast panoply of galactic combat play out around her in the echoing silence of interstellar space, watching armies maneuver and men die at Dex Draven's command, Kaia staggered under the sudden knowledge of this singular man's power.

From the moment they'd met, she'd done nothing but defy him. Not by design, but by instinct. At every level from the psychological to the intensely physical, something about him compelled her.

Now she knew she provoked him at her peril.

Why not admit it? Provoking him, challenging him, defying him might be essential to her own survival. But jerking the guy's chain also gave a thrill junkie like her a major adrenaline rush.

Simply stated, the man was electrifying—

"Stop thinking about Dex!" Nero snapped. "You need oxygen, and you just lost propulsion. Debug the thrust."

All that oxygen deprivation must be messing with her head. Despite the cabin's deep space chill, Kaia felt her face scorching. "Roger that."

Shoving her wayward musings about the First Indomitable into a box marked *Private* in the back attic of her brain, where she hoped like heck Nero would be polite enough not to pry, Kaia zoomed through cyberspace to the rear thrusters.

Where she found herself in a whole new world of trouble.

Because the Swarm cyber was still adapting. Now she could see the glowing strands that siphoned off her power and gummed up the works on her gear. A net of pure energy, taut and quivering, that stretched from the *Angel* all the way to the distant bot that stalked her. And instead of spiders—repulsive but at least killable—the offensive exploits tumbling down the glittering strands of cyber from the bot to her cruiser were eerily familiar.

A dozen samurai in jet and violet, sabers strapped to their backs, burgundy braids swinging as they backflipped down the lines. Fully realized avatars, glowing with gorgeous detail, dancing on empty air.

Betadroids.

I'm punked.

The singular danger of betadroids—offensive exploits designed and engineered to mirror with perfect precision her own weapons and avatar in the cyberverse—made zero sense. Not in this context. To clone a beta, you needed a fair copy of the original. An original who'd been imaged by a dendroid like the one that snapped her pic when she'd hacked into Mogadon cyberspace in her brain-damaged bid to tag Dex Draven.

So, yeah, the Mogadon had her blueprint. But how had her specs fallen into the hands of the Mogadon's mortal enemy?

Swarm spacebots in Mogadon airspace and Swarm cyber in the Mogadon grid? Looks like Dex has a spy or a traitor.

And those betas were almost aboard the *Angel*. In her weakened state, without access to a full-body cyberport, Kaia was simply no match for them.

"Ben!" she cried. "See that bot pacing us? Target it for me. Right the hell now!"

"Always happy to give you what you need."

The *Angel*'s psi-powered cannon hummed with a lurid burst of purple fire. In a spray of sparks, the bot exploded. Mouths gaping in silent screams, the samurai betas—wearing perfect replicas of Kaia's own face—tumbled soundlessly into the void and vanished.

Gone. They're gone.

But not forgotten.

Because her blueprint was out there. The Mogadon had it. The Swarm had it. For all she knew, every two-byte hacker in the Five Sectors had it.

A half-Kryll hybrid like Kaia commanded erratic foresight at best, but she had a nasty premonition those betas meant real trouble.

"Check my life support," she rasped, throat burning for oxygen. "And my thrust. Are we fixed? Or do I still have Swarm stowaways?"

Under Nero's impetus, her physical hand pushed a lever. The *Angel* hummed and exploded into hyperspeed, outpacing the swarming bots in a blink.

"You've got thrust and then some. And it looks like life support."

Kaia fell back into her body like a falling anvil and clawed the cyberjack from her throbbing temple.

Around her, the familiar confines of her cockpit crystallized. The sullen red orb of the Mogadon homeworld swelled to fill her viewport. Blessed oxygen hissed through the vents to repressurize the cabin. With a convulsive heave, her imploding lungs dragged in a head-spinning hit of pure air.

"Thanks," she panted, between deep gulps of precious breath. "Thanks for, uh, saving my bacon."

Which was way easier to say than the actual truth. *Thanks for saving my life. Thanks for not betraying me. Thanks for coming through for me.*

This time.

"Just another average, death-defying day in the life of a cyber samurai, is that right, angel?"

His barriers were jacked sky high. But with the psychic link of the lifebond still resonating between them, his acerbic tone told her more than he probably meant to project.

"That better not be judgment I hear in your voice, Ben Nero. Because you gave up any rights in that department for good a long time ago."

His tone through the comm link hardened. "You're still my lifemate. That's not a bond you just amble away from."

Which was easier for him than saying, *You'd better believe I wasn't about to lose you. Not on my watch. Which pretty much means: not ever.*

"And yet somehow you managed," she countered.

For some damn reason, he was still in her head. Which gave her the distinct impression her former lifemate was a scintilla less sanguine about her latest near-death experience than he liked to pretend.

It was a mistake to let herself believe he cared. Let herself believe he was motivated by *anything* other than the coldly political promise he'd made to her father and his stubborn sense of duty to his dying race. Let herself believe he loved her.

Those were lies she'd let herself believe before. Lies she knew in her bones were dangerous.

Gods, angel, he whispered in her head. *We really need to talk.*

Roughly she cleared her throat. "I have the helm. I'm good now. So, um, you can go."

Because the sooner Ben Nero was out of her head, the better. What with hating him and loving him and wanting him and despising him all at the same time, he didn't need any more exposure to know her head was a mess.

"I stand dismissed," he said dryly.

Like a flipping errand boy.

He might not like her latest edict, but he acceded to it like the ethical telepath he was and disentangled gently from their psychic link. She might've imagined the whisper of a sigh that brushed her cheek like a farewell kiss.

While she ran through her diagnostics and confirmed her operating status, exhaustion dragged at her leaden limbs. She'd nearly died of oxygen deprivation. And she'd barely slept since she bolted with the *Angel*. While she'd huddled in the shadow of one of Mogadon's moons, too tiny for Dex's fleet of surveillance satellites to eyeball, she'd cried herself sick for Kira.

Now she had the Tombola to face. Because she had zero intention of dooming her sole surviving sister Kylie to make the ultimate sacrifice in her place.

"Dex wants you on board the *Inevitable* five ticks ago," Nero said wryly through her comm link—a channel she vastly preferred to the intimacy of his voice in her head. "He sent his own flagship to get you. Just in case you're wondering where his head's at."

The last thing she needed was to be trapped on a Mogadon battleship, immobilized and helpless, with the Swarm coming and going from the sector at will and some spy apparently spoon-feeding them all the data they needed to stalk her.

And slaughter her.

"I have a better plan. I'm docking on the Mogadon homeworld. Same spaceport I left from. And I'm not asking for permission. He wants me back, and I'm coming."

Even to herself, she sounded sulky.

"Kaia." Nero sighed. "You can look forward to a personal interrogation from our mutual friend the moment you set foot on the planet. Right now he's a neutron bomb on a hairpin trigger—although, being him, he hides it. I wish to gods you'd stop provoking him."

I thought you wanted me to stop encouraging him. She fired off the thought like a laser to keep every living soul on the Mogadon channel from hearing her. *Isn't some charade of docile obedience just going to give him the wrong idea?*

A light flashed on her console as Nero toggled them to a private channel. She waited through his thoughtful silence. A silence that was far from typical for her quick-witted lifemate with his facile tongue.

Steady on, samurai. Probably best not to think about Ben Nero's facile tongue and what he can do with it while he's walking in and out of your head like a starbase mini-mart.

"At this point," he said at last, "I'm not sure it matters how you try to discourage him. You've more than caught his eye. After this latest death-defying stunt of yours, he's gone full-bore Mogadon."

"Meaning?" Stomach somersaulting with sudden nerves, she stared warily at her comm link.

"*Meaning* he's got six dead pilots who didn't survive your little skirmish. Six of his own who just died defending your shapely ass."

A tidal wave of remorse rolled over her. "Gods! I should have realized—"

"You intrigued him, you defied him, you escaped him—now he's killed to get you back," Nero forged on grimly. "You've flipped every switch he has. Right now every genetic instinct in Dex's Mogadon DNA is telling him to protect you. Which for a Mogadon male means to possess you."

Her tummy was still doing backflips. Because the thought of Dex Draven—protective… possessive… passionate—was more than enough to upend any girl's balance.

But he'd signed the Patriarch's contract and he valued his alliance and the war it was paying for way too much to break it. Those were Dex Draven's paramount priorities, and she'd better not forget it.

Even if the searing press of his hard body against hers turned her knees to treacle.

Stiffly she tilted her chin. "Let me assure you I have zero intent—"

Nero uttered a short laugh. "Don't even pretend you don't like it. Having him all over you. I've been in your head. Remember?"

Damn you for a meddling telepath, Ben Nero.

Her face flamed with fury. "Dex Draven may be running the Tombola, but he doesn't run *me*."

"That's not a message that's going to be well received," he said carefully. "Challenge him—fight him—and you'll only make him worse."

"Then what are you telling me to do?" she cried.

She suffered through another of those unNerolike silences.

Placate him, he finally sent, apparently unwilling to entrust this advice even to a private channel. *Keep reminding him you're safe. And make him believe it, angel. You're in his hands, he's got you, you're not going anywhere.*

"But I *am* going somewhere," she protested, too unsettled to project a clear thought. "The Tombola starts in, what, nine clicks? One of those five hundred suitors is about to buy his way into my bed. What do you want me to do about that?"

"You're the Patriarch's daughter, aren't you? The daughter of the Ninety-Ninth God in the Kryll pantheon? Maybe it's time to pray."

CHAPTER EIGHT
The Climax

The pop and flash of paparazzi cameras exploded in her face the instant the *Angel*'s hatch swung open. Squinting into a chemical billow of cooling vapor and a blinding blitzkrieg of light, Kaia barely held her ground on the exit ramp against the onslaught of shouted questions that erupted from the assembled Mogadon press.

"Maharani, what're you hunting for in a Tombola mate? You looking forward to the ritual?"

"Kaia, what's it like to see your lifemate again? Is Ben Nero here to bid?"

"Hey, Kaia, look this way! Let's have a smile for our readers at the *Kryll Caravan*."

She smiled vaguely toward the voices and a hundred shutters went *clickety-clack*.

Greatly to her discomfort.

Accustomed to living her life in the shadows, Kaia hated the press and all its attendant hubbub. Her picture-perfect twin had been a paragon and a saint for dealing with the scrutiny with her trademark unflappable poise.

It's enough to make a girl turn tail and beat it back to deep space. I'd rather face down another smack of Swarm spacebots than this circus.

Two hands emerged from the fog of cooling vapor—one cuffed in a Mogadon uniform, the other encased in a leather gauntlet. Seeing no graceful alternative, she gripped both and scrambled down to the landing bay.

Trapped between a mob of shouting press and a throng of spaceport staff, all contained by a grim cordon of helmeted Empire troopers, she glanced from Nero to Dex.

Nero she could never read, not with his barriers jacked from here to Parthon and his gloves securely in place to keep them from touching. But he *had* just watched her nearly die in deep space when the Swarm shut down her life support. Behind the dark heat in his eyes and the urgent press of his grip as he towered over her, she had the sudden staggering sense of being a breath away from kissing him.

Maybe he would've minded after all if she'd died.

It would have killed me, he whispered in her head. *I didn't leave the last time because I wanted to. Now remember what I said about Dex.*

Her gaze swung like a magnet to the First Indomitable. Only to feel his overwhelming physical impact slam through her all over again. Features controlled, uniform flawless, boots gleaming—even at weird o'clock at night. Every atom of emotion perfectly contained behind that icy composure he was famous for. But his battle-hardened grip was hot with temper and his incandescent eyes blazed with wrath.

Faced with that hurricane of barely banked fury, Nero's warning still ringing in her ears, a prudent samurai would know to keep her mouth shut.

But Kaia had never been known for being prudent.

Standing between the two of them, hands still linked, with these powerful currents of energy coursing among them, her entire body tingled with psychic voltage. She was seized by the strangest conviction: the strangest certainty of the three of them. Locked together as one against the whole flipping universe. Her soul rang like a bell with the resonance of an irrevocable bond—forged among all three of them. Anchoring them against the crushing forces of war and greed and ambition that tore the galaxy apart.

Goosed with a rush of giddy elation, Kaia cocked a hip and flashed a saucy smile. "Well, Commander, that was the obligatory escape attempt you so blithely dismissed as a threat. How'd I do?"

Beside her, Nero sighed in audible disappointment as she proceeded to ignore every damn thing he'd said. But to her utter befuddlement, Dex Draven actually laughed.

"You're not afraid of anyone, are you? Not even me. Do you know, I believe I may actually find that refreshing."

Braced for the resounding reprimand he'd all but promised her on the *Angel*—a reprimand she knew beyond doubt was still coming—Kaia found herself strangely unsettled.

And definitely off-balance.

Who knew the man could even laugh? Or look so devastatingly appealing when he did?

"I came back of my own free will," she pointed out. "I'm not a captive and I won't be treated like one."

"And I won't be given orders and ultimatums in my own Empire," he countered easily, but his eyes narrowed. "In this sector, all the orders and ultimatums come from me. The sooner you accept that fact, the easier you'll find me to live with, Kaia."

She couldn't even count the ways that comment unnerved her. She was still scrambling to compose a suitably scathing retort when his *optio* muttered something in Dex's ear and he pivoted to deal with the problem.

A soft sigh of relief slipped through her.

But instead of releasing her, Dex slid an arm around her waist, holding her at his side as casually as if she belonged nowhere else. Suddenly she couldn't seem to breathe. In the drafty chill of the hangar bay, the vital heat of his self-contained strength engulfed her.

"I see you still like living dangerously," Nero murmured. "Don't say I didn't warn you."

And there was the press corps madly snapping away as she stood practically in the First Indomitable's embrace. Under that buttoned-tight jacket, he was solid muscle. And she found it *really* inconvenient, the way tingling lassitude seeped through her limbs and slow heat built in her core every single time he touched her.

It's the pheromones, she reminded herself. *The Mogadon male is genetically designed to turn a girl on.*

Even though the only Mogadon male who seemed to have this effect on her was Dex.

She shivered against him and tried edging away, but his hand tightened in warning and drew her closer as he just kept on talking. Tucking her possessively right up against his hard heat.

To her sudden consternation, she found herself blushing.

Gods of the nine realms, what must they look like to the cameras?

Nothing like a ward and her Tombola master. Not with his hands all over you, angel.

"Maharani, Hector from the *Mogadon Hammer*!" an intense young man with spectacles shouted. "Any thoughts on the First Indomitable? Is he the Tombola master you wanted?"

Among the barrage of questions bombarding her, this one she decided to answer.

"I'm fully confident the First Indomitable will discharge his duties with meticulous precision," she said pointedly. "As you can see, he's very… protective."

"Careful, Kaia." Dex turned his head to murmur in her ear, warm breath sliding over her skin. "Unless you want me telling the press precisely how I feel about *you*."

All of which only made the tingling heat between her thighs spread through her whole body like a fatal case of desert fever. Gods, what was wrong with her?

Encouraged by her reply, an impudent urchin with curly red hair and a microphone pushed in. "Hey, samurai, any statement on *our* recent incarceration? Will you take a stand for freedom of the press?"

Beside her, Dex snorted and pivoted away, drawing Kaia with him.

Again she tried subtly without success to slip out of his deeply disturbing embrace. "You incarcerated them? The interstellar press? What, in your brig?"

Still flanking her, Nero made a disapproving noise. "Tsk, Dex, that's not very citizen-like. What about their galactic rights?"

"Hang their galactic rights," Dex said curtly. "They're a security threat and a nuisance. They're exceptionally lucky I didn't leave them all down there to rot."

"Spoken like a true dictator," Kaia murmured.

With Nero you could never be sure, but she thought he was hiding a grin.

Now the whole kit and kaboodle were streaming after them, the press shouting questions, the troopers bullying and herding, a dozen prefects trotting after Dex with tablets and harried expressions as they angled to catch his minatory eye.

At the exit, Dex pivoted to face them all down and pitched his voice to slice through the bedlam.

"The maharani won't be taking any more questions. And neither will I. My staff will issue a press release tomorrow at twelve hundred clicks. You're dismissed."

Over a collective howl of protest, he ushered Kaia into a narrow utility corridor, while the troopers kept the clamoring mob at bay.

When Nero slipped in after them, Dex spun sharply on his booted heel to block him.

"Precursor, we'll say good night," he bit out, every biochemical signal in his Mogadon makeup flashing electric with danger. "I do believe you've done quite enough damage to this compound for one night."

Nero's eyes went insolent with mockery. "Sorry about the mess in your hangar bay, Indomitable."

Dex's nostrils flared. Color climbed his corded throat. With her heightened hybrid senses, Kaia could all but see sparks flame and leap between the two men.

But faced with a wall of scowling Mogadon muscle poised to enforce Dex's every edict, Nero swept them both an ironic bow and melted diplomatically away.

While Kaia told herself she was glad to see him go.

Good luck handling him, her lifemate whispered in her head. *He's torqued pretty tight. Call me if you need me. You know I'll hear.*

"Don't hold your breath," she muttered.

Ben Nero might have just saved her sassafras, but you didn't erase nine years of betrayal in a night.

His elite guard flanking them front and rear, Dex propelled her along at a dizzying clip.

One of his hovering hangers-on dared to edge up alongside. "Sir, an update on the Syndax—"

"Centurion," Dex said grimly. "I've been on my feet for the past twenty-two clicks. I'm hitting my rack for the next four and I don't want to be disturbed even if the bloody Syndax invade, overrun this planet, and butcher us all in our beds. Do I make myself clear?"

The lackey paled and beat a prudent retreat.

Kaia had to admit a few clicks of rack time sounded heavenly. She could barely keep pace as Dex charged down the corridor, but the bracing energy of his arm around her kept her motivated.

"Almost there," he murmured, as if he could read her mind.

Or maybe she was projecting her thoughts at him, the way she did sometimes by accident when she was dead on her feet.

Although usually—given her telepathic limitations—she could only share thoughts with someone for whom she felt a strong connection. Which, if it turned out genocidal tyrant Dex Draven of all men in the galaxy was able to read her mind, would be a towering irony.

"Yeah, about that." She made a valiant effort to pull her head together. "Where exactly are we going? Because my berth's on the *Angel*."

His embracing arm hardened to steel.

She had no earthly clue how he managed it, being barely taller than she and armed with no obvious weapon but a blaster. Yet suddenly he was looming over her in that relentlessly possessive, utterly territorial Mogadon manner.

"Allow me to offer you a bit of direction."

She shot him a wary glance. "As my Tombola master?"

"As the supreme military commander of this planet and indeed the entire sector. The odds I'll allow you to set foot on the ship you just used for an unauthorized pleasure junket that nearly got you killed are precisely zero. As are the odds of letting you out of my sight with Swarm spacebots apparently stalking your entire family and some bloody Syndax pirate lurking in orbit just waiting for the chance to get his hands on you."

Damn if he didn't know how to get her back up.

"Let me remind you I'm here by *choice*," she fired back. "That means I make my own decisions. And I have a few orders and ultimatums of my own to lay down about how this Tombola's going to work. You don't own me, Dex Draven. And if you intend to keep me—and keep your precious alliance with my father—you'd better stop pushing me around."

Which was exactly what Nero had told her not to say, with the First Indomitable already going hardcore Mogadon on her ass. But the ritual was about to start, and it flat out needed to be said.

He jerked her to a halt and she spun to face him. His face was a study in ironclad control, but his gaze flashed with lightning.

He spoke with ominous softness.

"I do believe it's time for that clarifying discussion."

"Bring it on," she purred, spoiling for a fight.

He planted a palm against the wall panel. The door behind her shot open with a hiss.

He fired his next barrage of commands at their escort. "I want a four-man post on this door at all times. Make it happen. And I don't want to be disturbed."

"Ah, about the Syndax…" some valiant soul attempted.

"To be perfectly clear, the next man who comes through this door with anything less than a planet-wide emergency gets my blaster fired point-blank at his chest."

In the terrified silence that ensued, Dex gripped Kaia's arm and propelled her none too gently through the door. She slid free and strode in under her own steam.

Only to jerk to a confused halt as the door shot shut behind them.

She wasn't sure where she'd expected to be, but she definitely *hadn't* expected to find herself in a certain someone's deeply masculine living quarters. Dominated by dark wood, subdued light, gleaming leather, a massive bookcase filled with gleaming rows of antique tomes—and what had to be the biggest orgy couch on the planet.

"Um, ah, are these… your quarters?" she stammered.

"You're very perceptive."

Unbuttoning his jacket, Dex strode straight to the liquor cabinet that stood beside a curving wall of polyglass and a vast landscape of Mogadon night. A slice of turquoise moon and the ghostly shadow of three others floated low in the starry heavens.

As he passed the orgy couch, he dropped his jacket neatly over it. Leaving him clad in those form-fitting boots and trousers and some sort of black shirt that clung to the broad shoulders and powerful back his uniform worked hard to conceal.

"What are you doing?" she almost yelped.

"Getting comfortable. I've been wearing that damn uniform all day." Splashing tawny liquid into a pair of heavy tumblers, he sliced her an oblique look. "Assuming you've no objection?"

In fact, she objected violently to him undressing in any way whatsoever in her presence. But she couldn't figure out how to say so without sounding way too aware of him. And way too affected.

Which, of course, she was.

"Well?"

With a start, she realized he was actually waiting for her concurrence. All the while eyeing her as though he were far too aware of everything she wasn't saying.

She paced to the window to stare out without seeing the impenetrable Mogadon night. Somewhere beyond the reinforced glass, coated with anti-radiation polymer, lurked the damaged reactor whose meltdown eight years ago had driven the capital city's denizens underground, except for critical short-term stints, until the worst of the radionuclides decayed.

"As you yourself just observed, it's late." She sighed. "I need to ensure we're clear on my own conditions for participating in this obscene charade of a mating ritual before we go to bed."

"By all means," he murmured. "I'm all for clarity on your conditions before we go to bed."

She wanted to swallow her own tongue.

Diabolical man. He knows perfectly well that's the last thing I want.

The very last.

Face scorching with blistering heat, she accepted the glass without meeting his piercing gaze and took a hasty gulp of reactor-fermented Mogadon whiskey. The sweet fire of smoke and caramel seeped through her and loosened the knot of tension she was toting in her tummy.

They said a little radioactivity was responsible for the whiskey's potent kick. By the time she finished hers, she'd probably be glowing in the dark.

"My first condition is I wear what I want. No Tombola gowns. And *no* public viewings." The televised nudity of a Tombola bride during the ceremonial public viewing was an outright insult and categorically off the table, and she wanted him to know it.

"That will be a crushing disappointment for billions." Dex tossed back a swallow of liquid gold and unbuckled his belt.

Kaia's mouth went dry.

Calmly he settled the belt with his holstered blaster on a table in easy reach.

Gods of my father, how much more is he planning to take off?

Dex settled into the orgy couch with a soft exhalation of relief. "What else?"

With difficulty, she gathered her scattered thoughts. "I get to review all the bids. I want to know who's offering what and the conditions they want in the contract."

"That sounds reasonable."

He sounded reasonable—suspiciously so. Then he tugged his

collar open, and that searing sight of corded sinew and sun-bronzed throat distracted her all over again. "Anything else?"

She guzzled whiskey in a futile bid to wet her whistle. "I get a veto on anyone you—"

"Would you mind?" Stretching his booted legs before him, Dex hoisted his brows. "The boots? Otherwise I'll be obliged to summon a prefect. Then they'll all be in here with their tablets and briefings and crises."

Was he toying with her? The last thing she wanted to do was touch him, and he damn well had to know it. But his face was an impeccable study in courteous query as he waited with lifted brows for her reply.

"Fine," she said shortly. "Don't get used to it."

She tipped down a hefty slug of radioactive whiskey for fortitude and approached him warily, like the apex predator he was.

Watching him watch her through hooded eyes.

As she closed the distance between them, the air between their bodies seemed to heat. Struggling to control her face and steady her breathing, she folded to kneel before him.

Leaning in, eyes sedulously averted from the sinewed length of his thighs or anywhere else in that alarming vicinity, she gripped his boot in gingerly hands and started easing it off. This close to his dangerous orbit, the dark spice of his body invaded her nervous system. She let her hair fall forward to curtain her face.

On the couch, he pulled in a slow breath. His voice deepened to a timbre replete with masculine satisfaction.

"You smell like me."

Carefully she cleared her throat. "I thought that was the whole point. To keep your Mogadon sidekicks off me until we finish the ritual."

"Oh, I most definitely intend to keep them off you. All bloody five hundred of them. You can rely on me entirely for that."

Between the rough rasp of his voice and the wicked heat of his body and the inflammatory fact that she was basically kneeling between his legs to pull off his blasted boots—never mind how the hells she'd wound up in the position of undressing the man anyway— she just couldn't seem to catch her breath.

And she'd have to be blind not to notice from this superior vantage that the supreme commander of the Mogadon Empire was indomitable in more than name. If she got any closer to that impressive bulge between his legs, she was going to—

"Tombolas can be violent," she said breathlessly, setting one boot aside and turning to the other, hair still screening her face. "All that testosterone. Sometimes they turn into bloodbaths."

"I'm fully qualified to handle a bloodbath. It's a job requirement for First Indomitables."

She slanted an upward glance through her hair and found him grinning like the very devil. Not to mention sprawled way too comfortably on that orgy couch. It was far too easy to imagine herself crawling sinuously up the length of his body and unzipping his—

Barely in time, she brought that train of thought to a screeching halt.

Tugging his boot free, she said crossly, "Why are you smiling like that?"

"Just enjoying the view," he murmured, gaze sliding over her kneeling body, lingering on the curves encased in her cybersuit until she thought she'd go supernova. "And wondering if you've any idea quite how many of those mouthwatering mental musings you're projecting at me."

With a gasp of transcendent horror, she shot to her feet. He surged up to meet her, one hand locking around her utility belt to rivet her in place. With barely a handspan of open air between them, she stared straight into his blazing eyes. Her skin sizzled with shocking heat.

"Don't run away," he breathed. "I assure you the feeling is more than mutual. Enough so that I find myself resenting the hell out of this Tombola."

Her entire body was tingling with the electrical charge of his nearness. And that hot ache between her thighs made it *really* hard not to sway toward him and find out once and for all what it felt like to kiss him.

"Hold on a tick." She planted a warding hand on his broad chest. Which only made her hotter. "Let's not misinterpret what this is."

He tilted his burnished head to study her. "And what precisely do you interpret this to be? I'm genuinely curious to learn your theory."

"Well, obviously it's the pheromones! And it's not just some academic theory. Can't you… sort of… turn it down a few notches?"

His eyes narrowed dangerously. "Point A—it's involuntary reflex. So, no, I can't 'turn it down.' And point B—what you're feeling for me isn't some autonomic chemical reaction and I'm damned offended to hear you think so."

"I'm just being honest with you, Dex. Because for as long as I can remember, the only guy I've ever wanted in my bed was Nero."

She wasn't sure whether it was this injudicious reference to her lifemate or the fact she'd slipped up and said Dex's name like they were already intimate. But whatever it was pushed him hard over the edge.

He dragged her into his arms with a growl. "Let's see how I compare."

Heart thundering in her ears, she collided with the hard expanse of his chest and grabbed his powerful shoulders to stay upright. His hand closed around the back of her head to hold her steady. And when he leaned in to kiss her, by the Ninety-Nine Gods, she could only close her eyes and shudder.

The hot commanding press of his kiss sizzled through every synapse. That flare of intimate contact sent heat streaking through her like a cosmic ray bombardment. She sucked in a startled breath and clutched his shoulders in imminent mutiny. But the graze of his teeth against the tender curve of her lower lip made her breath rush out in a whimper that shocked all seven hells out of her.

He growled in response—the purely carnal aggression of a predator claiming his mate. His tongue dipped into her breathless mouth. And she gave way to the most potent blind instinct she'd ever felt in her life and leaned into his kiss.

She moaned under the molten slide of his tongue. He tasted like fire laced with caramel. He smelled like a scenting lion. The chemical thrill of his mating scent flooded through her and made her head spin. A shiver of surrender slid out and a flash of fire leaped between them. To ignite the inferno of barely contained sexual violence that had been simmering between them from the moment they'd met.

He kissed her the way he must kill men in combat—with utter authority, utter conviction, and utter determination to overcome all resistance.

He kissed her the way only one other man had *ever* kissed her.

Gods of the nine unknown realms, the way he kissed her.

And all she could possibly do in the face of this overwhelming onslaught on every sense and synapse she possessed was cling breathless to his shoulders while the world revolved around her and meet him kiss for frenzied kiss.

"Say my name," he groaned against her mouth.

"Dex," she breathed, swaying on her feet.

Nine years of near abstinence had left her flabbergasted and flat-out defenseless against this tidal wave of need.

Between deep drugging kisses that made her head whirl, his hard hands curled intimately around her hips and eased her against the straining heat beneath his trousers.

The electric sizzle of all that heat slammed through her. She voiced a throaty moan and writhed against him. Chasing something that hovered just beyond reach. Frantic to fill the vortex of aching need that sucked her under and drove her to clutch him harder.

"Gods, Kaia." He held her steady and gave her what she needed— the steady roll of his hips against hers. "Whatever comes of this infernal ritual, tell me I'm the only man you want in your bed."

"Mmmm," she agreed without thinking, turning her face into his sinewed throat and licking his salty heat and feeling him rumble with pleasure. His predatory scent was all over her and she loved it. "You and Ben."

Beneath her hands and mouth, he froze.

"Not together, I mean," she blundered, ducking her face against his shoulder. "Unless, um, you wanted that?"

He entertained an interesting silence, while his hand massaged the back of her neck. "That's what you think I want, do you?"

"Based on what I saw at the orgy tonight, it would be pretty typical for a Mogadon, wouldn't it?"

"Not this Mogadon, I assure you," he said grimly.

She wasn't sure she believed him. Until he eased her thighs wider and resumed the devastating thrust and rhythm through both their clothes that was slowly driving her insane.

"Although watching him make you come…" he rasped, breath heavy in her ear. "Watching you make *him* come… fancying you'll do the same for me… for that I'd pay real money. What are my chances?"

"Not good." She gasped out a startled laugh. "Ben and I are history."

"Are you really?" he whispered.

Her head snapped up from his shoulder, an indignant protest

bubbling to her lips. Hot and hard and hungry, his mouth fused with hers, stealing her soul all over again.

But the searing image his words evoked, coupled with the steady thrust of his rigid cock against her core, was making her brain go thermonuclear.

To say nothing of the rest of her.

In ways no guy had made her so much as quiver for years.

If she ever had both of them together—Dex and Nero—the way he was describing, she was pretty sure she'd spontaneously combust. Just thinking about it now was enough to… comets, was she *really* going to… ?

"Dex," she panted, clawing at him. "Oh gods, I think I'm… don't… don't stop—"

"Not stopping," he muttered into her mouth, "until I make you come."

She moaned into his words, her breath mingling with his. After all those endless years of feeling nothing, she didn't think she'd ever needed to come so badly. She was one vast chasm of naked need.

"Then we're going to do this all over again," he promised darkly. "In a proper bed. Repeatedly. Without these infernal clothes."

She fought like blazes to clear her head. He was her Tombola master, not an amorous suitor. And she'd promised… she'd promised…

"We can't!" she managed to gasp. "Can't do that—oh gods, Dex—please—"

"That's it," he urged with tender violence. The kinetic jolt of friction seared through her cybersuit against her soaked and aching core. "Let me hear you beg for me."

She never begged for anything. Which made this singular moment of utter surrender all the more shocking.

"Please—I need—*more*—more of you—"

"Darling." Her needy whimper wrenched a hoarse groan from his chest. "I'm going to give you everything you've ever needed. And that's a bloody promise."

The buzz of the comm unit barely registered, but it just kept on buzzing. Still devouring her with his mouth, he slid his hands beneath her thighs and lifted her effortlessly, backing her against the wall beside the door.

If only… he doesn't stop… I'm so… so close…

As the comm unit buzzed insistently away, he freed one hand to fumble the unit up and slam it back down. Ending the interruption by the simple expedient of hanging up on the caller.

If Kaia weren't hovering on the very brink of either the world's most explosive orgasm or a fatal heart attack—or both—she would've laughed.

Instead she clutched the muscled bulge of his spectacular derrière and rode him, head falling back against the wall, rhythmic cries spilling from her lips.

The unit buzzed again, this time right beside her head. Dex cursed savagely and yanked the wire from its socket. She caught a blurred glimpse of his face, brutal with need, tawny hair falling over his burning gaze, locked onto hers like nothing else in the galaxy would ever matter.

"I've got you," he gasped, driving into her. "Kaia… I'm dying here… I *need*—"

"Yes." She panted under the prod of her own raw need. "Do it—I want you to—it's just—we can't—"

The unit's incessant intrusion was replaced by the brisk rap of knuckles on the door.

"A thousand pardons, Indomitable." A mannerly voice intruded. "Your comm unit's malfunctioning. The Syndax leader Zorin—"

"Not now, damn it!" Dex snarled. "One more blasted word and I swear I'll vent the lot of you into space."

The threat that he would stop, that they would stop before she got where she was dying to go, was the nudge that finally drove her over the edge. A cataclysmic physical force poured through her like an avalanche.

She whirled apart into a million molecular particles and disintegrated.

Barely aware as she cried out to the heavens that he pressed a hand over her mouth to give her the only privacy possible from whatever lackey was lurking six cubits away.

Spent, shaking, shattered, she collapsed against Dex. Utterly undone, with all her defenses decimated. With tears of gratitude spilling from her eyes. Because it turned out it *wasn't* only Ben Nero, the man she'd been mourning for millennia, who could bring her to this pinnacle of pleasure.

She'd thought herself resigned never to feeling this way again. Until tonight.

Against her Dex too was shaking, arms clasping her in a desperate grip. Face pressed into her sweat-slick neck. Still hard to the point of bursting against the soft pulsing aftershocks at her core—holding onto the explosive force of his own release by his fingernails. Even after she'd given him permission to let go.

And the thought that they could just keep doing this—that he was willing and more than ready to blow every circuit she had—made her ache with impossible yearning.

A yearning that was downright dangerous. Because as far as the Patriarch was concerned, what she was doing here with Dex was blasphemy.

A defilement of Kryll's most sacred ritual.

To save little Kylie, the way her twin had saved *her*, Kaia needed to be falling for a man who wasn't her Tombola master.

Not to mention that promise she'd made her mother. The promise that kept every guy in the galaxy out of her pants.

"I trust," Dex panted against her skin, "we've decisively laid to rest… the question of whether I can… make you come. Speaking for myself, there was never a shred of doubt."

"I… I really don't understand… what just happened," she whispered, her voice stripped raw. "It's been a really long time since I…" She pulled in a shaking breath and gathered up the rubble of her shattered resolve. "Dex. You need to hear me when I say this. What we just did? This can *never* happen again."

CHAPTER NINE
The Ascent

It appeared his splendid little war was going rather badly.

Dex stood near the panoramic viewport of his living quarters, gripping a tablet of disastrous dispatches from the front, and watched the comet Chiron sear its smoldering score across the star-strewn heavens. In the north, above the jagged silhouette of the Mogadon mountains, the sky was paling to silver. Soon dawn would be upon him, and with it the day's unrelenting litany of demands.

All too clearly, he needed to be in the field, personally commanding the fleet combing the far reaches of the Omega Sector in a futile bid to corner that elusive traitor Zorin and compel him to combat.

The same fleet that had just lost a battleship to a Syndax ambush. The first engagement of the war—a hit-and-run commando raid that played to all the pirates' strengths.

And Zorin was the victor.

That bastard had captured his battleship.

"Damn you to hell," he said softly into the darkness. "Damn you, Zorin, for a coward and a snake."

Somewhere in the far reaches of space, that bloody-minded bugger was laughing at him. While the pirates' brutal raids on the outer colonies intensified. To say nothing of the unspeakable atrocities committed by Zorin's Swarm allies on helpless civilians.

Meanwhile, instead of restoring the virtues of the Pax Mogadon to the long-suffering colonies as duty demanded, Dex was trapped in the Alpha Sector for the next seven days running the Kryll maharani's mating ritual.

While every subatomic particle in his molecular makeup demanded he keep the Kryll maharani for himself.

"Which, if you do," he whispered, "will trigger a kill edict. And unleash the Patriarch's faithful hounds to compete for the honor of bringing him your head."

Think with what's in your head, soldier. Not what's between your legs.

Not to mention the infuriating fact that Kaia herself professed the most profound determination to keep him permanently at a distance. Which confused and confounded the devil out of him, given the gorgeous way she'd climaxed in his arms—her lush mouth breathless and gasping with passion, her supple form writhing and desperate with need, her expressive face flushed and transcendent with rapture—in that singular moment of her surrender.

A surrender she seemed hellbent never to repeat.

All of which amounted to one towering frustration.

And, for Dex, a sleepless night.

For the hundredth time, he scowled across the moonlit expanse of his quarters at the closed door of his bedroom. This time, he gave in to the elemental impulse he was bloody damn sick of fighting. Bare feet soundless on the silicon floor, he tossed aside his tablet of disasters and prowled across the room in his sleeping trousers. Deliberately he laid a hand on the biometric panel that warded his perimeter.

Softly the bedroom door *shussed* open.

Dex padded in, and the door whispered shut. He stood still in the darkness while his pupils dilated and his skin tingled.

At least tonight she was safe. He'd made damn certain she was safe. Of course she'd resisted, but he'd blasted well insisted.

Now every masculine instinct he possessed was roaring with satisfaction that Kaia slept in his bed. Even if he himself had been firmly relegated to the orgy couch next door.

Around him, the familiar contours of his bedroom took shape, shrouded in velvet night. The maharani lay in a blanket of lavender moonlight, nestled slim and graceful as a sylph under a snow lion's silvery pelt against the cold Mogadon night, one naked arm flung with abandon overhead. Her hair spread in a crimson tangle across his pillow, framing her delicate cheekbones and stubborn jaw.

Even in sleep, her brow furrowed in a troubled frown.

Dex breathed in deep, filling his senses with the sultry sweetness of night-blooming jasmine and the bracing tang of ozone from the cyberverse that rose from her tawny skin. Unmistakably laced with the predatory musk of his own mating scent.

His fists clenched with savage possession.

While she smells so indubitably like me, no Mogadon male who wants to keep breathing is going to come within ten cubits of her. Tombola or no Tombola.

And I intend to make bloody certain she keeps smelling like me.

Standing over her in the darkness, alone with the churn of his thoughts and the object of his obsession, his cock tight to bursting with sexual frustration and his chest tight to splitting with impossible need, Dex admitted in the privacy of his own inner sanctum that he wanted her for himself.

He wanted her sleeping in his bed, wearing his clothes and the treasures he gave her, mouthy and maddening and impossibly gorgeous on his arm at the endless parade of saturnalias and councils and gladiatorial games his status now demanded he attend. He wanted her crying his name deep in the night. He wanted her mindless and gasping with pleasure when he climaxed deep inside her.

And he had precisely seven days to talk himself out of the sheer suicidal idiocy of every damn thing he wanted before he was oathbound to hand her over to another man's keeping.

Seven days to get the rebel samurai—the interstellar scandal, the prime maharani and unconventional heir to the Kryll Corona—out of his head.

Seven days to convince himself, against the powerful pull of every genetic Mogadon instinct he possessed, to hand over the woman he wanted for himself to the strongest possible rival. Someone strong enough to keep her safe despite her reckless spirit and impulsive instincts and disastrous choices while the galaxy went up in flames around them.

But for the next seven days, a treacherous voice whispered in his head like a succubus, *no other man can touch her. For the next seven days, she's yours.*

Yours and Nero's.

Nero with his secret smile, his mocking whisper, his sultry eyes that always looked as though he knew exactly what Dex fantasized about doing to him. Which, being officially the galaxy's most powerful telepath, he undoubtedly *did.* And what the hells had Dex been thinking, telling Kaia what he dreamed about watching her do with Nero? And why the hells had she looked so infernally intrigued by the notion? She wasn't even Mogadon, yet despite her flustered protest, she seemed almost willing to entertain the incendiary idea of having them both.

Well, luckily for Dex, he was the galaxy's foremost expert at not thinking about Ben Nero. He'd had ten years' practice to perfect that skill.

He deployed it now with ruthless resolve.

Tight in the grip of a troubled sleep, Kaia moaned and thrashed in his sheets. Fighting every molecule of protective instinct he possessed, Dex resisted the overwhelming urge to shuck the trousers tented over his ferocious erection and crawl into bed beside her. Even if only to fold her tight against his strength and keep her safe from the Swarm and the Syndax and her fanatical father and especially her own catastrophic instincts.

Even asleep, she was half Valyrian and a telepath. He hadn't an electron of psychic ability, but for some damn reason she seemed to have no trouble at all getting inside his head. No more trouble, for that matter, than Nero himself seemed to have. Now, as if sensing his turbulent thoughts, she whimpered in her sleep.

"Easy, samurai," he breathed, a scrap of sound in the night. "I've got you. I swear by all the gods I've got you."

And I doubt very much it's going to be easy letting you go.

She sighed and settled into stillness.

Sleeping a wink on the orgy couch was all too plainly out of the question.

Pushing out a breath of frustrated acknowledgment, he stalked to the window seat that overlooked the bed and crawled onto it. Frigid air seeped through the viewport to nip his naked torso, but he'd slept in far worse places. Giving himself a clear view of the door and the maharani's sleeping form, he wadded a cushion under his head and willed the straining fullness in his trousers to subside.

Eased by the ebb and flow of her breath, Dex finally felt his lids grow heavy.

But sleep proved a dream as elusive as peace.

#

Psi fire burned until extinguished by its architect, and Nero didn't find himself in the mood. Wrathfully he stalked through the smoking ruin of the neptunium ore freighter—sluggish flames still flickering twelve clicks later—with cloak billowing in his wake.

Positively enjoying the way those swaggering Mogadon machos fell over their own big feet scrambling to stay out of his way.

Let them fear me. Let them regret they didn't finish the job and wipe us all out years ago. For five piddling creds I'd blow this entire Mogadon planet sky high, along with the Mogadon scientists and the Mogadon fleet and the whole Mogadon race.

Including Dex.

If the genocidal Draven biowar against his whole race weren't reason enough to be wrathful, he was still reeling under the revelation that his boyhood best friend had apparently just consummated all that sizzling chemistry that simmered between Dex and Kaia.

Nero's own lifemate.

A development Dex had to know couldn't fail to capture Nero's complete telepathic attention from anything less than a parsec away.

Never mind the long-lamented truth that Kaia had never let Nero properly consummate their own consuming passion way back when. Or the irrefutable fact that she'd rather make love with a rabid sand-runner these days than welcome Nero to her bed. Or even the fact that Nero himself was no more free to take a hybrid consort now than he'd ever been.

The fact that she and Dex were getting physical—without Nero—was more than sufficient to trigger his foul temper.

Well, why not admit it—at least to himself? He was jealous. He was jealous as all seven hells.

He was jealous of them both.

Before him heaved the pitch of ungodly turmoil Dex could command so effortlessly. His praetorian guard swarmed around a Sirocco-class shuttle, performing security checks and loading crates of Tombola gear onto the transport slated to ferry them all up to the *Inevitable* for the auction's ceremonial launch.

Except he sniffed out no whiff of the top dog himself.

And he glimpsed no sign of his lifemate.

Tugged by the pull of instinct he'd learned never to ignore, Nero prowled past the Sirocco to the hangar bay's darker, more remote regions. The nether regions.

Where he found the sleek, custom-built Hurricane fueling quietly near a utility hatch.

He pivoted toward the hatch a breath before it swung open and Dex climbed into view. Bristling with vigilance and tightly leashed violence.

Despite ten years spent carefully forgetting the way he'd felt about Dex and eight years hating him for the biowar, Nero felt his chest tighten and his cock heat.

Because Dex was a devil in his black dress uniform, with hair sternly tamed, ceremonial saber belted at his waist, a double row of platinum buttons edging broad shoulders and narrow hips, and those gleaming boots encasing the muscled length of his legs.

When Dex looked like that, every other guy in the galaxy paled to invisibility. Without even trying, he made the air around him combust with electrical energy.

Same as always.

While Nero watched from the shadows, diligently reinforcing every brick in his psychic stockade, Dex sliced a hard, wary look across the hangar bay, then pivoted to extend a hand for Kaia. But, being Kaia, she scrambled out under her own steam.

Looking everywhere except at Dex.

And the fact that she spurned her Tombola master's attentions so pointedly, and the shuttered look on his face when she did it, told Nero a few interesting truths about their current state of play. As did the carefully contained sexual tension that had Dex buttoned up tighter than his form-fitting jacket.

He might have blown every circuit Kaia had last night—in a way Nero once fancied only he himself could ever do—and the flame of fiercely masculine satisfaction blazed like a bonfire in Dex's psyche. But whatever damn thing had gone down between them had also somehow left him…

Thwarted.

Which would only make a guy like Dex more determined to prevail.

Then Kaia prowled into the light, walking not like a Tombola bride for sale to the highest bidder but like the fearless Prime Class samurai she was. And Nero forgot every desperate strategy of defensive barriers and distance he'd been coaching himself so militantly to impose.

Gods and demons, but he knew her. Knew she'd spurn the traditional Tombola gown's bare-breasted exposure for something that reflected her distinctive sense of self—something she could fight in. Knew her suitors would've already started bombarding her with exotic clothing and precious trinkets in a futile bid to curry favor. Knew his own gift would compel her and call to her fiercely independent spirit.

But even knowing all that, somehow he hadn't anticipated how he'd feel seeing her wear what he'd sent.

Or, gods of Solaris, the way she'd look wearing it.

The sleek black leather gown, inset with flashes of Valyrian violet, fit her lithe curves like she'd been sewn into it. But the thigh-high slit gave her freedom of movement, and the knee-high boots showcased her supple stride. The platinum torques that circled her bare arms were Valyrian tech—weapons worth her weight in precious metals she'd eventually learn how to wield. Because he'd always known she was a far stronger telepath than she'd ever believed. Even if none of those dolts at the Psi Academy had understood how to harness her hybrid gifts. Against all that black leather and sorrel skin, her cyber saber and utility belt looked right at home.

She'd scorned the ritual coiffure for a sleek copper ponytail that left her shoulders bare. And spurned the theatrical cosmetics of a Tombola bride for a sheer gold powder dusted over high cheekbones and a slick of bronze glitter over lush lips.

By the seven devils, she was *his*.

She was his.

Even if he'd made the bitter choice years ago to put duty to his dying race over love. No one in the galaxy knew her better.

But damn if she didn't stop his heart every single time he saw her.

And never more than now.

Now—when she was lit to burning like a torch by whatever the hell she'd done with Dex.

Now—when she was walking away from everything she could've had with Dex, and everything she used to have with Nero.

Now—when she'd made up her stubborn samurai mind to give her exquisite body, her extraordinary heart and her exceptional gifts to someone else.

Despite all his grim determination to keep his distance, something must have slipped through his barriers. Because halfway to the

Hurricane, she jerked to a startled stop and spun unerringly toward the shadows where he… supposed one could say he lurked.

"Ben?" Her head tilted, that quick smile he'd shift planets to see flashing forth in the instant before she remembered she hated him. "Why are you hiding there in the shadows?"

Because it's where I belong.

He didn't care if they both heard. He was surly and bitter and wrathful.

And when the Precursor was wrathful, someone always paid.

But for the sake of making things easier—one of those little social niceties telepaths learned to cultivate—he swept them a bow steeped in irony. "Seems it's a day for hiding. Or else why this elaborate charade with the decoy Sirocco and Dex's toy soldiers over there?"

Dex was briskly detaching the fuel hose and briskly releasing the docking cable. Briskly doing everything Dex could to ignore him, in fact. Which did absolutely nothing to sweeten Nero's temper.

So it was left to Kaia to stride toward him, her confident saunter revealing a truly mouthwatering stretch of supple thigh. "Dex doesn't seem to trust his own guard. Which is apparently nothing unusual for a First Indomitable. Especially since I've told him he has a spy skulking around here somewhere who's selling me out to the Swarm. Now his security goons are on a manhunt for the mole. Meanwhile, we're ascending to the *Inevitable* in a way the spy won't expect. We hope."

She looked up at him with those mischievous lilac eyes he'd never forgotten. Because even in her platform boots, Nero still topped her lithe acrobat's body by a full cubit.

"I have you to thank for this gown—not to mention the Valyrian tech. Don't I, Ben?"

As he strode up the gangway, Dex sliced him an unreadable look. But it wasn't hard for anyone with a particle of telepathy to suss out that Nero wasn't the only one who was wrathful.

The First Indomitable of the Mogadon Empire wanted Kaia wearing *his* clothing.

And if that was a wildly inappropriate impulse from her Tombola master, Dex didn't give one flaming damn.

"I thought it would suit you." Nero kept his face closed and his tone impersonal. "We've never understood hybrid telepathy all that well. It's pretty much a neglected field in the Senate. But what I do know is this. The more you wear those torques, the better they'll eventually work. Once you master the trick of using them, you'll be a goddess."

As if you weren't one already.

But he kept that thought locked down tight. And watched her recoil from his distant coldness.

Only to parry with her own saber-sharp sass.

"Arming me to fight off some overly amorous consort? That's a fitting gift for a Tombola bride." Her mocking tone hardened to ice. "But mine won't be like that. My father knows if I don't favor his choice, I won't conceive. Then he won't get his heir for the Kryll Corona."

Before the bitter flash in her lavender eyes, his heart clenched in a fist of pain. She was steeling herself for another man's bed.

Somehow, gods help him, he had to do the same.

"There are five Valyrians among your suitors." He managed an indifferent shrug, like his chest wasn't splitting at the prospect. "Before the war, there would've been a lot more. But these five are strong telepaths. I'll rank them for you—"

"Don't bother." She spun away and marched toward the Hurricane, but his legs were longer and he easily kept pace. "Been there. Done that. Over it. The last thing I need is a Valyrian consort."

Even through his barriers, that barb stung him like a scorpion. He gripped her arm—safe enough through his glove—and swung her around hard to face him.

Wishing he could shake some sense into her stubborn samurai head.

"So you'd prefer a Mogadon? Maybe one who's willing to share you with his First Indomitable? Someone willing to stand behind Dex and cheer while he launches his next biowar?"

"Don't you get it? I need someone strong enough to *stop* him." Her face twisting, she wrenched free. "When I find him up there—whoever he is—I'm his."

Spinning away, she scrambled up the gangway in a flash of leather boots and sleek golden legs to vanish into the cockpit.

Leaving Nero alone on the ramp, gaping after her like a moonstruck schoolboy.

You've underestimated her again, haven't you, buddy? Along with

Dex and her dad and probably every single suitor on that ship. She hasn't given up. Not even to save her kid sis. She's made up her mind to save Kylie and the whole flipping galaxy from this Mogadon war. And Dex doesn't have the first flipping clue—

Beneath his boots the gangway hummed and rose, folding in for launch. Nero pulled his head together and ran lightly up the ramp.

"What, no twelve-man honor guard escort? And none of your butcher boys to do your dirty work? Don't tell me you're actually…"

His words trailed into silence as Nero absorbed the stylized cockpit. A full-body cyberport dominated the aft wall, with an admiring Kaia already swarming all over it. Another wall featured a weapons console with all the options, complete with solar cannon, bio-armed bomblets and tactical nukes. Off to starboard, the navigational array was designed to impress. Digital star charts and sat-nav monitors framed a three-dimensional holograph of the galaxy, its spiral arms studded with the massed icons of the Mogadon fleet—currently combing the far fringes of the distant Omega Sector for the elusive Zorin.

While right here beside him in the Alpha Sector, Dex stood on a utility box, blocking the entrance. Tinkering with something behind a dangling ceiling panel.

"Stars and comets," Kaia enthused, already jacked in through the port at her temple. "You've got every cyber exploit in the samurai playbook loaded onto this bad boy."

"I'm pleased you approve," Dex muttered, tightening something with a wrench. "I designed this ship myself. For my thesis at the Empire Academy. She's part fighter, part scout ship, part weapon of mass destruction. Welcome to the *Ascendant*."

Unable to slip past with Dex blocking the way, Nero said the decent thing. "Want some help with whatever you're doing?"

"No," Dex said curtly.

"I see we're still not over my minor display with the ore freighter," Nero drawled.

"You put eighteen of my people in the infirmary with your 'minor display.' So, no, we're not 'over it.'"

Hearing the casualty count, Kaia stopped playing with the cyberport to shoot Nero an unhappy look. Confronted by the guilty chagrin invading her pretty face, coupled with Dex's over-the-top rudeness, Nero felt his temper slip.

Dex was still standing squarely in his way. Instead of waiting on the stoop like an errand boy, Nero squeezed into the tight passage behind him. Deliberately he gripped Dex's waist as he eased past. At the touch, his former best friend went rigid. Color climbed the back of Dex's neck. Even through the protective insulation of his gloves, his trim muscled heat made Nero's palms tingle.

And, inevitably, that instant of forbidden contact roused all his sleeping demons. It was indecent, the guy feeling so good under his hands after all the bad blood between them. Not to mention smelling halfway between a predator and a god.

Indulging his impulse to devil the man, Nero flexed his fingers against Dex's waist and breathed in his ear, "Still ticklish?"

"No." Dex's tone would have frozen mercury. "And if you don't mind terribly, Precursor—"

The muffled *whoom* of a nearby explosion made the *Ascendant* shudder. By instinct Nero steadied Dex for the tick the guy needed to grip his shoulder and spring down. One swift assessing glance through the viewport wrung a soft curse from Dex.

Then he was strapping into the pilot's seat.

While Nero and Kaia stared through the polyglass at the flaming wreckage of the Sirocco that was supposed to have taken them aloft, flaming debris rained down around the scattered forms of what were clearly Mogadon casualties. Nearby, an emergency alarm broadcast the disaster with its shrill wavering siren.

"What the *hells*… ?" Kaia whispered.

"Sabotage." Dex raced through his preflight checklist with brutal efficiency and the *Ascendant* came alive—engines humming, lights flashing, data scrolling across the command console. "Nero, I need you on weapons."

The lightning charge of adrenaline jolted through him with a kick. The same kind of kick he used to get brawling back-to-back with Dex against the ashram's local toughs.

Back when he used to trust him.

Still, as he strapped into the weapons console and Kaia harnessed herself to the cyberport, Nero's psychic senses vibrated with danger.

Sure, Dex had been a hotshot pilot before his ascent. And he enjoyed the well-earned reputation of having the galaxy's coolest head in a crisis. But even for him, he seemed suspiciously prepared for this near-death experience. Prepared beyond the ruse that had them sneaking off on the *Ascendant* in the first place rather than flying the doomed Sirocco with the rest of Dex's entourage.

Across the hangar bay, booted feet thundered and men shouted orders. Amber lights flashed over the scene as a fire crew converged, spraying a fan of chemical vapor to smother the flames.

Unnoticed in the shadows, the *Ascendant* lifted from the tarmac and coasted toward the exit.

Although the layout of the weapons console was unfamiliar, it wasn't all that hard to figure out. Nero switched off the safety on the solar cannon and wrapped his hand around the joystick.

He supposed this wasn't the time to remind Dex of his unfortunate tendency to get violently space-sick during aerial maneuvers. Still, he felt obliged to give them both a heads-up about another tactical issue.

"Unless these are psi-powered weapons, I'm, uh, not much of a marksman—"

An agitated voice crackled through the comm unit. "Hurricane fighter, you are not—repeat *not*—cleared for takeoff. Stand down and present your identity credentials."

"Look alive." Dex gunned it for the sunlit exit, whose double-hulled titanium doors were already starting to groan closed. "And if you can avoid slaughtering any of my men, Precursor, I'd be profoundly obliged."

"Shields are up and—looks like your identity beacon's disabled." From her perch in the cyberport, Kaia's voice had the distracted, not-quite-present sound of someone who occupied two places at once. "I assume that's by choice."

"Hurricane fighter, stand down!" the comm unit barked. "We have an unauthorized intrusion in the bay. Stand down or you *will* be fired upon. This is your final warning."

Directly ahead, the closing gates bracketed a narrowing slice of sunlight under periwinkle Mogadon skies. A line of armored guards toting blasters raced to get between the Hurricane and their freedom. Nero's finger tightened on the kill switch.

"Leave off that solar cannon," Dex said tightly, swinging the Hurricane on its axis from horizontal to vertical, their starboard wingtip nearly skimming the ground. "Those troops report to me."

"I exist to serve your every tyrannical whim," Nero said with crushing humility, the sarcasm thick enough to choke him, strapped tightly in place as the force of gravity pushed him sideways toward the floor and his gut gave a sickening lurch. "But since you wanted me on weapons—"

"Mars! Are you or are you not a bloody telepath?"

Nero uttered a soft curse.

Mere heartbeats before collision, he stripped off a glove and clenched his fist. Orchid-purple light spilled between his fingers. Crushed by a vise of psychic force, troopers tumbled against the wall in a knot of flailing limbs. Painful—but not fatal.

Which was really too bad.

Because as any Valyrian could tell you, the only good Mogadon was a dead Mogadon.

Directly before them, the doors slammed shut. But a steely-eyed Dex opened the throttle, face hard and fearless as disaster loomed. Nero swore again and squeezed off a desperate round on the solar cannon.

A globe of orange fire *thwomped* from the muzzle and seared through the doors.

The *Ascendant* shot through the smoking hole and soared into amethyst Mogadon skies. Straight toward the flaming crimson orb of the Mogadon sun. Targeting alarms blipped as ground artillery lobbed laser rounds in their wake. Dex twisted the *Ascendant* into a tight evasive spin that sent all the blood rushing to Nero's head and wrenched a nauseated groan through his clenched teeth.

With dizzying speed, the ground fell away.

"Hurricane fighter, return to base! Blast you, that's an order—"

Dex flipped a switch and the frenzied voice fell silent. Then he flipped something else and the G-force pressed Nero hard into his chair. Grimly he ordered the contents of his churning stomach to stay put.

The skies darkened to indigo. They punched through the stratosphere into orbit.

"You've got a transmission in the hopper," Kaia called from the cyberport. "Looks like a pre-recorded message in your outbox?"

"One I very much hoped I wouldn't be forced to deploy," Dex muttered. "Yet here we are. Relay transmission on all frequencies."

"Roger that." While Kaia smoothly did whatever she did in the cyberverse, Nero couldn't help noticing how instinctively Dex gave the orders and how reflexively they both scrambled to obey.

Which would certainly make for an interesting dynamic in his bed.

And either the thermal shields in this glorified getaway vehicle were on the blink—or the fever that shivered through him was attributable to that unrequited torch he was still toting for their pilot.

Abruptly the cockpit filled with the controlled cadence of Dex's recorded voice.

"All Mogadon bases, this is Mogadon One. As all media outlets will shortly report, the Kryll maharani and I have just survived an assassination attempt, very likely perpetrated by Syndax agents, who detonated explosives on a Sirocco-class shuttle delivering security forces and Tombola gear to the *Inevitable*. This despicable act of cowardice is an outright violation of the armistice to which the Syndax swore for the duration of the Tombola. But rest assured—once the perpetrators' identity is proven, this outrage shall not go unpunished."

Hearing the bleak promise of vengeance in that dispassionate voice, Nero's blood iced with the chill of certain violence.

Because when a Mogadon Indomitable like Dex promised vengeance, that typically meant murder.

"Meanwhile, know this." His recorded voice gained resonance. "The traitor Zorin and his Syndax lackeys have utterly failed to achieve their obvious objective of voiding the Tombola and assassinating me. The ritual begins at twelve hundred clicks as scheduled. Code Alpha security protocols will now be initiated to secure public safety and bring the perpetrators and their accomplices to justice. I require your full compliance with these security protocols. Continue to discharge your customary duties and await further instructions. This is Mogadon One out."

And that's why they call the Empire a dictatorship.

Nero chuffed out a chuckle of dry appreciation. "You're mighty prepared for a guy who just barely survived an assassination attempt."

"It's a survival trait for First Indomitables," Dex said shortly. "We always land on our feet—or we don't land at all. Of late, I've had the hunch one of my loyal guard was plotting to move against me. Even without concrete intelligence to validate, it's an instinct I've learned to ignore at my peril."

Kaia unplugged from the cyberverse and hunkered forward, elbows propped on her shapely knees. "How do you know your guard was collaborating with the Syndax?"

"I don't. But this gives me all the pretext I require to ban all incoming Syndax candidates from bidding for your bed. In fact, it's a pity the strictures of your Apocrypha forbid me from disqualifying the lone Syndax candidate who's already bid. I'll have to find some other pretext for getting rid of him."

Oh, well played. Nero shot him a look of grudging approval. *In a single tyrannical act, you've managed to cock-block the Syndax from a Kryll alliance and throw a serious wrench in Kaia's plan to choose a powerful rival for her bed.*

A selfish flicker of satisfaction knifed through him. *She'll have to consider the Valyrian candidates now. And I don't intend to rest until she takes a Valyrian consort.*

"You're impossibly presumptuous." Color rising in her face, Kaia was glaring blue murder at Dex. "If you'd bothered to ask, I would have told you I happen to want Syndax candidates among my suitors. And so will my father."

"The Syndax have very likely violated their pledge of Tombola truce," Dex said blandly, frowning over the star map. "My intelligence organs will assemble the evidence required to prove it. I'm afraid my course as Tombola master is inscribed in your own Apocrypha. While this inquiry remains open, there's really nothing I can do except disqualify new bidders from the contest."

"Whereas if the Syndax turn out to be innocent, you've just violated the Apocrypha yourself by lying—"

The ping of a warning bell sliced through her indignant protest. Dex assessed the sat-nav monitors with an arctic gaze. His face hardened to ice.

"Those are Zephyrs. A full bloody wing of them." Dex reached for the yoke. "Blast."

"Mogadon fighters?" Nero arched a skeptical brow. "Gunning for their own Indomitable?"

"They don't realize I'm aboard. The base undoubtedly launched those fighters to recover our stolen Hurricane. We're a nuclear-armed vessel. They'll want to retrieve the warheads."

"Then it sounds like we're pretty much punked." Kaia reached for her cyberjack, then hesitated. "Assuming they can track us."

Dex spared her a cool nod. "Even without our transponder, they'll use the planet's defensive satellites to track us—unless we hide behind something bigger than we are. Hold tight."

He pushed the yoke forward. The *Ascendant* pitched into a stomach-jarring dive. Never a fan of this sort of aerial tomfoolery, Nero gripped the arms of his chair and ground through gritted teeth, "*Dex. Why don't you just tell them who you are?*"

"Because we haven't found the saboteur. Confirming our location and identity will be precisely the intelligence he's hoping to acquire." Dex sliced him a narrow glance. "My profound apologies, Precursor. I'd forgotten you don't care for combat flying."

His words were unimpeachable, but devilry lurked in his tone. No doubt paying Nero back for that little moment with the tickling.

"Don't mention it," he muttered.

Which only gave Dex all the excuse he needed to flip the Hurricane into a series of head-spinning wing-over-wing revolutions that sent the blood rushing straight to Nero's brain. A cold clammy sweat broke out on his brow, and a fresh surge of sickness squirmed in his gut.

"Hey, knock it off!" Kaia called sharply. "You know Ben doesn't like that."

Dex steadied the shuttle and shot him a probing look. Nero scowled right back at him and watched something like contrition finally flicker in his hard face.

"Sorry, Ben," Dex said softly. "I can be a Prime Class bastard, can't I?"

Nero willed himself to loosen his death grip on the armrest and managed a surly mutter. "Not that I've noticed."

Brow furrowed in concern, Dex studied him until Nero waved an annoyed hand to signal he'd survive.

"Sorry," Dex repeated with a sigh. "But I wasn't simply pulling your chain. Charting a random trajectory makes us harder for the satellites' search algorithms to track."

Yeah, I know. But you're also showing off, Nero fired back silently. *You may be the Empire's star jet jockey. But you'll need more than flashy flying to impress a Prime Class samurai like Kaia.*

Or me.

Dex's gaze flashed with winter lightning. "I don't need to impress you. And I told you to stay out of my head."

Neatly, Dex leveled the Hurricane.

To his intense relief, Nero finally felt his gut unclench.

Now an ominous shape filled the viewport, etched against the dark expanse of space. The fierce raking lines and laser-scored hull of a last-gen battleship that had clearly survived more than a few close calls. Haphazard patches, soldering seams, and sheer desperation held the rust bucket together. Ranks of jury-rigged solar cannons glowed a sinister scarlet, locked and loaded for violence.

Battered or no, that battleship meant business.

"Gods of my father," Kaia breathed. "Check out the farking size of that thing. Is that… ?"

"The Syndax envoy." Dex's profile was edged with fastidious distaste, his tone with grim resolve. "That's the *Relentless*. She's the biggest ship in this quadrant until the *Inevitable* arrives to collect us. Big enough to cloak us from Mogadon satellites, even if our saboteur can access the feed."

"Don't you think the Syndax might be a little jumpy about this neighborly fly-by after that bombshell you just lobbed?" Nero asked. "You know, that nationalistic broadcast where you accused them of trying to assassinate you—without evidence—and swore bloody vengeance on the whole tribe?"

"Couldn't be helped. Not unless I want the entire Empire to know I've lost the requisite ability to intimidate my troops into a state of terrified compliance." Dex shrugged, but his jaw was tight. "We'll look like a common scout ship to the Syndax, and we'll do nothing to disabuse them. With any luck, the captain's with their candidate on the *Inevitable*—"

"Hey, Mogadon." An insolent voice crackled through the comm unit, distorted by the aging tech but all too understandable. "This is the Syndax ship *Relentless*, flying under a flag of truce for the Kryll chick's Tombola. Gimme your call sign or I'll blow you outta the sky."

"So much for luck," Kaia murmured as the fire-scored hulk blotted out the stars. "I'm with Ben on this one. Maybe we shouldn't be flying quite so close. You know, show a little respect?"

"Showing the Syndax we're intimidated would be a grave tactical error." Dex thumbed open a private channel. "*Relentless*, this is the Mogadon scout ship *Ascendant* completing an assigned patrol of this quadrant. We're reimposing order after an unauthorized incursion last night into Mogadon airspace by a smack of Swarm spacebots. We require—that is, we *request* permission to scan your hull for stowaway spacebots."

Despite this ludicrous effort to pass himself off as some average Aurelius, the clear expectation of obedience edged Dex's voice in iron. He sounded precisely like the tyrant he was, demanding instant obedience to his every whim.

Kaia rolled her eyes. Nero turned his head to hide an unwilling grin.

"Huh." Together they suffered through a nail-biting pause. "Hang tight, *Ascendant.*"

"If you insist," Dex muttered, tucking in the Hurricane beside the Syndax ship's battle-scarred flank.

A leaden silence settled over them like gravity. Kaia uncoiled to her feet and sauntered over to prop one sleek leather-clad hip against the command console. Dex leaned back in his chair, his electric gaze sliding slowly down her body with a smoldering appraisal that brought heat flooding to her face.

Driven by a few possessive instincts of his own, Nero lifted a casual hand to run her silken ponytail through his naked fingers. Because he just couldn't seem to keep his hands off her. The sweetness of jasmine and the tang of ozone rose from her golden skin, spiked with the potent musk of Dex's mating scent.

Dex's sizzling gaze slid to Nero. Suddenly Nero's heart was thundering. Liquid heat pooled and pulsed in his cock.

We make quite the trio, he thought, steeling himself against the guy's physical impact. *Kaia pretending like hell not to want Dex. Dex pretending like hell not to want me. And me pretending like hell not to want them both. All three of us spectacular failures at pretending.*

If it gets any hotter in here, we'll be wiping steam off the windows.

By the dusky glow of starfire and Mogadon's green moon, Dex's eyes locked on Nero—eyes so blue they were practically fluorescent. And if Dex with his battery of inherited hang-ups was picking up how hard the whole setup turned his crank, Nero didn't give a flip.

Kaia angled her head to slide her ponytail from Nero's grasp. Leaving his skin tingling with a sudden sense of loss. "Go back to what you were saying before, Dex. You knew the Sirocco was rigged to blow?"

Dex frowned and wrenched his gaze from Nero.

"I suspected," he said tightly. "After the Syndax raid against my fleet in the Omega Sector… having suffered those… losses, an attempt on my life by my own men became a virtual certainty. After all, the primary reason one becomes a praetorian guard is to have a fair shot at killing the First Indomitable and ascending oneself."

"Gods, what a system." Kaia's booted foot tapped out her impatience. "Sounds like you need a different kind of guard. You know—the kind you can actually trust?"

Face shuttered tight, Dex studied the Syndax ship. "There is no one I can trust."

Unexpectedly Nero felt his throat close.

You trusted me—once. We were oathsworn brothers. And I'm not the one who violated that trust by launching a genocidal biowar to exterminate an entire race.

Kaia cleared her throat, telling Nero without words he was projecting again. "You slaughter thousands for sport in your gladiatorial games. Why don't you tell those poor yahoos in the fighting pits you'll pardon them if they swear allegiance to you? You'll have spared their lives. They might actually mean it."

"Those men are condemned criminals. I may be the executioner, but I'm not the judge." Dex swiveled his chair to face Nero down and nailed him with another burning stare. "And I didn't launch the biowar, damn it. My father commanded the scientists who developed the novicide, and he personally gave the order that deployed it. In point of fact, I nearly came to blows with him trying to prevent it."

"Then you should have tried harder, Dex." The minefield of buried anguish in his own voice appalled him.

"Do you think I don't know that? You think I don't know six billion Valyrians died on my watch? Because *I* failed to stop him?" Dex's voice splintered. His jaw knotted and his fists clenched. "Blast it, Ben! There hasn't been a day since that I… that I haven't…"

"Save it," Nero scoffed. "Save it for someone who'll believe it. Pleasing him mattered more to you than saving me. That's the bottom line. I would've died for you."

Dex stabbed an accusatory finger in his direction. "Easy for you to say. You're the one who ran."

"He does that," Kaia chimed in, her words dripping acid. "It's a bad habit. He's a stud pony for the Senate of Psychics and their barbaric breeding program. Any time some pedigreed Valyrian mare needs servicing, the Senate crooks its finger and their prize stallion comes running."

"Breeding program?" Dex arched a sardonic brow. "Oh, is that what happened? When you lit out in dead of night and jetted offworld without a single blessed syllable of farewell to a living soul—"

"You shut me out!" To his shock, Nero found himself shouting. Through sheer force of will, he lowered his voice and throttled his chair in a white-knuckled clench. Apparently they were going to venture onto this forbidden terrain after all.

Even with it rigged to blow beneath their feet.

"Didn't you know I came to your room?" Nero gritted out, low and bitter. "I mean—after? I can hardly believe I actually intended to apologize. For making *you* uncomfortable. You with your Mogadon hang-ups. You walked in on me, remember?"

"It was an *accident*," Dex pointed out, color creeping up his neck.

As Kaia's wide-eyed gaze swung between the two of them, Nero tried like blazes to rein in the billowing sail of his own out-of-control emotions. But after a lifetime of suppression, the words howled to be freed.

"I'd obviously appalled you! Appalled you the one farking time I let you see how I—" Roughly he wrenched himself away from a lifetime of stifled confessions he'd always known in his bones his best friend never wanted to hear. "Every night that summer, your door was open. We were always coming and going. That night, you locked me out."

"You came to my room?" Dex looked astounded. "Why in Ceres didn't you just knock?"

Kaia uttered an eloquent snort, but left it to Nero to answer in words.

He dragged an agitated hand through his hair. Aghast to realize his fingers were trembling. "Gods and demons, I wasn't about to beg! I'd already humiliated myself once that night—"

"*Ascendant*, this here's *Relentless*." The comm unit hissed with static. "Looks like it's your lucky day. The big guy just okayed your sweep."

Nero snarled with frustration. "Damn it."

"Saved by the Syndax," Kaia murmured, looking far too fascinated by this whole farking mess.

"About bloody time," Dex muttered roughly, and toggled the channel open. "Acknowledged, *Relentless*."

Before Nero could even begin to sort out the anger and loathing churning in his gut—anger and loathing that burned for an outlet—that impertinent Syndax voice was back, every word edged in menace.

"You better believe we're targeting your Mogadon ass. If that solar cannon or those missile tubes on your underbelly even look sideways at this vessel, you'll be space dust before you can salute. Acknowledge *that*."

"Arrogant little prick, isn't he?" Dex said.

"Apparently you don't hold a monopoly on the arrogance market." Kaia looked like she was trying not to laugh. "You'd almost think you'd just declared war on them or something. Want me to acknowledge for you?"

Dex glared at both of them—clearly fighting to master his own anger—and grated into the comm link, "Acknowledged."

While Dex nudged the *Ascendant* into a credible search pattern along the Syndax hull, Nero thought about what he'd just said. So Dex had made some token attempt to talk Maximus Draven out of exterminating Nero and his entire race like a nest of termites. So what? He'd failed. Failed when Nero needed him most. Now here Dex was again, threatening to launch a whole new biowar against the Syndax.

And this time Maximus Draven had been dead for years.

While he chewed over these unpalatable thoughts, Kaia hopped up to sit on the console between them and crossed her legs. Which did really interesting things to her slitted skirt. Nero found his train of thought abruptly sidelined from brooding over Dex to wondering if Kaia was wearing anything at all under that sexy dress.

Hells, she was going to kill both of them—Dex and Nero—if she didn't stop teasing them and sit properly.

"I don't know, Dex. You seem awfully hostile toward the Syndax." Blithely Kaia swung her booted leg, while the two of them watched her like moorcats eyeing a particularly provocative sparrow. "With your brand-new novicide and all? I know they're pirates, but I'm an outlaw myself as far as the Quorum of Four's concerned. What exactly have the Syndax done that's so reprehensible?"

"What have they *done*?" Dex's voice stretched tight. "If you'd been to Epsilon Four or Beta Prime or any of a dozen colonies after the Syndax and their Swarm allies paid one of their neighborly visits, you'd launch a biowar yourself. You do realize that the Swarm are cannibals?"

Kaia kept her voice level. "Yeah, I've heard as much. The same people say I'm an abomination. Like those racial purists in the Valyrian Senate. To them, I'm a half-Kryll hybrid who should never have been born."

"They're wrong about you. But not about them." Dex shifted his fierce gaze from the looming megaship to rivet her. "Kaia, I've seen the colonies after a true Swarm attack—not a peppering by their spacebots, but a full-on feeding raid by the humanoids themselves. Rest assured the Swarm are indeed cannibals. And their preferred entree is children aged six or younger. Preferably consumed while the poor souls are alive and screaming."

Kaia sucked in her breath and swallowed hard, while Nero felt queasy all over again. Because he could see all too clearly the graphic images inhabiting Dex's head.

"They're utterly voracious," Dex finished grimly. "And they'll take whatever they can get. Pregnant women. The elderly. Household pets."

"Gods of my father," she breathed. "Where the flip did they come from? I've always wondered."

Nero shifted uneasily in his seat. "A distant galaxy. That's what our prophets say. A galaxy they've already laid to waste. Now, like a virus, they're spreading to this one."

"But what do you think they want?" she pressed.

"To feed," Nero whispered. "I've felt it. They *hunger*."

Kaia wrapped her arms around herself and shuddered.

Catching the reflex, Dex frowned and adjusted the climate controls. "They've troubled the outer colonies over the ages from time to time. In exploratory forays—never in force. This time, they're different."

"Different?" Her head tilted. "How so?"

"It seems they've a new leader." Meticulously Dex edged the *Ascendant* around the Syndax ship's glowing red thrusters. "The one they call Proteus. Supposed to be a shapeshifter. They seem to believe he's some kind of god."

Kaia made a scornful noise. "I know a few gods myself back on Kryll. My father's one. I'll be one too if I ever ascend, though that's the last thing I want. Divinity doesn't equal omnipotence. You can trust me to know."

Dex hesitated, face unreadable as he scanned the *Relentless*. "This particular god is… different. I've seen what he drives them to do. And Zorin's Syndax are their ally. That's why I declared war. To put the pirates in their place, send the Swarm packing, and restore the Pax Mogadon."

"The Mogadon peace." Now it was Nero's turn to scoff. "You think *that's* what's best for the galaxy?"

Dex's golden head lifted with conscious pride. "We are the galaxy's master civilization. Mogadon justice and Mogadon strength bring order and enlightenment to all civilized races. Even if you Valyrians ruled differently in the dark days when you were the galaxy's dominant race. Your ancestors never grasped that the good of the many outweighs the good of the few."

"Unless you're one of the few," Nero gritted out.

Kaia swung herself down to prowl the cockpit. "I can't agree— I'll never agree that majority convenience outweighs personal freedom. That's why I ran off to the circus in the first place. Why I fled the flipping Tombola."

"Yet you're submitting to it now for the good of the many?" Dex watched her with lifted brows.

"I'm submitting to it now to save my sister!" Fiercely she spun to face him down. "The same way my twin submitted years ago to save me. And I'm doing it to end *your* war, Commander. Which is precisely why I'll *never* choose a Mogadon consort."

Dex's voice dropped to a growl that sent a shiver shooting down Nero's spine. "What if you fall for one anyway?"

"I won't!" she fired back, eyes flashing.

Dex looked more than tempted to march over there and prove her wrong.

"Comets, Kaia." Nero sighed. "Have you forgotten everything I told you not to say to him? Or are you deliberately taunting him just to spite me?"

"This isn't about you," she shot right back. "You made sure of that years ago when you left."

Nero expelled a hiss of sheer frustration. "No. This is about Dex. Who hasn't exactly been forthcoming about his own motives—have you, flyboy? Because for you this war's personal. Yet you haven't said one living word about your *hero, Zorin.*"

He knew he was pushing it when Dex's jaw clenched. But the man maintained a steely silence that got under Nero's skin.

Even after all this time, there was no guy in the galaxy who turned him on or flipped him off as well and as thoroughly as Dex.

Nero forged on, reckless with wrath. "You remember Zorin, don't you? That paragon among men you used to idolize? You'd make me sick going on and on about your hero—the commander, the legend, the First Indomitable. You were determined to grow up to be just like him! Until he murdered your father and betrayed everything you admired him for. Now you'll launch another biowar just to punish him."

"As I've stated repeatedly," Dex bit out, every word bristling with danger, "I didn't launch the last one. And my personal views toward that reprehensible traitor are none of your bloody business."

"Just tell me one thing." Nero gripped his chair and laid it all on the line. That hideous, unaskable question that had been eating him alive for years. "About that war. Did you let your father slaughter my entire race just because it meant you'd finally be well and truly rid of me?"

"Zowie!" Kaia gasped and leaned forward to peer through the viewport. "Is *that* your flagship?"

Seething with frustration, Nero wrenched his gaze from Dex's appalled face to the pale wedge of the Mogadon battleship slowly sliding into view as the *Ascendant* circled the Syndax ship's ugly hull.

Nero dragged in a shuddering breath and forcibly unknotted his fists from the chair. Some questions were better left unanswered.

Even if the guilt of wondering *what if* was eating his soul like a cancer.

"That's the *Inevitable*. Right on schedule." Visibly battening down his own powerful emotions, Dex busied himself at the console. "And no sign of patrolling Zephyrs. Precisely as I'd hoped, they're giving the *Relentless* a wide berth. We'll be aboard shortly—just in time for the Tombola."

As if Nero needed any reminder of that looming ordeal. The same ordeal that required him to observe with magisterial detachment while his lifemate met and measured five hundred eager rivals to replace him in her bed. Five hundred men determined to seduce the Kryll maharani and sire the Kryllian theocracy's next god. And despite his own coldly strategic motives for doing the Patriarch's bidding, he doubted Dex was very happy about it either.

"Oh yay," Kaia said glumly. "I can hardly wait."

Well, that officially made three of them. All three dreading this monumental disaster.

And all three powerless to stop it.

CHAPTER TEN
The Patriarch

"Gods of my father! It *reeks* in here." Nervous as a caged tiger, Kaia paced before the curtained entrance—wide enough to accommodate an armored troop transport. "Smells like something between an orgy den and a fighting pit."

"Telepathically it feels even worse," Nero muttered, doing some restless prowling of his own. "There are enough Mogadon pheromones blasting from that amphitheater to launch every one of those five hundred suitors into a rutting frenzy. I can tell there's already been bloodshed."

Standing quietly near the ready room viewport on his flagship *Inevitable*, as perfectly contained as Nero was restless, Dex frowned down at his briefing tablet and rapidly tapped out orders.

Calmly sparing some lives and ending others with every keystroke.

"You can blame the Syndax for that. Two of their candidate's honor guard—if you want to call them that—ambushed one of my Indomitables. Butchered him like a banquet steer."

"Good gods!" Kaia's anxiety level shot through the starship ceiling. "You mean to tell me we haven't even started this thing and they're already killing each other?"

"Auction or no auction, our two civilizations are at war." Dex lifted a tawny brow at her seething agitation. "No need to worry. The miscreants have been detained. I've the situation well in hand."

Her skeptical retort was drowned out by the deep, shuddering toll of a bronze bell that sounded once and shattered the air. A throbbing baritone chant knotted Kaia's tummy in an instant fist of dread.

"I know that sound," she whispered, lost in the rhythmic rise and fall of a hundred voices fueled by fanatical devotion. "It's the Kryll candidates. They're worshipping my father." Her pulse hammered in her ears. "The Patriarch. He's out there."

"Only his avatar," Nero countered, swift as breath. "If there was a god out there, you can believe I'd know it."

He stripped off both gauntlets and tucked them in his belt. She'd feel a lot less nervous if she didn't know *he* was nervous. Nero himself was a god among men—yet he was nervous. His fingers danced with the purple flame of lethal violence.

"The Patriarch's due to hologram in for the opening ceremony," Dex confirmed, pausing to mutter orders into his wrist unit. From the corridor, someone bellowed a command, and booted feet tramped toward them.

"I should never have agreed to this." Because for the first time since she ran away years ago, she felt the presence of her father.

Who wasn't a god.

Not really.

But the psychic impact of billions of overzealous worshippers, all channeling through him the raw energy of their devotion, fueled the aura of omnipotent divinity he projected to such soul-shattering effect.

Awe.

Fear.

Power.

The drive to subdue and control.

The lethal impact of the Patriarch's presence crashed over her with the cosmic force of an exploding star—

"Kaia." The hard heat of Dex's hands gripped her bare shoulders. His piercing gaze—level with hers from a cubit away—shattered the ice that encased her.

Helpless to speak through the dust of fear that caked her throat, she stared into his eyes. Clearly sensing what she couldn't say, he tightened his grip. A frisson of energy raced tingling down her arms and coiled low and tight in her belly.

For a heartbeat, hidden currents surged between them. The powerful riptide of things unsaid. She found herself swaying toward him.

For protection.

Toward the strength that ruled half the galaxy with a fist of iron.

If anyone could keep this nuclear bomb from blowing up in all their faces, it was Dex.

"I've got you," he said hoarsely. "I'll protect you. I swear it. From five hundred suitors and a thousand Swarm spacebots and even a bloody god."

Desperate for reassurance, she searched his face. He was the most powerful man she'd ever known. Last night he'd proven he could rock any girl's world. And right now his neon eyes were locked on her like no one else in the universe even existed.

If he wasn't my Tombola master… and if he wasn't about to launch a flipping biowar… he's the one I'd pick.

The knowledge seared through her at a molecular level. Bitter in her mouth as mining acid.

Because that future could never be.

I want him. That means we'd conceive. And the mating would hold. With the Kryll and the Mogadon as allies, we might even hold off the Swarm.

But he is who he is. He might blow every circuit on my motherboard, but he's still the galaxy's premier tyrant. And he's about to launch a genocide.

I have to find someone to help me stop him.

"This is bigger than either of us. And no one can protect me." She swallowed hard to bring some moisture to her fear-blasted throat and stepped out of his grip. "Not from this."

The cold mask he wore for public consumption snapped into place and turned him inscrutable.

"We'll see about that." With sharp precision, he tugged his uniform straight and primed the blaster at his hip. "Nero."

"Right here."

Like a dark angel, her lifemate materialized beside her in all his barbaric splendor, with fur-lined cloak and belted tunic and the shining platinum of Valyrian tech gleaming at his throat. Hot gusts of psychic wind stirred the ends of his hair.

"If a single one of those suitors steps out of line, I'll blast him all the way to the Beta Sector." Nero smiled grimly into her frightened face. "By all the gods, I hope someone does cross the line. I'd positively relish a little destruction."

Buttressed by the two of them, both sworn to protect her, Kaia put pride in her shoulders and steel in her spine. She was no helpless Tombola bride. Time to stop acting like one. Her sister was counting on her. Her choice could change the future for billions.

Her choice could mean billions *had* a future.

She could do this.

She could take a consort who'd end the war.

Still, she couldn't resist reaching out to both of them—these two men she was walking away from forever. She slipped one hand into Dex's calloused grip and entwined the other with Nero's deft touch. For a single desperate breath, she clung to them both while the current of Nero's quicksilver talent and Dex's steely strength eddied through her.

"You'll blow them all away," Dex promised, low and fierce, his potent heat warming the air between them. "And I will protect you. Never doubt it."

Nero bit out an oath. "Try not to be such a damn Mogadon. She's your ward here—not your consort. It's bad enough having your mating scent all over her. None of those suitors is going to come within a parsec of Kaia with you looming over her like that."

"You're looming over her yourself," Dex pointed out. "And every man out there knows exactly what you were to her—and what you still are."

Over her head, they glared at each other. But the outcome was they both released her and edged back. Shifting restlessly from foot to foot, system pumping fight-or-flight adrenaline through every synapse, Kaia loosened the saber at her shoulder.

The outer door shot open to admit a double column of Dex's armored guard, brutal strength backed by stun rifles, fixed and ready. Ominous and anonymous behind their helmets. They wheeled into place and formed up smartly, a wall of faceless menace.

All waiting for Dex to lead them.

Though she had to admit it added a certain kick knowing one or more of them was doing his level best to have them all killed.

"On my command." Dex pivoted sharply toward the entrance. "Nero—the curtain, if you will."

Ultraviolet light spilled from Nero's eyes. "My pleasure."

A telepath with Ben Nero's technical competence and unparalleled training could wield psi fire with enough exquisite control to cauterize a wound a breath from a patient's eye without collateral damage.

But Nero was smoldering with contained tension.

The force of the psychic wind that gusted from him blew Kaia's ponytail into her eyes, knocked over a staging table and sent it skidding into the wall.

Purple fire poured from his outstretched hand and incinerated the curtain to ash.

While the charred doorframe still flickered with violet fire, Dex clipped out the order to advance. Swept along by his utter certainty, Kaia found herself striding between them through the curtain's smoking ruin.

The *Inevitable*'s amphitheater yawned below, its immensity magnified by the vast walls of polyglass that arced above, framing the cloudy silver spiral of the Apollo nebula and the fiery triple suns of the neighboring system.

Together they marched across a walkway suspended in space.

Her five hundred suitors stood ranked below, order prescribed by ritual, faces hawkish with intent, eyes avid with lust. A hungry growl rumbled from their chests, adding a savage undertone to the chant. Even with the chill of space seeping through the polyglass, the atmosphere was humid with sweating bodies, rank with blood and rage. The heavy spice of Mogadon pheromones and the musk of male arousal made her dizzy.

And there before her, looming at the head of a shining steel stair, stood a tall spare figure. Her father.

Her first instinct was to flee. Even though stars shimmered through his transparent vestments and the *Inevitable*'s crossbeam shone through his towering crown.

Steady on, samurai. It's only his avatar. A digital projection through a distant cyberport.

Besides, she knew better than to show fear to a predator.

Much less five hundred of them.

It would be easy to cower behind the ranks of armed Mogadon muscle. Easy to hide behind Dex's erect frame and Nero's sweeping cloak.

Too easy.

Which was why she quickened her stride.

Side by side, the three of them climbed straight toward the demon she'd been fleeing for years. Gaze fixed forward, chin held high, fists clenched at her side, she strode like a woman who fully intended to draw her sword on that staircase and slit someone's throat.

From on high, the elemental force of her father's will beat down like the heat of a million suns. A force that threatened to crush her against the gleaming stairs like an insect.

Steeling herself against the radioactive burn of all that raw power, she stopped three steps from the top and glared up at him.

The father she'd worshipped with tearful devotion. The lover who'd wooed a Valyrian consort in a political match so successful that Kaia's mother had fallen in love and conceived three times despite herself. The tyrant who'd hunted his daughter through the galaxy like a runaway hound and brought her at last to heel.

All the vast distance of interstellar space seemed to bend toward him. As though he dragged the physical matter of the galaxy and all its screaming souls straight into his gaping maw.

Beneath the towering structure of the Kryll Corona—half royal crown, half papal miter—her father's severe face blazed with a true believer's holy fervor. Light poured from his silver eyes to cast shuddering shadows over the hall. One hand gripped the barbed spear of his divine office, ten cubits tall and gleaming with violence. The other swept forward to fix her with a finger of condemnation.

When he spoke, his merest whisper crashed through her ears and crushed her skull. His words echoed and rang like tolling bells.

"Daughter, thou shalt kneel before Me and worship Me as My due."

Grimly unbowed, she gritted out her rebuttal. "I'm here to save Kylie—not worship you. Where is she?"

"Kneel to signal thy submission to Me and I shalt summon her."

Hating him with a rancor that turned her stomach, Kaia scowled up at him. Even while knowing in her bones that defiance, at this juncture, was a useless impulse. If she hadn't already submitted to her father's edict, she wouldn't be here.

"Kaia," Nero murmured at her side. "You're not helping. Give him what he wants so we'll be rid of him."

That was classic Nero, a political animal all the way down to his DNA. Strategy unsoftened by sentiment. Ruthless with practicality when he needed to be ruthless.

Which happened to be exactly why he'd left her.

"I suppose you think I should kneel too?" she said bitterly to Dex's icy profile.

"Up to you," he muttered. "But if he expects me to kneel, he'll be waiting until those triple suns go supernova."

And that was classic Dex.

"You're not helping either." Nero pushed out an exasperated breath. "For gods' sake, be reasonable! Do you want to see Kylie or not?"

Well, she couldn't say her lifemate didn't know what would sway her.

Burning with resentment, she lowered herself to one knee. Defiant to the last, she unsheathed her saber and stood it blade-down before her.

An unsubtle reminder that she came before the Patriarch as a warrior, not a pawn.

She swayed under the tidal wave of her parent's vengeful satisfaction. He'd loved her once—or claimed to. But her rejection of the sacred duty that dictated his entire existence had demolished whatever affection he'd once felt. She'd made him the galaxy's running joke. The so-called god who couldn't control his own daughter.

For that, he would never forgive her.

The more bitter her submission, the sweeter he'd find his triumph.

His voice boomed out, clashing against the titanium superstructure and splitting the cavernous space.

"Behold the obeisance of Mine own daughter. The outlaw, the rebel, the runaway who now heeds My divine will and submits to her sacred fate as prime maharani and heir to the Kryll Corona. So does she step into the slippers of her sweet-souled twin, the martyr Kira— best-loved of all My daughters—who sacrificed her life to Mine own service."

From the pack of hyenas below rose an ugly growl of ambition and avarice. He might have embargoed the news, but of course they'd all suspected. Heard rumors of her sister's slaughter.

You couldn't keep a secret like that in times like these. Not for long.

Now the weight of speculative eyes crawled over her kneeling body like a cornucopia of slugs. Wondering what she looked like under all that leather and how eagerly she'd welcome them to her bed. Indifferent to her own desires, they were betting their fortunes and their futures for the power and prestige she'd bring and for no other reason.

And for that, she despised them.

Which was going to be a problem. Because she doubted she'd have much luck hiding it.

"Whosoever among thee takes Kaia of Kryll as thy consort and sires thine heir on her holy flesh—that man shall rule the Gamma Sector as My successor and wear the Kryll Corona." Her father's voice smoothed to a gut-churning croon. *"Woo her with thine ardor. Seduce her with thy wealth. Compel her with thy merits. And make haste."*

He ground his barbed spear into the quivering floor and leaned forward. *"Five hundred suitors become two hundred at midnight tomorrow."*

An ominous rumble rolled through the theater, and Kaia's heart turned to stone. She scrambled up, saber slanted at the ready. Beside her, Dex snapped a sharp command. Ranked on the lower stair, his phalanx pivoted outward and fixed their rifles on the shifting mob.

Tense as a coiled spring, Nero spun to put his back to hers. Silent lightning crackled and the metallic scent of ozone hung heavy in the air.

Because all of them knew what the Patriarch had done. By compressing the bidding timeline, by eliminating so many suitors tomorrow at midnight instead of the customary four days later, by flinging the entire collective into a mad scramble to present their bids and win her fancy before the clock to the first culling ran down in thirty-six clicks, he'd thrown them all into a feeding frenzy.

And made her position exponentially more dangerous.

Even with the full force of the Empire army at his command and the galaxy's most powerful telepath at his back, this was one bloodbath the First Indomitable would be hard pressed to control.

One they'd all be lucky to survive.

Fearless of her father's looming menace, Dex sprang up to command the platform and fixed the muttering mob with unsparing eyes. She didn't have the first clue how he managed it, but the overwhelming aura of utter command he projected so effortlessly permeated the vast chamber more effectively than fallout from a bomb blast.

Before his crackling vigilance, the dangerous undertow of imminent violence subsided.

"As your Tombola master," he stated with cool precision, "I expect and require full adherence to all rules of order as prescribed by the Kryll Apocrypha—to whose terms you committed when you paid the munificence and signed the compact. The principal rules are three. First, I guarantee every man a fair and equal opportunity to present his bid and make his case—in my presence, of course, and that of my neutral second."

He nodded courteously toward Nero, who acknowledged her suitors' sullen glares with a sardonic bow.

"Successful bids will be forwarded to His Holiness at the end of each bidding cycle, along with my own commendations." Dex straightened his broad shoulders and clasped his hands behind his back. "Second, the maharani herself chooses which candidates advance."

A rustle of shock swept the crowd. But Kaia's eyes were on her father. A barely there blip in his avatar told her he too had been caught flatfooted by that condition.

A reaction that spiked her blood with savage satisfaction.

Stars and comets, how did he think I was going to play this? He knows how it was for my mom. I may be only half Valyrian, but Kira's cycle worked the same way, and I'm her twin. If I don't desire my consort, I won't conceive.

Dex raised a hand that commanded instant silence. "Each of you will be rated based on the financial and political features of your bid, the terms and conditions of your Tombola contract—and your personal appeal. As assessed by the maharani herself."

Only Kaia stood close enough to see his jaw clench. She didn't think he relished the prospect of her assessing the personal appeal of men his Mogadon instincts must perceive as sexual rivals.

Even though they weren't. Not really.

The Tombola had been designed eons ago to marry off a dynasty of pureblooded Kryll maharanis who'd been bred for docility in the Patriarch's harem. Given the way her fertility worked, the entire premise for a hybrid like her was fatally flawed. She wanted nothing to do with any of these would-be suitors. And whatever assessing of the masses she did wasn't going to be a physical thing.

No matter how hot to trot they all were down there, thanks to those Mogadon pheromones.

Brusquely Dex swept them all past that perilous precipice. "Two hundred candidates will be selected to advance at the end of day two, one hundred of these at the end of day three—with further proportional reductions thereafter until the winner is chosen among the final ten candidates on day seven."

The winner.

Kaia swallowed a surge of bitterness. Before she agreed to board Dex's shuttle that morning, she'd finished the negotiation her steamy encounter with the First Indomitable last night had interrupted. Bargained her way into choosing those final ten. Secured her right to send packing four hundred ninety of the five hundred sweating aspirants crammed cheek-to-jowl below, horny and stinking.

But the Patriarch himself would choose the winner. Kryll tradition demanded it—to say nothing of his own tyrannical instincts.

And she'd known exactly how far she could push him.

I just have to find ten guys in this room who don't turn my stomach. Ten aside from the two I actually want—who happen to be the two I can't have.

Has to be doable. Right?

From the heights, Dex's glacial gaze scanned the sullen crowd. He edged his words in ice. "Allow me to compel your attention to a final requirement for these proceedings of supreme importance to me personally. No man touches the maharani without my express permission."

Silence hollowed the air around her. A silence so profound she could've heard a mouse hiccup.

"That'll be the trick, won't it?" Nero breathed in her ear—irreverent even in a crisis. "Getting Dex's permission to let some other guy touch you? Some other guy than me, I mean—which I'd like to imagine he'd find a way to tolerate. What's your plan for that, angel?"

Dex was never part of my plan, she told him silently, heart aching. *Neither were you. But if you're asking what it would take for Dex to let you touch me… that particular topic's already been addressed.*

"Has it really?" he murmured.

His tone implied idle indifference, but his body at her back was taut as a wire.

Don't get excited. It's purely hypothetical. A thought experiment. But… I think he'd be up for it, she acknowledged, having a little trouble with her own detachment. *If you let him watch.*

His barely audible reaction was a single swift inhale. But the throbbing ache that flared to life between her legs nearly buckled her knees.

Great gods. The visual he was sending her—the inflammatory image of Ben Nero burying his cock deep inside her while Dex Draven watched them both lose it under his electric blue stare—fueled the same potent high for Nero that it did for her. They'd climax when Dex told them they could.

And she bet he'd be ruthless.

She barely bit back a moan.

"Gods, Kaia," Ben whispered hoarsely. "I think I could live with that."

Somehow she pulled her head together.

Too bad I couldn't, she sent back tartly. *You blew your one chance with me to subatomic smithereens ages ago. I'm not a forgive-and-forget kind of girl.*

On the platform Dex was watching Nero whisper in her ear. And the flash of heat that kindled in his gaslight gaze told her he knew exactly what they were discussing.

Behind him, upstaged for once in his divine life by a mere mortal and his own Tombola master, the Patriarch was preparing for his trademark showy exit.

Without showing her Kylie.

Getting her head back in the game, Kaia planted her boot on the next step up and rested the tip of her blade against the floor with casual violence.

"Not so fast, Your Holiness," she said softly. "Where the flip's my sister?"

Beneath the spiked monstrosity of the Kryll Corona, the Patriarch measured her strength with eyes like liquid mercury, toxic with menace.

"Thou hast grown insolent in thine absence. I doth not envy the man who wins the honor of bringing thee to heel."

She voiced a short laugh. "Neither do I. Where is she?"

His flowing sleeve swept out. Beside him, a slim figure coalesced. Kaia's heart lodged in her throat and choked her.

Because her twelve-year-old sister's tomboy slimness had abruptly ripened with the curves of nubile adolescence. Showcased in a parody of a Tombola gown. Instead of the nonexistent bodice that exposed the wearer's breasts, a sheer panel of silk barely preserved the child's modesty.

If not for that scant nod to decency, Kaia would have gone for her father's head.

Even if it took her another nine years to kill him.

"You slimy, sadistic son of a bitch. You're giving her the shots. *Why?* I'm doing your farking Tombola."

"Thy twin didst perish three weeks past, and thou didst agree to this Tombola yesterday." Her father leveled his spear at her chest. *"I ordered the little one's treatment halted—for now—before she ripens to fertility. Easy enough to resume, dost thou defy Me."*

The threat couldn't be clearer. Beneath the copper hair piled high under a coronet neither one of them had ever wanted, her sister's freckled face was white with dread.

"Kylie." Her chest split wide with heartbreak.

"Hiya, sis," Kylie whispered, waving a transparent hand that tried to be jaunty but wasn't.

Kaia scrambled up the steps, sword forgotten at her side.

Stupid to do this. It's just her avatar.

But the instinct to comfort and protect her scared little sister was way too powerful to deny.

"Hey, kid," she whispered, two cubits from Kylie's wavering hologram. "Don't be afraid, okay? I'm gonna do what he wants."

"Yeah, well that's pretty much what I'm afraid of." Kylie pitched her voice too low for anyone else to hear. "All these gnarly dudes? They really suck."

She's afraid for me. Kaia's heart swelled to shatter her chest like glass. *And she knows if I screw this up, they'll be hot after her.*

"Don't sweat it. They won't bother you. I'll keep them off you." Kaia's voice shook as she swore away her freedom. "Every last one of them. And that's a punking promise."

Six cubits away, her father spread his arms as though he'd spawned the entire spectacle like the god of creation—the five hundred suitors, the two desperate sisters, the First Indomitable and his army, the cloaked and deadly telepath, and all the vast span of interstellar space.

"Behold! See how I honor Mine oath to Mine heir. So shalt I honor My pledge to thee. Seven days hence, one man aboard this vessel shall claim the Kryll Corona. To that man doth I say—the spoils of victory are sweet. All the great wealth of My merchant empire deeded as thine inheritance. All the Kryll faithful of My vast congregation kneeling at thy feet. And all the sweet pleasures of My beauteous

daughter chained in thy bed. Wild and willful is she, but lo! How thou shalt enjoy the taming."

Her stomach dropped to her boots and the blood drained from her face.

Chained.

The Tombola chains.

According to the Apocrypha, a Tombola bride went chained to her consort's bed. It was supposed to be a symbol of submission, but the chains had been known to serve the practical function of physically restraining a reluctant bride. Only her consort possessed the key, and the chains only came off once she'd pleased him.

For a woman to appear chained in public the next day was the ultimate humiliation. A public proclamation that she'd failed to satisfy or balked at some sexual act required by her new consort, and therefore required more rigorous instruction. A consort who appeared chained in public became available for any man's pleasure—the ostensible purpose being to train her to obedience. Until the rebellious bride showed utter submission to her unpalatable fate.

She'd adamantly resolved to negotiate away that odious custom in the conditions she gave Dex for agreeing to the auction.

Then he'd kissed her and she'd lost her flipping mind—

The Patriarch's heavy spear slammed against the floor with a deafening peal of thunder. Lightning forked and flashed to blind her. When Kaia's vision cleared, her father and sister had vanished.

Leaving Kaia alone to face the five hundred men he'd just baited to a foaming frenzy to do whatever it took to claim her.

And then chain her.

CHAPTER ELEVEN
The Pinch

"… tell you what went down with my brother's Tombola bride." The Kryll spice merchant's jocular voice was phlegmy with satisfaction. Above the piped-in clamor of tribal rhythms, two other candidates pushed close to hear. "Kept her chains on after the mating night, he did! Virgin, you know, like any Tombola bride. And brother's a back-door man, if you know what I mean?"

Lewd laughter heaved the gourd of the merchant's belly under his straining tunic. "Bride didn't like that so much, did she? Well, he sends her out to bazaar next day wearing her chains and a neat little sign saying what's the problem. Comes home that night to find her lubed and spread for him sweet as you like…"

The hearty guffaws of his audience mercifully muffled the rest of the nasty anecdote, right up to the Kryll's gleeful climax.

"Just begging my brother to take her that night, wasn't she? She wanted those chains off!"

From her hidden post behind a pillar, Kaia squeezed her eyes shut and shuddered, sick all the way down to her boot soles. After six grueling clicks meeting suitor after suitor in rigidly structured interviews under Dex's militant eye, she was desperate for a respite.

But not desperate enough to stay where she was and listen to this self-satisfied pig give gleeful voice to her worst nightmares.

"And did he?" the avid listener demanded. "Take her chains off?"

Knowing she'd lose her lunch if she heard another unsavory syllable, Kaia pushed off and slunk deeper into the shadows that edged the amphitheater. Enormously aided by the entertainment on offer from three dozen dancing acrobats Dex had miraculously magicked up to mollify her five hundred horny suitors.

Angels and asteroids. Thirty-six acrobats. And every living one a redhead in a cybersuit.

Not to mention masked—which to Mogadon sensibilities signaled sexual willingness to explore any taboo. Acrobats were already starting to slip away with one or two… or three or four… of Kaia's ostensible suitors to the curtained *cubicula* behind the viewing tiers that ringed the austere expanse.

The whole setup would be farking brilliant.

If it weren't so farking obscene.

Obscene or no, she had to admire Dex's unorthodox tactics. Somehow the paid performers were blunting the dangerous sexual edge the Patriarch's provocative prodding and all those Mogadon pheromones had honed—an edge to amp up the atmospherics and goose her purchase price. Not being the only sentient being with cleavage and a vag in circulation at this circus with five hundred overstimulated suitors was a blessing for which Kaia could hardly overstate her appreciation.

Nearby, Dex was trying unsuccessfully to extricate himself from a knot of eager Indomitables all clamoring for advice on their bids. After six clicks of interviews, he'd actually loosened his collar. Now his corded throat gleamed with sweat.

Which didn't help one bit to suppress her renegade fantasy of popping the gold buttons of Dex's dress uniform one by one and dragging her tongue down his naked chest.

Now she too was sweating.

Catching her stealthy escape in his peripheral vision from ten cubits away, Dex sliced her a harassed look. *Don't you dare run off. I mean it.*

She stopped dead in her tracks and stared. He wasn't even a telepath, so how in the seven hells…

It's all right, space cadet. I've got her.

This from Nero, who'd been watching her entertain her five hundred despicables all afternoon from a discreet distance. And who seemed to have plucked her own irreverent nickname for the First Indomitable effortlessly from the most intimate nooks and crannies of her brainbox.

Along with who knew how many other intimate tidbits?

Since we all seem to be sending and receiving now, she told them, *and never mind how weird that is—you know, with Dex being Mogadon and all? I need to get out of here for ten ticks or I'm going to blow. I'm ducking into this little cubby. Keep everyone out.*

And she wasn't waiting around for a royal dispensation. Despite her appreciation for their shared surveillance, she prayed neither of her self-proclaimed protectors followed her.

Deftly she darted behind a curtain into one of the private alcoves.

Because she desperately needed solitude.

Behind her, the heavy curtain slithered shut. Wrapping her in a womb of warm dark silence.

With the curtain drawn, the only light seeped dim through the viewport. Already the sullen red planet of Mogadon and its ringed indigo neighbor had receded to coin-sized discs circling a rubescent sun in the *Inevitable*'s interstellar wake.

Spurred by the imperatives of his splendid little war—a war it didn't look like he was winning—Dex was gunning his battleship straight for the heart of the Gamma Sector. Where the Tombola would be celebrated—if that was the word for it—in seven days on the Kryll homeworld. A planet whose prime location between the upper and lower spiral arms of the galaxy was directly responsible for the indecent wealth of Kryll's merchant princes.

Not to mention her father's indecent power.

At which point Dex and his *Inevitable* would be well on their way to the hinterland. The Omega Sector.

And his next regularly scheduled genocide.

This time with the Syndax.

Shaking with nerves and exhaustion, Kaia tossed aside a stray acrobat's mask, crawled into a cushioned chair, and tucked her knees to her chest. She wrapped her arms around her legs and lowered her head. For the next little while, she poured herself into just breathing.

In.

Out.

In…

Out…

And slowing her anxious heart.

Releasing a slow sigh, she lifted her head and lost herself in the glittering span of stars. She wondered if Dex had ordered the *Angel* stowed in the *Inevitable*'s landing bay the way she wanted. She hoped like hell her speedy little psi-powered cruiser hadn't been left behind on Mogadon.

"I wish I could fly away from here," she whispered, just for the comfort of hearing her own voice. "I wish I could ditch this Tombola, fly straight to the Omega Sector myself, and never come back."

"Actually, so do I." Across the way, a low baritone rumbled from the depths of a high-backed chair cloaked in darkness.

That voice startled her so badly she shot to her feet with a gasp.

The shadow in the chair stayed comfortably put. Which was the only reason she didn't haul tail right out of there.

"Don't scamper off just yet," that deep voice rolled on calmly. "I'm sorry for startling you. You look like you could use a breather from that three-ring solar circus out there even more than me."

"You've got that right," she muttered, poised on the edge of flight.

Whoever the guy was, he wasn't blocking her exit. Even if he was one of her suitors—which seemed extremely likely—he couldn't pose any major danger. Not with Dex and Nero both in reach, only a telepath's whisper away.

Besides which, she had her cyber saber.

And she wasn't shy about using it.

"You go ahead and take a load off." A casual hand waved her to her chair. "I'll stay right where I'm at. We don't even need to palaver."

While she hovered in place, undecided, a burst of bawdy laughter invaded their shadowy refuge.

"… and then I told brother, I said, if she loves sucking cock so much, we better *both* indulge her. Let her suck us both at once!"

Thankfully, the music blotted out the rest of the sordid tale. Shuddering, Kaia dropped into her chair and hugged her knees.

Any tick now, he'll start talking. Either presenting his bid or trying some ham-handed seduction. The moment he does, I'm out of here.

But her shadowy companion was as good as he'd promised. Silence opened up between them.

A weirdly comfortable sort of silence she gradually realized he wouldn't breach.

After a while, her galloping pulse slowed and her clenched muscles unknotted. She even found herself growing curious about Mr. Dark and Silent over there. As her eyes adjusted, she snuck a few peeks.

He was hard to see, but he looked like a big guy. Not fat like that Kryll blowhard with the brother, but solid. He sure filled the chair—a substantial piece of furniture. The uncertain starlight gleamed on a thickly muscled thigh clad in a gunmetal-gray cybersuit, gleaming with some sort of anti-blast armor. One large hand rested quietly on his knee. Square-fingered, blunt-nailed.

The hand of a fighting man.

Dimly she discerned a craggy profile and a proud head of unruly hair cropped in the militaristic Mogadon style.

Cautiously she cleared her throat. "Um, thanks for the no-talking thing. I appreciate it."

"Yeah. You're welcome." His eyes stayed where they were, gazing out to space. Which gave her no view at all of his face.

"Are you Mogadon?" she ventured.

He pushed out a breath that might have been amusement. "Technically, yeah."

Curious. She'd met so many Mogadon over the past six clicks she was pretty sure Dex had dutifully introduced her to all of them. Although with Dex looming protectively over her and scowling catastrophic threats at every conceivable candidate, nobody was venturing very close.

Which suited her just fine.

"And you're a candidate?" she probed.

"Yep."

Cautiously she lowered her booted feet to the floor. "But you're not going to press your suit?"

"Would you like me to?"

Now he definitely sounded amused.

"I'll have to hear it at some point, whether I want to or not." Hearing how grudging and ungracious that sounded, she felt heat climb into her cheeks. "What I mean is, uh, you've been decent. I'll hear you now if you want. Although I should tell you in all honesty I have no intention of choosing a Mogadon consort."

And why in the universe she'd *told* him that, when she hadn't told any of the others, she couldn't begin to fathom.

"Doesn't surprise me a bit," he murmured.

She leaned forward. "It doesn't?"

"You're half Kryll, ain'tcha? Wouldn't be a big shock if you're looking for some kinda counterweight. Someone to oppose the kid—I mean Dex—with his army and his nukes and his misdirected drive for vengeance."

She was gobsmacked. Mogadon males had been blustering and swaggering past her all day. Not to mention cowering whenever Dex looked particularly menacing. Which Dex was very good at doing. But not one of those candidates had been perceptive enough to figure out what this guy just had.

Or confident enough to say it.

Which made her even more curious.

"You're actually right," she admitted with a laugh, leaning closer. If he'd only turn his head a little. "If you're honest enough to say it, I'm honest enough to admit it. Are you disappointed?"

"Nope. Pretty much the opposite."

Now—finally—he did turn. Just enough for the slate starlight to pick out broad cheekbones, rugged jaw, the narrow slice of a scar through one thick eyebrow, the blade of a nose that had once been broken. Sandy hair, silver-tipped and salted with maturity, spiked over a furrowed brow. Not a young man by any means. And clearly he'd lived a hard life.

But still a good-looking guy.

By any girl's measure.

"You're not? Disappointed, I mean?" Gods, she sounded like a Prime Class idiot. Still, she couldn't help asking. "Why not?"

"Kaia," he said patiently. And the sound of her name, spoken so gently in that deep rumbly voice, did strange and disturbing but not at all unpleasant things to her fluttery tummy. "Lucky for me, given your aversion to all things Mogadon, I'm the Syndax candidate."

Damn if her heart didn't stop. Because she figured Dex had found some pretext—the way he'd threatened—for driving away the lone Syndax.

But also because of the guy.

She couldn't tell what color his eyes were in the twilight. But something about the way he was looking at her made it hard to breathe.

She cleared her throat and tried like blazes to pull her head together. She needed to think. Badly. She'd wanted to find him—the Syndax candidate. And now here he was.

With Dex nowhere in sight. A reprieve that can't possibly last. Get it together, angel.

"Right." She hoped she didn't sound as breathless as she felt. "I'll hear your bid now. If you want."

"Then I better seize my moment," he said easily. "Gods know I'm not the richest of your wannabes or anybody's odds-on favorite. In fact, I guess you'd say I'm kinda notorious. But you're kinda notorious yourself, ain'tcha?"

"Yeah, kind of." She laughed. "I like it that way."

"So do I, actually. That's why I'm here. I never woulda offered for your twin."

"Oh, wouldn't you?" she flared, stung on Kira's behalf.

"Now don't get all spun up. I'm sure she was outta this world. But she was a conventional gal at heart, wasn't she? A guy like me wouldn't have stood a chance." He chuckled wryly. "And even if I did, I'm afraid she woulda bored me in a week."

"You're wrong about Kira. *Dead wrong.* There was a whole lot more going on behind that polished, perfect façade she cultivated so carefully than most people ever realized." She tried to leave it there. She really did. Yet she couldn't seem to stop herself from asking. "But you think I wouldn't, ah, bore you?"

He pushed out a chuckle. "Haven't you heard enough blarney from your army of admirers, princess?"

"More than enough." She scooted to the edge of her seat. "And you can call me Kaia. But I'd actually like to hear your take."

"Sure it won't scare you off?" He gazed through the viewport, eyes narrowed and distant in thought. "Been a while since I've had a consort. Lotta women, I find at this stage of life, tend to be kinda predictable—at least in my world." His head swiveled to fix her, firing with sudden intensity. "When I saw you face down your old man today like a wrathful goddess... ferocious as a tiger protecting a cub... challenging a goddamn tyrant with nothing but a samurai sword and enough raw courage to fuel a battle fleet? Well, that was pretty much it. I figured you're the woman I want in my bed."

"Oh," she whispered. "Wow."

Amazed she could manage that much.

Because the dark undercurrent of desire that vibrated in his voice made craving pound through her blood and burn in her nipples and throb between her legs until she ached to be touched.

And because the thought that he admired her for doing what

she had to do opened a gaping fissure in her bruised and guarded heart.

"I knew I wouldn't rest," he said low, big hands easy on his chair, "till I won you for myself. And I can offer you something none of those wannabes can top. Absolute freedom, with no rules and no conventions and no accountability. Give me a son or a daughter, and they'll have the same freedom.

"And unlike those yahoos out there with their swagger and their egos and their insecurity, I don't need to chain a woman to keep her in my bed. If the time ever comes you decide I'm the one you want, you'll come to me more than willing.

"Or else not at all."

It was like someone had looked inside her head, saw what she'd dreamed of but knew she'd never find, and programmed a man in the cyberverse who'd fulfill her every flipping fantasy.

And all she could seem to do was stare.

"I'm, ah, half Valyrian." Good gods, she was actually stammering. And blushing to boot. "We need to… desire our consorts or we won't conceive. And then the match won't hold. How do I… how do I know I'd… well… ?"

His scarred eyebrow hitched. "How do you know you'll desire me?" His deep voice dropped an octave. "Kaia. Don't you know already?"

She couldn't seem to stop babbling. Or blushing. "My love life— my, um, romantic history? It's kind of an open book in the media, right? Ben—Ben Nero is my lifemate. But we can't ever… and then there's this thing with Dex."

"Yeah." He sighed. "I've seen the three of you together. You're all pretty young. What you three kids are trying to do—it almost never works. Not for more than a night or two."

"We're not trying to do anything," she rushed to assure him. "I mean, Ben's wanted Dex for years, but Dex won't—and Ben wants *me* but *I* won't. I've told him I'm never letting him anywhere near me."

"Unlike others of my race, one woman's enough for my bed," he told her with quiet finality. "And I figure I'll be more than enough for hers."

She struggled to get her head straight.

"What you're offering—it's appealing," she had to admit. She'd been honest with him so far, hadn't she? "I'm not a traditional Tombola bride. Someone like you is… more than I expected to find, actually. But I—I need to think."

"That's what these seven days are for, ain't they?" he said easily. "If you wanna talk, you'll find me on my ship. The *Relentless.* We're pacing the *Inevitable* till the hootenanny's done. Or till you turn me down and give me the old heave-ho, I guess. That's when my truce with the Mogadon ends."

Big-boned and rangy as a Kryllian sand wolf, he unfolded to his feet. And the way he towered over her, head nearly brushing the ceiling, just made her body go haywire.

She jumped up to… stop him from leaving, she supposed… and gripped his arm in an urgent press. The cold scaled starmetal of blast armor grazed her fingers. Underneath, the powerful swell of his biceps seared her palm.

He stood still beneath her touch, patient as a wolf with a newborn pup, head angled to look down on her in the shadows. The expanse of his cavernous chest rose and fell a handspan from her face. She wanted to touch him—touch more of him—and find out if his big body was really as powerful under all that metal as it looked.

I wonder if this could actually work, a voice whispered in her brain, on tiptoe with desperate hope.

"What else can I answer for you?" he said softly.

You can kiss me. It was all she could manage not to say it out loud. *You can kiss me and show me once and for all if this thing between us could possibly have a chance.*

But she could hardly say that, could she? Not after she'd known him all of five ticks. "Your name? You can tell me your name. Because I can't go around calling you the Syndax candidate, can I?"

"Nah." Finally he grinned, which softened the stern nobility of his battle-scarred features. "You want the gods' honest? Cuz I'm afraid once I spill the beans, you'll just up and skedaddle."

"I'm not the skedaddling type. Tell me your name."

Acting on their own recognizance with zero guidance from her brain, her hands slid up his bulging arms. She had to reach above her head to rest her palms on his mighty shoulders. A predatory scent swirled through her senses—a dangerous whiff of wolf and steel. Darker and more raw than Dex's mating scent, the bracing spice she herself was still exuding from every pore. She tilted back her head to meet his searching gaze.

His eyes were silver-blue—Mogadon blue—blue as winter seas. And he *was* going to kiss her, she realized with a shiver.

And she was going to let him.

But even now, poised on the edge of a moment, with the air between them throbbing with held breath and expectation, he let her set the pace.

"Mosey on over here," he rumbled low in his chest. "Show me what you want. I don't want there to be any mistake."

She swallowed hard and rose on tiptoe. His big hands settled on her waist, and a bolt of raw need shafted through her.

"Tell me," she whispered. "Your name."

"Well, you asked for it." He lowered his head and she lifted hers to meet him halfway. "I'm actually, uh—"

A brutal hand dragged the curtain back. A harsh yellow glare, strident as a spotlight, spilled over them. In the doorway Dex's black-clad frame stood riveted, light trapped in his tawny hair.

His thunderstruck silhouette bristled with violence.

"What in the name of the seven bloody devils—?" Dex went rigid like he'd been lasered. *"Zorin?"*

#

Nero was engaged in a futile effort to coach the Valyrian candidates—none of whom had sparked even a flicker of interest from Kaia—when the psychic impact of her silent scream blasted through his brain.

Without a word of apology, he muttered a curse and shoved headlong through a clump of laughing acrobats toward the alcove where his lifemate had vanished. His blood pounded with the urgent pulse of danger. Below the raucous clamor, through the closed curtain, someone was shouting.

When he tore in there, he nearly ripped the fabric from the rod.

Dex stood braced with his back to Nero, blaster leveled squarely at someone's chest from six cubits away. A massive stranger encased in a starmetal cybersuit stood riveted in dangerous stillness, one hand extended in a plea for calm, big body protectively angled between

Dex's blaster and Kaia hopping up and down behind him. She was trying desperately to get between them, of course—being Kaia—but somehow the big guy managed to keep her safely behind him and out of harm's way.

A protective impulse Nero thoroughly approved.

But one that he could already see was driving Dex berserk.

"Take it easy, kid." Whoever he was, the guy projected rock-solid authority with every syllable. "She's fine. We're all fine."

"Like *hell* we are," Dex clipped out. "Get away from him, Kaia, so I can blow him to the next galaxy."

"I'm under a flag of truce." The target of Dex's rage had a remarkably cool head in a crisis. Rather like Dex himself—at least under normal circumstances. The guy kept his steel-blue eyes locked on Dex's face, not his blaster. "And I'm pretty sure you promised the Patriarch not to butcher his cash cows. Think it through, kid."

Even in extremis, his tone was threaded with a chord of dry humor. But Dex all too clearly wasn't in a laughing mood.

Particularly with Kaia jumping up and down, straining to see over the big guy's shoulder. "He's the Syndax candidate, Dex! And he's right about my father."

"He's an execrable traitor to his race and the blood-sworn enemy of his people. Not to mention my father's murderer," Dex gritted out. "You get away from him, Kaia. You get away from him right now."

Abruptly the pieces dropped into place. Only one man in the galaxy could get under Dex's skin this way.

"Zorin?" Nero exclaimed, so startled he actually spoke out loud. "Good gods, man."

"And you're Ben Nero." Zorin spared him an easy nod, but his eyes stayed on Dex. "Come on, Dex. You know what Max was. He was my best friend, wasn't he? Before the biodrugs ate his brain. Then he was just an addict and a sadist. By offing him when I did, I performed a public service—as I'm sure your Valyrian buddy here would agree."

Thus called upon for support defusing the crisis, Nero had to admit the truth. "Your father was a monster, Dex. Maybe he didn't start out that way, but he turned into a genocidal psychopath."

"If it wasn't me who did it, you'd have had to put him down yourself." Something like pity surfaced in Zorin's gaze. "Sorry, kid. You know it's true."

"I'm properly addressed as *commander*," Dex said tightly. "And my father was admittedly no saint. But he was your friend, your comrade-in-arms, and a war hero. All of which one might have expected to preclude you from slaughtering him unarmed and naked in his bed like a coward, instead of the soldier you were supposed to be. You dishonored and betrayed all three of us that night! You—who were once the best of us."

And Nero didn't like the sound of his voice. The coolest head in the galaxy was about a whisker away from losing it.

Clearly Zorin too read the warning signs. He kept his armored body still and his deep voice level. "Max was psychotic. Capable of anything. He'd stockpiled enough novicide to kill every living thing on Mogadon ten times over. And he woulda used it, Dex. Believe me." The Syndax pushed out a heavy breath. "I spaced him the only place I could find him where he didn't have his hand on the kill switch."

"I don't believe you. I've never believed you. Nor does any of that poppycock explain what in the seven hells you think you're doing here. Or why *you*—" Dex fired at Kaia "—were standing there kissing him! Of all five hundred bloody men at this Tombola, *he's* the one you're noticing?"

"Ah." Nero sighed in weary comprehension. This was a Zorin thing. But it was also a Kaia thing. If she'd been reckless enough to kiss Zorin of all men anywhere within a hundred parsecs of Dex, she would've punched all his buttons. "Dex, he's their candidate."

"And I wasn't kissing him—yet," Kaia fired back, peeking out at him around Zorin's massive shoulder. "But I'm allowed! I believe you called it 'assessing his personal appeal'?"

"He'll find it rather difficult to be personally appealing once I blow his brains through the back of his head," Dex snarled. His hand wasn't nearly as steady on that blaster as Nero would have liked.

And Kaia's defiance wasn't exactly helping defuse the tension.

Zorin himself clearly sensed the battle shifting to dangerous terrain. The furrow deepened between his sandy brows and his eyes flickered with the cold gleam of battle. And the space pirate looked more capable of handling himself in a brawl than any guy Nero had ever seen.

When Dex's shoulders tightened, Nero knew he needed to intervene—and fast. Or there'd be blood on those velvet curtains, and lots of it.

Gliding in close, he wrapped his arms around Dex's chest from behind and fought without success to ease down the blaster.

"Come on, Dex. You'll thank me for this later," Nero murmured.

"Not bloody likely. Stay out of this."

Nero barely knew what he was saying. Because it had been half a lifetime since he'd held Dex in his arms—one of those brotherly hugs at the ashram he was always hoping against hope would morph into something more. Now the hard muscled strength of Dex's back and thighs against his body for the first time in ten years flooded Nero's entire body with heat.

"Damn it, Dex," he whispered under his breath.

But he couldn't let go until the guy lowered that blaster.

"Take your infernal hands off me." Dex tried irritably to shrug him off.

And for the very life of him, Nero couldn't help himself. He leaned in to put his mouth against Dex's ear. "You sure that's what you want?"

"Oh, for the love of Juno!" Far too provoked to exercise his trademark restraint, Dex made another exasperated attempt to shake himself free.

Which gave Nero all the excuse he needed to prolong the contact. With the inevitable physiological effect he somehow hadn't seen coming. Pressed against Dex's powerful frame from shoulders to thighs, Nero felt a tight coil of heat gather in his cock.

"Dex, for gods' sake, stop struggling," he said hoarsely. "Because I can do this all night."

An electric jolt of shared awareness arced between them. Triggered by the hungry heat of his cock pressed between them. Dex went suddenly still, breath audible and a tad too rapid in the supercharged silence. A flush crept up the back of his neck.

Has to be something there, Nero thought, fairly distracted himself by this point. *Whether he wants there to be or not. Every time I touch the guy, he blushes.*

A reaction that—considering that Dex ruled half the galaxy with a fist of iron—completely charmed the hell out of him.

That was always the problem for him with Dex. If he'd just wanted to get the guy in the sack, he could've gotten him liquored up and seduced him years ago, never mind his Mogadon hang-ups. Nero knew without conceit he was a world-class master of seduction. The trick was he wanted Dex still talking to him the next morning. He wouldn't have run home to Valyria like a scared schoolboy that summer if all he wanted from his best friend was a quick romp in the hay—

"All right," Dex said hoarsely, and lowered the blaster. "I promise not to blow a hole in the bugger's chest. At least not tonight. For tomorrow, I offer no assurance whatsoever. Nero—let go."

A directive that would be far more convincing if Nero wasn't breathing in the head-spinning musk of Mogadon mating scent. Kaia and Zorin between them had done more than enough to make Dex go full-bore Mogadon. But Nero couldn't help wondering if this time, he hadn't managed to trigger Dex's mating instinct himself.

A prospect that only made him harder.

He'd pay real money to slide his hands down Dex's trousers and find out for himself whether he was the only one getting hard.

If not for the indisputable fact that Dex would kill him where he stood.

Not to mention Zorin himself watching the byplay and looking bemused. Clearly drawing conclusions about the state of affairs between them that would horrify Dex to the core if he knew.

But at least the deadly tension of imminent violence was draining from the space pirate's big body.

Zorin eased aside to let Kaia scamper out from behind his protective bulwark.

Nero whispered to Dex, "Behave yourself," and carefully loosened his grip.

"I could say the same to you." Dex freed himself in a hurry and straightened his uniform with brisk, furious motions.

But at least he holstered his blaster.

"Gods of my father, Dex. That is *not* how this Tombola's supposed to work." Kaia looked more than a little annoyed herself, but she came forward to straighten Dex's collar for him. That small gesture of intimacy did more to settle him down than anything Nero had managed with his hands all over the guy.

Dex wrapped a protective arm around her waist and tucked her against his side. Absently Kaia twined her arm around his torso and leaned into him—the first time she'd done anything like that in Nero's presence. And he'd bet she didn't even realize she was doing it.

Glorious. She's always had a soft spot for any wounded warrior. As if Dex needed any more leverage to hold her interest.

Whereas I might as well be dead for all she cares.

Reclaiming the bastion of his accustomed authority, Dex scowled at Zorin.

"I want you off my battleship in five ticks, you bastard. Or I'm throwing you in the brig and charging you with murder and high treason. And since I'm the presiding official over any judicial proceeding on this ship while in transit, I assure you a trial won't end well for you."

"He's a Tombola candidate," Kaia said firmly. So much for appeasing him. "You can't lock him up. I want him on my shortlist."

"I'd rather see a Swarm spacebot on your shortlist." Dex bristled.

A mutinous flame kindled in her eyes. "It's not up to you."

"You want her for yourself," Zorin said on a soft exhale of comprehension. "Of course you do. That's why your mating scent's all over her. And as the emcee of this shindig, you can't bid for her, can ya? That's a tough break, kid."

"That pretty much sums it up," Nero agreed, earning a hostile look from Dex. "Hells, Dex. If he bids and she wants him, you can't throw him in the brig. And you definitely can't have him tried and shoved out the airlock. You're oathsworn. And maddening as I happen to find you, I'd rather not see a death warrant land on your stubborn Mogadon head."

"Listen to your friend," Zorin said with gruff sympathy. His eyes wandered thoughtfully over Nero.

An unexpected tingle zinged down Nero's spine and settled in his groin.

No wonder Dex hadn't been able to stop talking about the guy back in the day. Even if, being Dex, he was clueless about the fact he was crushing on his boyhood idol. And even if Zorin was Maximus Draven's contemporary and observed a strict hands-off policy toward his best friend's son, far as Nero could tell.

If he even leaned that way.

And he found himself really wondering if the Syndax leader leaned that way.

It was the deadly combo of all that physical mass and all that unapologetic power, his hard face and his pragmatic lethality, leavened by flashes of humor and compassion. He was a killing machine with a notorious image, but he was steady and solid as a mountain in a crisis. His battle scars and the silver sprinkled in his dark blond hair gave him gravitas. He was deadly the way a blaster was deadly.

And he was sex on a stick.

Gods of Solaris, Nero thought in a daze. *I'm crushing on him myself.*

"I've heard about you, Ben Nero. For once, looks like the rumors might even be true." One corner of the pirate's mouth lifted in a wry smile, and Nero found himself suddenly breathless. "No wonder they're both in love with you, huh?"

And for perhaps the first time in his life, silver-tongued Ben Nero actually found himself at a loss for words.

"You want my advice?" Zorin went on calmly. "I'd take the Commander here to bed tonight and make him come so hard he can't remember his own name, much less any of this mess, including my presence on this ship. You can both thank me later."

And while Dex stood paralyzed with outrage, the pirate said casually, "See ya around, kid. You'll have my bid in the morning."

With the graceful tread of a hunting lion, the Syndax slipped past and was gone.

Kaia stood riveted, staring after him with lips parted and eyes wide. And just the look of her flipped Nero off.

She was his lifemate—she was *his*—even if he hadn't seen her in years. He'd handled her with kid gloves when they were both, well, kids. She'd been a year younger, she'd made some crazy promise to her Valyrian mom, he'd been protective and indulgent and out of his head with love. He'd learned every way there was to make a girl climax with her clothes on.

Kid stuff. All of it.

Now she was all grown up. Over the years she'd had the occasional lover; he'd made it his business to know. He was aching for everything he'd been denied. And he had exactly seven days to get it.

Yet she'd been ignoring him for Dex since the day he turned up on Mogadon.

Now it looked like she was going to ignore him for Zorin.

"Damn it all to hell, Kaia," Nero ground out.

And the thwarted bitterness in his own voice astounded him.

He was the Valyrian Precursor, wasn't he? No one in the galaxy thwarted him.

Not anymore.

"Don't," Dex rasped, pulling free of Kaia. Moving stiffly, he crossed to stand before the viewport with his back turned squarely to them both. "Just—don't."

Nero didn't need to see the rigid set of his shoulders or the fists clenching and unclenching at his sides to know the guy was hurting. He didn't even need telepathy. Max Draven's madness and murder and monumental disgrace had been the formative events that chiseled away Dex's shining, idealistic, hero-worshipping youth and left this aloof, distrustful, self-contained loner to rule the Empire in his place.

And Zorin had always been an open wound for Dex.

Clearly sensing the minefield they were standing in the middle of, Kaia practically tiptoed up behind him.

"Dex, I'm so sorry. About Zorin and your dad—I didn't know. Are you… are you okay?"

His voice was scraped raw as skin dragged over rubble. "I want both of you to leave."

"I don't want to leave," she whispered, a tentative hand touching his shoulder. "I don't want to leave you alone—"

Dex lifted his wrist unit. "Marcus. I need a security escort for the maharani. Take her to my quarters."

Kaia whispered a curse as the Mogadon military machine wheeled efficiently into motion. The curtain slid aside and Dex's *optio* marched in.

"This way, lady. If you don't mind." Deferential but firm.

Clearly recognizing the inevitable when she saw it—even when she didn't like it—Kaia shot Nero an unhappy look. He profoundly hoped she wouldn't seize this ill-timed moment to air her grievance about sharing Dex's quarters, even if it was a devilish unseemly arrangement—to say the least—between a ward and her Tombola master.

I'll stay with him, he sent silently, holding her pleading gaze. *He's going to need a little time to wrap his head around you and Zorin.*

And, just in case you're wondering, I'm not exactly thrilled with you and Zorin myself.

Annoyance flared in her face. *You don't get a vote, Ben.*

A slow wrath kindled in his blood. *Yeah, about that—*

"Lady?" the *optio* urged, beefy hand gripping her elbow. Which Nero could've told him was a mistake.

"All right!" She shrugged his hand away. "You don't have to manhandle me. And don't call me 'lady,' for gods' sake. I'm going! But we need to talk about this, Dex. I have to choose someone, don't I? And it won't be a Mogadon."

"Comets, Kaia! Don't do this now." Nero urged her with his eyes. "Go."

Because Dex's ominous silence was really starting to worry him.

"All right." Exuding reluctance from every pore, she slid one last worried look at Dex's stiff back. "I'll wait up for you, okay? So we can talk."

Dex said nothing, and Kaia had to live with it. She slipped out unhappily with the *optio* on her heels, and the curtain whispered closed behind her.

Leaving him and Dex alone.

Eyeing his forbidding back, Nero cleared his throat. "Listen. About this Tombola..."

"Yes, about that." Dex's voice was acid, and Nero couldn't help wincing. "We might as well cancel the whole bloody thing. Zorin's as good as got her. At least until the Patriarch chooses the winner from the final ten. That Syndax bastard's a wretch and a traitor—but what he has, he holds. He'll make damn certain no other candidate has a chance."

Nero admitted Dex was undoubtedly right. The Syndax pirate would make a formidable rival, and he looked like a man who knew what he wanted.

But it was going to be pure hell on Dex.

Uneasily Nero shifted. Wishing the guy would at least look at him. "She has to choose someone—though I know he's the last man you want. This entire business is an unmitigated disaster, but you promised her father and now you're stuck with it."

Dex said nothing, and Nero pushed out a frustrated breath. "You think I don't know how it feels to watch her walk away, knowing it's your own damn fault she's leaving—"

"Get out."

"Not happening." Nero planted his feet and stayed right where he was. "Look, man, you're a wreck. I just want to—"

"Get. Out."

Nero clenched his fists. "Gods, Dex. Are we *ever* going to talk about this?"

Dex drew in a long breath. When he spoke, he sounded as defeated as Nero had ever heard him.

"I just stood here watching her all but kiss my father's killer. The man I swore I'd haul in to face Mogadon justice. The man I've spent the past eight years hunting. The man whose perfidy I've launched an interstellar war to punish. I just stood here listening to her tell me she wants *that man* for a bloody consort. Then I let him walk out the door— free as a renegade comet.

"You... Ben..." His golden head dropped. "I can't do this now."

Nero felt a burn in his chest and a pressure in his throat. Dex was upset. Genuinely distraught. And as much as he wanted to hate the guy for the biowar, he was under no delusion about his true feelings for Dex Draven.

Hells, even Zorin could apparently see the state of his heart.

"Look." Nero squared his shoulders. "I'm not going to—do what he said to you. I'd have to be brain-dead not to know how you feel about it. I just... You're hurting. Let me just... be here with you for a tick."

Dex stood silent, proud head resting against the viewport. Fighting the inconvenient sting of sentiment in his eyes, Nero waited him out.

Then Dex said, barely audible, "All right."

His heart pounding so hard in his lungs it threatened to burst through his chest, longing so strong it threatened to choke him, Nero stepped up softly behind him and laid a hand on his rigid shoulder. Bracing himself against the blow of being shrugged off at any moment.

Dex let his hand stay where it was.

Gently, Nero tightened his grip to turn him.

Head lowered, Dex let himself be turned.

Moving slow as a hunter stalking a jungle cat, Nero eased into his space and carefully put his arms around him. For an endless interval, Dex stood stiffly without moving. Then his hands rose clumsily, almost gingerly, to rest on Nero's waist. Nero leaned into him, feeling Dex shaking so violently he felt like he'd fly apart.

Cautiously Nero tightened his grip, but he was afraid to hold him too hard.

Dex released an uneven breath and slid his arms around him. Nero made a conscious effort to breathe. Which only made him more aware of the dark musk of Mogadon pheromones and the dizzying scent that always meant Dex to him.

Dex's hard hand slicked over Nero's long hair. "Soft," he whispered, barely audible in the darkness. "Just like I always knew it would be."

Nero closed his eyes and shivered. "You think I don't know I'm the last thing you want? I just… I have to know. Would you really rather see me dead?"

Dex clasped the back of his neck in a gentle squeeze meant to comfort.

And Nero's knees nearly buckled.

"Jupiter. I never wanted you dead. I always wanted—what I wanted. I just couldn't let myself want… *this*." Dex's head turned toward him and their mouths met.

Nero thought his heart would stop. Because the head-spinning hit of hesitation and hunger trapped between Dex's mouth and his would've undone a harder man than Ben Nero. When Dex's strong hand closed around his head to ease him closer, it was all Nero could manage to keep his legs under him.

He was terrified of moving too fast, going too far, driving away the very thing he'd craved with hopeless longing all these years. But he was no more capable of resisting the hot hard press of Dex's mouth against his than he was of stopping a planet's spin around the sun with his bare hands. His mouth opened with a groan to that insistent need.

He felt Dex shudder with a hoarse echo of the same raw need. His arms clenched around Nero and fused their bodies together.

Dex tasted like wine and wanting and every erotic dream he'd ever had. And the electric slide of Dex's tongue meeting his blew every neuron in his body. Despite his desperate effort to rein himself in, hold himself back, let Dex set the pace, Nero tightened his grip against the powerful muscles of Dex's lower back to clutch him tighter.

He *needed*. Gods of Solaris, how he needed.

Dex growled in his chest and backed Nero against something—a wall, a bulkhead, a flipping moon for all he knew—calloused hands closing around Nero's face to hold him in place. Like he was going anywhere. Those commanding hands and the bulkhead behind him anchored him in a madly tilting world as Dex devoured his mouth with deep desperate kisses that demanded a surrender he was more than ready to give.

Stars were exploding in his head. And the only problem Nero had with this entire mind-blowing arrangement was that their current placement did nothing to ease the urgent swell of need in his cock.

Despite the jumble of cautionary words jangling around in his head, his hands slid of their own accord over the hard bulge of Dex's ass and dragged their hips together.

A whimper, raw with hunger, spilled from his throat.

"Easy, love," Dex whispered against his lips. "Just let me… be with you, just this once. Just for a moment. Wanted you so long. The way you sound… the way you taste… the way you kiss…"

Nero panted his name and tried to form a sentence. "Gods—Dex—I need—"

Dex's fingers skimmed the lacing of Nero's breeches, and he nearly lost his mind.

"Is this what you need?" Dex murmured.

"Yes." The word tore from his chest with a naked yearning that should have appalled him. "So much. Please. Anything. We can stop whenever you—"

"I beg your pardon, Commander?" A mannerly voice just beyond the curtain barely made sense to his reeling brain. "Would you mind terribly if I have a word?"

Dex breathed a curse against his mouth. Somehow Nero loosened his desperate grip and broke the kiss before Dex could do it for him. Because he didn't think he could survive getting pushed away again.

"Bloody hell." Dex cleared his throat and called, "Ah, Titus—a moment."

He pressed his brow against Nero's.

"And here's the problem," Dex said softly. "If we ever started something like that, I don't think I'd want to stop."

"And that's a problem why?" Nero rasped, licking his tingling lips. Wanting nothing more than to lean in and kiss him again.

But he knew.

He knew.

Dex's accursed Mogadon conditioning, courtesy of his accursed father—that ingrained, soul-deep conviction that same-sex unions were somehow *less*, that they could only ever be a cheap kinky thrill, that they demeaned whoever shared them, especially whoever wasn't in the pilot's seat—might've been briefly in abeyance.

But now, like the immortal hydra of Mogadon myth, those deep-rooted convictions were rearing their ugly heads.

"You know why." Dex squeezed his shoulders once and released him. "I'll bet you a thousand creds this is about Zorin. That man causes trouble just by breathing."

"To the seven hells with Zorin." Nero pushed his fingers through his tousled hair, amazed to realize his hands were shaking. "Don't you think we should talk about what just happened?"

"No time." Dex ran a hand over his own burnished hair, electric eyes sliding over Nero's hurried grooming. His voice dropped an octave. "Just tell me this. What we just did. It's what you wanted, wasn't it?"

Nero managed a noncommittal noise. Because he wanted so much more than that from Dex.

But he was afraid if he admitted what he really wanted—admitted just how far his dreams of Dex extended—the guy would just bolt.

"Was it…" Dex cleared his throat. "Worth the wait?"

By now, Nero had his head together.

"Want to know if you're worth it? Jury's still out. I know all about your Mogadon baggage." He swung his cloak over one shoulder and returned Dex's wary look with a dark promise. "Next time you've got your hands on my body—assuming there ever *is* a next time? We're not stopping till we both see flaming rockets."

As he flung the curtain aside and stalked past the blandly incurious eyes of Dex's subordinate, Ben Nero swung between the seething tension of a decade of dammed-up sexual frustration and a spike of supreme satisfaction.

Because he had, once again, managed to make Dex Draven blush.

CHAPTER TWELVE
The Virgin

Kaia slithered out of Dex's quarters through a ventilation shaft at midnight.

Because Dex was definitely avoiding her, and the scarred hulk of the Syndax battleship was keeping pace as they streaked through space, and maybe they'd start shooting at each other, and if they did it would be her fault, and it flipped her off being locked in the First Indomitable's quarters like a flipping felon while four of his elite guard—any number of whom were doing their level best to kill him—played cards in the corridor.

Besides which, her head was going to erupt like a volcano if she stayed cooped up any longer, with thoughts of Dex and Nero and Zorin shuttling through her brain on play-rewind-repeat and short-circuiting every synapse in her body.

"Blast these Mogadon pheromones," she muttered around the penlight she gripped between her teeth to light her way as she wiggled on her belly through the snug metal chute. "For years I'm like a farking robot. I go through the motions and run through every girl-on-guy maneuver in the pre-sex playbook, but no one makes me feel *anything*—umph. Tight corner here. And now look at me."

So thermonuclear I feel like I'm going to explode if I don't get horizontal with one of them... or all three of them. Despite what I promised my mom.

Blast these pheromones!

She swallowed down a groan as a metal grate opened up below. A potential outlet from the shaft's increasingly snug confines. Cautiously she bellied up and peered through.

The last two grates had opened directly over the busy corridor. Not an option if she wanted to keep her escape from incarceration quiet.

And she definitely wanted it kept quiet. Pretty sure she'd provoked Dex enough for one day.

This time, she peered into the shadowy confines of a guard dorm lined with tiers of tidy bunks. Mostly empty.

But a few held blanketed lumps that looked suspiciously like sleepers.

Especially given the seesaw snores.

Instantly she switched off her penlight. The snores sawed on without a hitch. After a nerve-racking wait, she released a cautious breath.

But she didn't feel much relief. Because she'd already seen that the shaft ahead was sealed. Her options were to retreat to her stifling prison—which was *so* not an option—or lower herself into the guard dorm, tiptoe past the sleeping Mogadon, and hope like hell she didn't sneeze.

Working grimly by touch in the drafty dark, she wiggled a screwdriver from her utility belt, unscrewed the grate, and eased it aside. Then she slithered through the hole like an eel and dropped gently to the floor.

The snorer snuffled. A sleeper mumbled. The sour scent of dirty laundry corrupted the air. Kaia breathed shallowly through her mouth and crouched. Poised to bolt for the door whose dim outlines she could barely see.

After an agonizing wait, the snoring droned on. Heart hammering, she eased to her feet and ghosted for the door. A beat later, the corridor erupted in a burst of male laughter.

Right before the door shot open.

A spill of fluorescent light poured in to expose her. Silhouetting a massive pair of armored troopers, blast helmets tucked under their arms, stun rifles slung over their shoulders.

Kaia was already running, three strides launching her into a lightning-fast sequence of front flips.

"Hey! What the devil—?"

Her fourth flip slammed her feet-first into a trooper's chest. The guy dropped like a stone, stun rifle skidding out of reach. A pained grunt exploded from him as Kaia's knees landed squarely on his diaphragm.

"What the flip? It's one of them whores!"

While the guy beneath her wheezed for air, his buddy dove to grab her. She scrambled free and dropped, booted foot shooting forward in a crescent sweep.

The blow knocked Trooper Two's legs from under him. He collapsed with a shout, helmet rolling across the floor. She followed up with a leaping side kick to the sternum that put Two on his back, empurpled and winded.

Kaia shot to her feet and darted around the first corner she hit before anyone caught his breath and started shooting. An explosion of confused questions and breathless complaints spewed in her wake.

As she fled, she adjusted the acrobat's mask she'd purloined at the Tombola more securely over her nose.

A dizzying ellipsis of twists and turns later—spurts of running punctuated with periods of purposeful walking when she encountered occupied corridors—Kaia finally dared to pause and get her bearings.

Lucky for her she thought ahead. Before she'd been locked in Dex's quarters, she'd wheedled an abbreviated tour of the *Inevitable* from Dex's *optio*.

And the guy's carefully neutral face while he dealt with her spoke volumes.

Dex might think he was getting away with the flimsy deception of housing her in his quarters to secure her personal safety. But she didn't think he was fooling his own men. Those sidelong looks of rampant speculation she kept intercepting told her they firmly believed she was sharing not only Dex's quarters.

But also his bed.

Maybe they thought the First Indomitable planned to pull a fast one on the Patriarch by seducing his royal daughter right under the old codger's nose. Or maybe they guessed what was really happening— that the inconvenient chemistry between the two of them was so off-the-charts combustible they could barely keep their hands off each other.

Either way, she didn't think she was doing Dex's Mogadon reputation any damage.

But if the Patriarch ever caught a whiff of that dangerous rumor about his daughter's desecration, that misplaced speculation would get them both killed.

Her skin tingled with nervous tension. All too aware that tonight, in her acrobat's rig, she lacked Dex's protection. She'd dressed as conservatively as subterfuge would permit, in a stretchy red leather cyberdress—long-sleeved and high-necked—with only a handspan of sleek golden thigh visible between her high boots and short skirt.

The cyber saber was a calculated gamble.

Recognizable.

But the whole gimmick Dex was playing on with these redheaded acrobats was to impersonate her. To ease the pressure.

He'd set them up as lightning rods, drawing off the lust of her pheromone-fueled suitors. And the clever tactic was actually working.

Except now, disguised as an acrobat herself, it would work against her.

Still, the girls were paid courtesans with the freedom to choose their own lovers. She'd made sure of that. If anyone hit on Kaia in her acrobat's disguise, she had the right to say no.

She gave a wide berth to the bridge, the Tombola hall and the ready room—all places she was dangerously likely to encounter Dex. Whose reaction to finding her roaming his battleship fancy-free she didn't care to contemplate. When she talked to him about today's encounter with Zorin—an encounter that still made her chest ache— she wanted him calm with no distractions.

You're falling for him. When you saw him all torn up over Zorin and his father's murder, it split your chest wide open. You would've killed to take away his pain.

You're definitely falling for him.

But falling for the First Indomitable of the Mogadon Empire emphatically wasn't part of the plan. Falling for the First Indomitable was, in fact, the exact opposite of the plan.

So she shoved the disturbing prospect of falling for the First Indomitable firmly into her mental closet and barred the door.

Just. Not. Happening.

Nope.

At this hour, the gleaming silicon corridors were mostly silent. Except for scattered security patrols and a few scattered packs of Tombola candidates roaming the halls, too restless and sexed up to sleep.

These, too, she gave a wide berth.

Dex had set something up in the Tombola hall for evening giggles that was the interracial equivalent of a saturnalia, complete with orgy couches and the acrobats on a pay-to-play basis. Part of his continuing strategy to keep the ritual's sexual frustration, with its ominous potential for violence, to a slow simmer rather than a rolling boil.

She was sedulously careful to go nowhere near the place.

Her destination was the Blind Tiger.

Part speakeasy, part gin joint, part disco, the Blind Tiger was where the *Inevitable*'s crew went in their downtime to blow off steam. An indulgence that wasn't officially sanctioned by a militant Empire whose crew could be called to battle stations in an eyeblink—but this little deviation from the Mogadon Codex was tolerated. They'd wandered past the place on her tour, and she'd winkled the secret from Marcus.

Because after the day she'd had, and given the massive overdose of Mogadon pheromones wreaking havoc with her hormones, she too needed to blow off steam. And she figured the Blind Tiger might be the best place on this battleship for a make-believe courtesan to do just that.

She slipped through the unmarked portal without challenge. And the impact of the place hit her like a bucket of ice water flung in her face.

The throbbing tempo of tribal drums.

The murky dusk crawling with holographic images.

The digital flashes of verdant jungle and tropical heat and stalking beasts with amber eyes.

The solid wall of flesh, in and out of uniform, packed along the bar's serpentine swirl.

The slow heave of writhing bodies behind an energon curtain of vines and moss in the tiny grotto devoted to dancing.

Kaia slid through the crowd to find an empty corner at the crowded bar. Careful to keep her eyes down and her hands to herself. Under the probing impact of wary eyes, her telepathic senses tingled with caution.

Because she still smelled like Dex.

Nothing much she could do about that.

Except roll the dice and gamble their alpha's mating scent would incline these off-duty troopers, technicians and engineers to give her plenty of space.

Too bad the wiry bargirl with the close-cropped hair and fighting leathers wasn't playing the game. The bargirl shot her an unfriendly scowl. "Sorry, sweetheart. Blind Tiger's for crew and guests of crew only."

Kaia's heart dropped to her boots. Because she didn't need telepathy to know this hard-as-nails gatekeeper wouldn't be budged.

"She's with me," a voice said quietly. "Kryllian firewater for the lady, if you please. And the same for me."

Braced to fend off some randy Indomitable, Kaia spun to face him. And the gent standing at the bar beside her was definitely Mogadon—blond hair, blue eyes, tidy uniform. Even if he lacked the razzle-dazzle of the Empire's senior officers.

Not to mention their armed and menacing physical mass.

In fact, this one wasn't even armed. And the cryptic sigil that glittered gold at his collar was pretty much the only adornment on his slender frame. A sigil that made her blink with a flicker of recognition.

"Whatever you say, Doc." The barkeep backed right off. "Double draw of firewater it is."

Kaia had the barkeep pegged for a tough customer. But as she scurried to fill the order, what surfaced and sank in the girl's eyes was naked fear.

"Doctor, is it?" Warily Kaia's gaze shifted from the scientific symbol stitched to her neighbor's collar to his clean-cut, kindly, unremarkable face. "That's decent of you. But I should tell you I'm, uh, off duty. Not looking for paying customers, I mean."

"I should think not," he murmured, eyes crinkling as he met her suspicious look without offense. "One presumes five hundred suitors would be more than sufficient for any woman. Even one as famous as the Kryll maharani."

"Oh, I'm not—" Kaia paused as the bargirl slid two glasses of firewater down the bar and found urgent business somewhere else.

Clearly, the game was up. Least as far as the doc here was concerned.

Kaia heaved a sigh of resignation. "Am I that obvi?"

"Only to me." Her neighbor smiled down at his glass. "I'm more… observant than most."

"Are you a suitor? Because I'm only hearing bids in the formal Tombola."

"Which troubles me not at all, as I haven't entirely determined how to bid. I believe I'm what you'd call a bit of a dark horse candidate." He took a thoughtful sip of his glass's incendiary contents without a wince. "I'm Dr. Cato. Pontius Cato. The First Indomitable's chief scientist."

Well, that explained his observational skills. She tossed back a swallow of her own firewater and felt the burn hit her throat with a satisfying shudder.

Without much interest, she asked, "You a rocket scientist? Aeronautics engineer? Physicist?"

"Oh, none of the above. I'm a physician. I oversee Commander Draven's biological research laboratory and the test facility," Pontius Cato said calmly. "And his production sites, of course."

After the day she'd just had, Kaia was a tad slow on the uptake. Comprehension, when it came, hit her in the gut like a sledgehammer.

"You head the *biowar* program?" She pushed away from him violently, like he'd infect her just by looking at her. "Gods!"

"The program's vision and strategy are entirely Commander Draven's, I assure you. My own modest contribution is merely to oversee the execution of his research and developmental directives." Pontius Cato lifted his blond brows. "I collect you find this information disturbing?"

"I'm half Valyrian! You have to know that if you're a candidate." She stood five cubits away from him and felt sick to her stomach. "You did your damnedest to exterminate my mom's entire race. She was one of your victims, you bastard!"

And thanks to your novicide, she died rabid with madness. With her brain turned to pulp.

And all I could do was grieve.

"In point of fact, *Valyrensis novicida* was the brainchild of my unpleasant predecessor in the chief scientist's post. At the time, I counseled him that the entire operation was ill-advised. But Maximus Draven was never the sort of master to whom one offered 'no' as an answer." His mannerly face tightened in a grimace of apology. "No more so than his son, I'm afraid."

Kaia stood stranded in space and stared. All the Ninety-Nine Gods knew she wanted nothing to do with the creep. And the revelation that the head of Dex's bioweapons program actually planned to compete for her bed turned her stomach. But the fact that the villain appeared so innocuous and comported himself so courteously somehow made the entire affair even more obscene.

He's a monster. He should look like one. Not like some… university professor.

Cato studied her rigid frame and a small sigh slipped out. "Somehow I perceive you'd be ardently opposed to my courtship? Due primarily to my profession, I take it?"

"You think?" She sidled cautiously to the bar for her drink. He hadn't touched it, and she needed it like blazes. She tossed it back and signaled to the bargirl for a top-up.

"Alas." Cato's slender hands spread in resignation. "Thus are my hopes dashed and my heart broken. Although, truly, perhaps this regrettable development is for the best. You see, for better or worse, I know Commander Draven rather intimately."

"Because you work together so closely?" The firewater churned in her empty belly.

"Because I've made it my business to know him. He is the dominant power in this sector." Pontius Cato spared her an ironic smile. "I'm not entirely a fool, my dear. You're sharing his quarters and his bed, are you not?"

Heat flooded her chest and scorched her face. "I'm *not*… sleeping with him."

"If indeed you're not already doing so, I doubt very much that rather remarkable restraint on his part will persevere. Our illustrious leader has made his interest in you abundantly obvious. Every man on this battleship can smell him on you. To speak with complete candor, we've all begun to doubt Commander Draven has any intention whatsoever of seeing you complete your ritual."

A thrill zinged through her that she didn't understand. A thrill suspended somewhere between paralyzing fear and dizzying exhilaration.

She caught up her newly filled glass and gripped it tight. "What do you mean?"

Cato arched a knowing brow. "I believe you comprehend perfectly well what I mean. There's a rather lively betting pool in this very bar that places the odds at two to one that either Dex will challenge Zorin or Zorin will challenge Dex for the pleasure of your bed within the next twenty-four clicks. And theirs is an old and bitter rivalry. Any challenge between those two will only end when one of them—or both of them—are dead."

She shuddered with a visceral dread. A dread she couldn't capture in words.

She only knew with the blind certainty of Valyrian foresight that somehow, someway, she had to stop that from happening. "Dex can't challenge Zorin or anyone else for my bed. He's my Tombola master. According to the Apocrypha, if he bids himself, it's blasphemy."

"What's a little tribal superstition to the First Indomitable of the Mogadon Empire?" Cato made a rueful moue. "Commander Draven makes his own rules. Surely you've discerned that much about his character. Eliminating Zorin—the most talented and successful Syndax Voortrekker in centuries—will of course eliminate the prospect of any organized resistance to the next Draven biowar. Eliminate Zorin, and the entire Syndax civilization—such as it is—well, our piratical tribe of parasites is as good as dead."

For some damn reason, she still couldn't seem to wrap her head around the idea of Dex launching a biowar against anyone. He'd been so adamant about his opposition to the last one.

But she was reluctantly forced to concede that Pontius Cato, of all Dex's many minions, would be in the position to know.

"You sound like you admire him," she said softly. "I mean Zorin. Even if he is a parasite."

Pensive, Cato studied the writhing dancers behind the shimmering screen of jungle. "When he ruled the Empire as First Indomitable, Zorin was the man we all aspired to become. Did you know he was born a member of the plebeian class? In point of fact, a freedman's son."

Despite the gin joint's humid heat, Kaia's skin prickled with sudden chill. Briskly she chafed her arms through her thin cyberdress. "You telling me Zorin's father was born a slave?"

Over the music's frenetic tempo, she could almost hear the chink and chime of harem chains. Her own homeworld's happy spin on slavery.

"Born and raised in chains," Pontius Cato affirmed. Like he was reading her flipping mind. "Until the last Imperator abolished Mogadon's slave class, after the uprising, in a bid to ease social tensions. An experiment that has proven somewhat less than fully successful—and which, in certain ways, has brought ancient resentments and inequities among the classes into even sharper relief."

"Well, they're still under the imperial boot, aren't they? Your plebeian class? Can you blame them for being resentful?"

"Be that as it may—" he shrugged "—our slaves became freedmen. Zorin himself was born free. Still, any son of slaves bears a certain indelible… stigma."

"Yet Zorin became First Indomitable anyway?" Kaia cocked a curious brow. "Stigma or no stigma. I'm guessing that was a first."

"Indeed," Cato said dryly. "We've had perishingly few Indomitables in Mogadon history who aren't patricians' sons like Dex, trained from birth for war—and none at all descended from the former slave class. Most of those stay planet-side like their enslaved ancestors and tend the smelting reactors at the core, or ship offworld to man the mining asteroids."

"Except Zorin."

"Correct. He ascended through the ranks, fueled solely by his own considerable merits. Even my father respected his achievements, despite his humble antecedents. And Dex was his most promising protégé."

Her skin tingled with interest. "Until the day Zorin killed Max Draven."

"Precisely. Many of us felt Zorin should have been lionized for exterminating a sociopath instead of condemned. Even if the act itself was an unsanctioned combat—an ambush, technically speaking, of an unarmed soldier—and therefore illegal under the Mogadon Codex. A tactic one expects from a surly servant or vengeful lover, but never from a senior military officer toward a peer."

One scholarly hand lifted in a slight gesture, steeped in old regret. "But Dex turned on his former mentor and petitioned the Imperator for the legal right to fight Zorin to the death—and the Imperator granted his consent. The night before their combat, his loyal subordinates abetted Zorin's escape and joined him in exile. He fled to the outlaws— the Syndax horde, the flotsam and jetsam of the galaxy—and rose through their hardscrabble ranks like a rocket."

Cato fiddled with his glass. "I confess, I have sometimes… regretted… that I wasn't among them."

"Why?" she asked in a small voice. "Don't you admire Dex?"

One shoulder lifted in a diffident shrug. "I trust it's not unduly disloyal to admit Dex is a difficult man to serve. And an even more difficult man to know. Our current First Indomitable is a hard and troubled man who rules only through fear and never love. But Zorin… well, he was a different sort. A living legend. We'll not see another of his ilk."

Stubbornly Kaia shook her head. "I don't think you understand Dex as well as you think."

"Perhaps you're the one who doesn't understand him," he said gently.

Disconcerted, she frowned over her glass, then cleared the space junk from her head. "Let's cut to the chase. If there *were* some sort of rivalry between Dex and Zorin for my bed—which there isn't—it sounds like you'd advise me to choose Zorin."

"Only if you want to be happy." Pontius Cato gave her a mordant smile. "And on that cheerful note, my dear, I really must return to my laboratory. I'm in the midst of overseeing a rather delicate experiment and dare not leave the protocol unsupervised for long."

She sure wasn't sorry to see him go. But she found herself more confused than ever once he'd left.

How can I be falling for a monster? Because clearly the galaxy's dominant tyrant is a monster. Has to be a monster.

Yet Dex seems anything but.

All of which was entirely academic, wasn't it, since Dex was her Tombola master and couldn't compete for her bed?

Even if she wanted him to.

Which she didn't, because the plan was to stop him. Not join him and make him stronger. That was why she'd chosen Zorin for her shortlist. Not because the Syndax Voortrekker intrigued her—even though he did—but because he was the only counterweight she'd found who might actually resist Dex's methodical drive for galactic dominion.

And every syllable Pontius Cato had spoken only reinforced the wisdom of her strategy.

Stars and planets, I'm going in circles. More agitated and unsettled than ever, she bolted another shot of liquid fire and pushed through the crowd to the dance floor.

Her entire body was humming with Mogadon pheromones like a live electrical wire. Restless heat pooled and pulsed in her core. Under her stretchy red cyberdress, her breasts felt full and swollen. Her skin oversensitized, almost too stimulated to touch.

In simple terms, she *ached*.

Her body was a vortex of throbbing need, and she knew exactly what it was she needed. That explosive release from spiraling tension she'd only known that long-ago summer with Ben, then again last night with Dex. She was strung so tight she'd explode at the first touch.

And taking care of business herself—as she'd learned to do over the years through unromantic necessity—wasn't going to get it done.

Not this time.

Now she was dancing madly, trying to work it off that way, sweating with exertion and desire, hair flying free, limbs grazing the writhing bodies around her. Every glancing contact sparked a flash of heat that shot straight to her clit.

But she knew none of her oblivious, utterly ordinary neighbors could quench the burn that consumed her.

Until she lifted her head and saw *him*.

Ben Nero.

Standing three cubits away on the crowded floor, with a pocket of empty space around him. Entirely separate from the jungle chaos, but gorgeous and deadly as a stalking predator. Striking all in black, tunic and boots and breeches thrown carelessly over his tall slim frame, his chiseled beauty framed in a mane of tumbled raven silk. With his brooding eyes locked right on her.

And a dark purpose burning in their depths that shot straight to the pulsing tension between her thighs.

"Ben!" she said breathlessly over the pounding beat, tossing back her sweat-damp hair. "What are you doing here?"

He closed the distance between them step by step. Stripped off his gauntlets one by one. His eyes held her paralyzed. He hummed with high-voltage power.

"You called me," he said low. "You woke me. With your need."

An electric jolt of awareness sparked through her. "Oh! I—I'm sorry."

"No you're not," he growled. "And neither am I."

And there in the midst of the Blind Tiger, with a hundred clueless

Mogadon writhing in a frenzy around them, he dragged her against his lean supple strength and swooped to fuse her mouth with his.

Kissing Ben Nero was like kissing a tiger. He was darkness and heat and hunger. He coaxed, compelled, demanded, dominated. With lips smooth as watered silk and hands light as thistledown dancing down her back, making her tingle through her cyberdress like he stroked her naked skin.

Giving her absolutely no option but to yield and open to the urgent press of his kiss. The slick slide of his tongue against hers made the floor spin beneath her feet.

Comets, she was lost. The way she was always lost when Nero kissed her. A lifetime of loss and loneliness obliterated in a breath. She was a kid again, out of her head in love with the most powerful young telepath in the Psi Academy, the one they all crushed on, irrespective of gender.

Reeling—then and now—with the giddy knowledge that he was *hers* and hers alone.

"Love you, angel," he'd breathe in her ear as they lay on the beach late at night, sticky with sweat and languid with longing, entwined under the six moons of Hegemon. *"There'll never be anyone else. Not for either one of us. When we graduate, I'm taking you back to Valyria with me."*

But when the time came and the Quorum ruled against their unsanctioned union, he'd gone back to Valyria without her.

The world of the Blind Tiger blurred and revolved around her until she clutched at him for balance. Trying less to pull him closer and more to push him away.

And he was having none of it. His bare hands tightened and dragged her hips to his. The violent shock of his fiercely aroused body wrung from her lips a moan of desperate hunger. She wanted to climb his tall sinewed frame and wrap her legs around him and let him sink deep inside the wet ache at her core.

The way she'd never let him do nine years ago.

"Missed you," he sighed against her mouth. "Gods, Kaia. I've *missed* you."

She fought a desperate rearguard battle to clear her head. "You left me."

"Not by choice," he muttered between hard hungry kisses. "Leaving you nearly killed me."

"Poor you." Somehow she dragged in a breath. "But it *was*—your choice. Ben… I don't… I don't want…"

"Yes, you do," he said with brutal candor, eyes gone ultraviolet with passion. "You can't lie to me. I won't let you."

His mouth found her sweating throat, where her pulse slammed against his lips like a trapped and frantic animal. She'd never been any good at all thinking with his mouth on her skin, those soft lips fierce with hunger, making her shiver and burn to feel his sinful mouth on the rest of her. Claiming her needy flesh one aching atom at a time. Making her admit with her body what she'd always known in her heart.

That she'd never stopped being his.

She wound her hands in the sleek tangle of his hair. "Listen, Ben. I need—"

"I know what you need. I've always known."

His growl vibrated deep with sexual hunger. His eyes burned heliotrope with deadly fire. And all she could do was shiver. Even when he swung her into his arms and strode from the crowded floor with brooding purpose.

Fractured images of wary faces and averted eyes flashed past. He was the Valyrian Precursor. The Mogadon sensed his hatred. And they feared his power. One look at his wrathful face and no one would stop him from carrying off a masked courtesan.

Especially one who wasn't exactly fighting to get free.

Because you don't want to get free. You're going to fly apart if he doesn't touch you. One touch of his hand or—gods help me—his mouth is going to be enough to send you over the edge. You just need to—tell him—before—

But when he swung into the narrow cell of an unfamiliar room, when he sealed the door behind them with a casual gesture and a smolder of psi fire, the vitally important truth she needed to tell him spun right out of her head.

She caught strobe-light flashes of a bed, a mirror, a porthole overlooking the club's writhing chaos. Pulsing green light leaking through dirty glass. A rented room, pounding with the music's sonic shock, that existed for exactly one purpose.

Which meant she *really* needed to tell him…

Without slowing, he strode to the bed, long booted legs eating up the ground. Kaia made a supreme effort to recall all the reasons she hated him. Even while her body throbbed with a raw hunger only he could satisfy.

"Blast it! You left me—"

"I had to. I would have lost everything—"

"Except *me*."

"I was doing it *for* you. For us. For all of us."

In a flurry of limbs and cybersilk, he flung her on the bed. And just this hint of the dark menace that was Nero in a temper tightened the coil of need in her belly. Before she could breathe, he slid between her legs and climbed her body like a panther.

"Just wait a tick, will you?"

"I've been waiting a lifetime." Deftly he plucked off her mask and tossed it aside. "You don't need to hide who you are. Not from me."

He was moving way too fast. Somehow she got her leg up and planted a booted foot against his chest.

"Let's go back to why you left, Ben Nero. You're telling me you rejected me and humiliated me and abandoned me for my own flipping good?"

"Come on, Kaia." He was a man on a mission, and annoyance at the interruption smoked in his chiseled face. "You're smart enough to know why I left."

She kept her foot where it was. "Why don't you spell it out for me."

His eyes slid down her body to where her skirt rode high on her thighs. And despite her own tight-leashed anger, her body burned under his possessive stare.

"I'm the strongest telepath of my generation. The strongest to survive the war. That's why they made me Precursor, decades ahead of the curve. I have a duty to my race—a duty to propagate my gifts through the breeding program. A duty to rebuild our strength."

"How patriotic of you." Old envy twisted in her gut. Envy she'd thought she'd exorcised eons ago. "Exactly how many gifted offspring have you sired?"

"Enough," he breathed, sensing danger and skirting it like the agile telepath he was. "Enough to have the Senate of Psychics eating out of my hand. A few more genetic favors and I can take whomever I want for a consort. Even the Kryll maharani… if she's the consort I insist on having.

"And I do…" He gripped her booted knee and eased it aside. His dark head bent and his lips seared the naked skin of her inner thigh. "… insist."

His touch incinerated every wisp of her smoldering anger in a cloud of ash that swirled away in the cosmic storm raging through her body.

Her eyes fluttered shut in surrender.

His hands slid up the sensitized skin of her inner thighs, easing up her skirt and spreading her wide. Now only the stretchy red silk of her panties stood between him and all her secrets.

Exercising the very acme of her will, she got her hands on his shoulders to hold him. "Why didn't you tell me you'd survived?"

"Because you're my lifemate! I knew if we ever reconnected, I'd never be strong enough to walk away. Doing it once nearly killed me." His voice sank to a whisper. "You're my greatest vulnerability. My only vulnerability. You have to know that."

Deep in her chest, her battered heart twisted tight. She wanted to believe him. Didn't dare believe him. Still, she fought like blazes to clear her head. To remember all the reasons they needed to stop.

"You're my neutral second. So you can't… you can't bid."

"I won't need to bid," he sighed, hot breath and silken lips grazing her skin as he tugged on her panties with his teeth. "A blind man can see where this auction is going. Either you're going to Zorin, or you're going to Dex. Either one of them will be… persuadable… when it's me doing the persuading."

Breath rasping in the darkness, he raised his head to rivet her. "Show me how much you'll like it. Sharing your bed with me and Zorin. Or sharing with me and Dex."

Already stretched tight and aching with need, she felt the visual explode in her body like a hand grenade. A throaty moan spilled from her lips, and her hips rolled beneath him on a rising tide of wanting.

"Gods, Kaia, I can smell him on you," he whispered, breath licking the damp gusset of her panties. "I can smell how hard he made you come. Just like I can smell *you*. Both of you driving me out of my mind. You're already wet for me, aren't you? Show me how much you want me inside you."

Here was another ideal opening to say what desperately needed saying. But she was as incapable of stringing words together in a sentence as she was of flying. Instead, her thighs spread wide and her fists clenched in his hair to drag him closer.

His mouth nuzzled the pulse of need beneath her panties. When his lips brushed her clit through the silk, she arched into him with a wordless cry.

"Angel," he panted against the damp silk. "You're going to make me come in my breeches. Give me a tick…"

The slither of cloth beyond her closed lids told her he was dealing with his lacings. She told herself they'd finish this the way they had so often during that distant summer of discovery and frustration and frenzy—through their clothes, with his hand or hers. But they veered wildly off script when his hands skimmed her out of her panties. Cool air hit her slick flesh.

"Ohmygods, wait!"

"I told you. I'm done waiting."

His deft fingers spread her wide in the darkness. And the sweep of his tongue down her soaking wet slit made stars explode in her head.

After that she was beyond saying anything except *Ben* and *please* and *gods* and *oh.* Beyond knowing anything but the unprecedented slide of his sinful tongue teasing the aching nub of her clit—circling, rubbing, dancing away, never giving her quite enough friction to ease the coil of spiraling need. Beyond doing anything but rocking and begging and vibrating like a drum beneath his mouth.

When he eased a finger into her tight heat, she almost lost her mind.

"You're so ready for me, aren't you?" he groaned, easing the digit deeper into her pulsing pussy. "I want you right on the edge. Right till I'm inside you."

"Nothing…" she panted, clenching and releasing around his finger until her world went white. "Oh, Ben, please. Nothing's changed…"

"*Everything*'s changed. I've changed. Now no one in the galaxy is strong enough to take you away from me." He played her like a maestro, tongue teasing her desperate clit while her slick heat rode his hand, breathless cries spilling from her lips, begging for a release she needed more than breath.

"That's it, Kaia. Ride me. Beg for me." He worked a second finger into her aching passage and she begged in earnest, heels digging into the mattress as her hips bucked against his hand.

"Oh gods oh gods oh gods Ben *please*—!"

An instant before she shattered into a million pieces, he eased off. "No coming without me, angel. When you fall apart, I want you wrapped around my cock."

In the rhythmic flash of lasers from the club below she caught a single searing glimpse of him kneeling over her, cock in his fist, staring straight into her eyes and giving himself a long leisurely stroke she felt like an electric current between her legs. Precum glistened in the pulsing light. Her tongue traced her tingling lips. She couldn't breathe.

Lashes falling over his nuclear gaze, he rubbed his rigid length along her soaking slit. Explosions of shock and pleasure went off in her clit like fireworks. Helpless in the vise of need, her hips undulated against him and her thighs pulled him closer. She shook like an earthquake under the pull of diametrically opposing drives.

The potent physical need he stirred in her so powerfully.

Set against the truth that howled to be spoken.

"I want you to scream my name when you come." He fitted his cock to the mouth of her channel. "Do it now."

"Ben, wait!" The words were wrenched from her gut. "Nothing has changed. I'm still…" She sucked in a breath and blurted out the truth. "Intact."

His head jerked up, eyes glazed and blind with passion. And, gods help her, *all* she wanted him to do was push forward and bury himself deep inside her.

"I know you've had lovers. The master samurai in Gamma. That rotten little thief in Epsilon." He leaned in to claim a dark hot kiss.

And the taste of her own musk coating his tongue made her moan into his mouth, the sound husky with longing.

"I swear to gods," he muttered, "I wanted to kill every man who ever touched you for taking what's mine. Now I'm going to make you forget those other men were ever alive."

She was never any good at thinking with Ben Nero's mouth on hers either.

"Those guys…" She pulled back and did a little panting herself. "My, um, lovers? They respected my boundaries. We never… you know… finished."

She suffered through a beat of stupefied silence.

"Kaia." Braced over her and trembling with restraint, Ben looked

thunderstruck. "You—you can't honestly mean to tell me—you're still…?"

"A virgin," she whispered, closing her eyes. "Yeah."

"No."

"Yes." Gods, this was mortifying. She felt like an utter ass. Not for her choice—which was her choice to make—but for not telling him sooner. "I kept trying to tell you."

"What about all those infernal lovers? You telling me they were okay with that?"

"Why not? You were. Or, at least, you respected it." Her eyes opened to search his face in the darkness. "Once I explained about my mom, the samurai was. The thief… wasn't. He didn't stick around long."

"I respected it because I fully expected to be the consort you chose. Delayed gratification is something I'm quite good at." His lids dropped over his smoldering stare as he rocked gently against the clamoring need at her core, slick cock sliding against slippery flesh. A shiver of anticipation jumped between them to shudder down her spine.

"You and your mom and that farking promise. I always figured it didn't last past her death."

"Why not? A prophecy's a prophecy." She lifted trembling fingers to graze his face, rigid with the tension of restraint. "She was purebred Valyrian. And foresight was her gift, remember? She said if I saved myself for the guy I mated, I'd bring peace to the galaxy. I promised her I'd wait."

Not that I cared a molecule about peace at that age, but I kept the promise because it mattered to her and I loved her.

"Though I never understood how a vision like hers could be real. Because I was nothing. Everything was always about Kira." She swallowed hard. "Until now."

He crouched above her, braced and panting, cock lodged hard against her sweet spot.

"Are you saying," he said carefully, "you want me to *stop*?"

She chuffed out a breathless laugh. "No. I think I'll die if you stop."

"Then…?" He eyed her grimly. "You'd better spell this out for me, angel. Use small words."

"I'm not a kid anymore. I think I can make this work for both of us." She blushed hot enough to glow in the dark. "Just… no penetration, okay?"

Between them stretched a breathless silence. Never had she strayed so close to the edge with any of her handful of pseudo-lovers. It wouldn't have been fair—and she wouldn't have trusted them. Dex alone had held himself back long after any other man would have broken.

But Nero was her lifemate. She'd always trusted him.

Somehow, when it came to this, she still did.

Now she watched him wrap his head around her offer and ease back with exquisite care. Scrambling to accommodate this new reality.

More than ready to explore her boundaries.

He pressed his mouth to her ear and whispered, "Why don't you show me exactly what you have in mind."

He was the galaxy's most powerful telepath. He'd probably sired a hundred pedigreed offspring with a hundred pedigreed women. He'd humiliated and abandoned her to face an interstellar scandal alone.

But tonight he was at Kaia's mercy.

Under the pulse of tribal music downstairs, she unspooled the rope from her utility belt and whispered, "Strip."

His breath quickened in the darkness. But he peeled off his tunic, taking his time, giving her every opportunity to appreciate the sinewed power of his shoulders and the sleek plane of his chest and the taut column of his abs, illuminated for an eyeblink whenever strobe lights flashed. He shucked his boots without caring where they fell.

When he slid out of his breeches, his eyes locked on hers like a heat-seeking missile.

His fully aroused length sprang free and slapped against his belly with a soft *thwack* that brought the blood rushing to her cheeks.

She'd never seen him like this. Not really. Too shy to look when they fooled around as kids, and he was too protective of her to push. Now the thought of all that cock in her hands, between her lips… wherever she chose to put him… made her mouth water.

"Well?" he said huskily. "Like what you see?"

"Um." She swallowed hard.

He grinned and eyed the rope hanging slack from her grip. "You have a plan for that?"

Somehow she got her head together. "See that pipe above the bed? Grab it for me."

He pushed out a breath that sounded like appreciation and crossed his arms overhead. Forcing her trembling fingers to obey, she tied his wrists snugly to the pipe. And kneeling on the bed next to his naked length while she did it—without touching the part of him she ached most to explore—made her entire body tingle.

"Not too tight?" she whispered.

"You know I can get out of this any time I want." His breath teased her face, the sweet scent of cloves laced with the musk of her own arousal. "There isn't a rope in the universe that can hold me, no matter how you tie it. And I need to tell you—when I'm with a woman these days, I'm always the one calling the shots."

"Too bad I'm not one of your pedigreed brood mares," she fired back. "All tame and docile and broken to the saddle. Your ego have a problem taking orders from a woman?"

"Maybe." His eyes glinted. "It's never come up."

"Well, it's coming up now." She leaned in and whispered in his ear, "Just close your eyes and pretend I'm Dex."

He groaned and turned his face into his upraised arm. "Comets, Kaia. You're going to kill me."

"That's the general idea."

The heavy pulse of arousal throbbed between her legs. She wasn't sure how much longer she could prolong this—or delay her own explosive climax. But he'd kept her waiting for years, hadn't he? Now, by all the gods, she was going to make *him* wait.

She was going to make him beg.

"Let's see." She tapped a finger on her chin. "What can we use for a blindfold?"

"No." He nailed her with a burning look and a warning flare of psychic fire. "If you're going to do this, I'm going to watch. And I want to see all of you. Lose the dress." His voice dropped an octave. "The boots you can keep."

His peremptory tone sent a visceral shudder streaking through her system.

"You're not giving the orders." She wound her hand in his long silky hair and tightened her grip in a threat. "I am."

He leaned in and claimed her mouth in a hard kiss that made her shiver even harder.

"It's called 'negotiation,' angel. You haven't done this before, have you? It's okay. You're a quick study. And I'm glad I'm your first."

Even bound and naked, he was way too dangerous.

She scrambled out of reach and crouched on the bed to watch, fingers unsteady as she slipped off her utility belt, breath quick and rough with anticipation. In the pulsing light, he was dark and beautiful as a chained demon, summoned straight from the abyss to beguile her. All supple skin and hard muscle, honed by a barbaric culture on an ice world that relied on horsepower and hard labor for anything their psi-powered batteries couldn't fuel.

Fighting for control, she eased her dress slowly off her shoulders and over her bare breasts. Her face burned in the shadows. The friction of leather against her taut nipples sent twin currents of pleasure zinging through her.

Straight to the tight ache between her thighs.

She left the dress just beneath her breasts, lifting and thrusting them forward, and heard him moan in appreciation.

"That's all you're getting," she whispered, licking her dry lips.

"We'll see about that," he said, low and throaty, lids falling over the smoking heat of his gaze. "Get over here."

"Not yet."

This was a game too sophisticated to play, not when he was so clearly a master. Even so, her impulse to tease him, fueled by instinct and nine years of anger, seemed to be working. She slid her hands over her tingling breasts, fingers teasing the tight buds of her nipples—tweaking them to make her breath hitch and his cock twitch. She watched creamy liquid collect at his slit and swallowed again.

She wanted to taste him.

She would die to taste him.

"I said come here," he grated, eyes locked on her upthrust breasts. *"Now."*

Catching her lower lip between her teeth, she crawled sinuously across the bed, breasts swaying with every step. A handspan away and just beyond reach, she stopped and looked up.

From below he was a fallen angel with shackled wings, psi fire glowing in his eyes, breath rasping in his lungs, fists clenched and muscles tensed against the rope that bound him. Cock rigid and trembling for her attention. She wanted to lick him. She wanted to devour him. She wanted to suck him until he lost every last particle of control he possessed and exploded in her mouth.

"You seem to have trouble taking orders, Ben Nero," she purred. "We're going to have to change that."

Panting audibly under the grinding music, she leaned in to run her tongue around the tip of his cock, spreading saliva across hot trembling skin stretched taut over sinew. He moaned her name and rocked urgently, trying to sheathe himself in her mouth.

"Say please," she whispered against his flesh, savoring his salty taste, his craving coating her tingling lips.

A strangled sound clawed from his throat and he thrust into her mouth. But she backed away, legs trembling beneath her as she rose to her knees.

You will beg for me, Ben Nero, she sent him silently, meeting his blazing look. *And I don't give a flip about your ego.*

He snarled in warning and lunged for her, rope creaking and pipe groaning as he tested the bonds that held him. But she tied a mean knot, and his struggles only torqued it tighter.

She wrapped one hand around his throbbing length and eased her fingers down his shaft, spreading his own precum down his length. He felt as good as she remembered from those endless summer nights, smooth and hot and tight in her grip. And he arched into her touch just the way she still dreamed of, his head falling back and his mouth falling open, a hungry groan rising from his chest.

"What do you want?" she whispered.

"Anything," he said on a breathless laugh. "Gods! Jack me off."

"You mean like this?" She gave him a few leisurely strokes, from base to tip and back, pausing with head tilted to study the effect.

He pumped into her fist. "Faster. And harder."

She eased closer, still kneeling before him, the tips of her breasts grazing his chest. And just that glancing contact made her moan. Her thighs grew slippery with her own need.

"I want it slow," she whispered. Hardly recognizing her own voice. "And I'm giving the orders."

She prolonged the foreplay, long slow strokes sprinkled with observation, resisting all his efforts to quicken the pace. Relishing his increasingly tortured breathing, the moans and curses he couldn't contain, the frustration that made him sweat and jerk in her hand, straining for more contact and slick in her grip.

"Kaia—by all the gods—*harder*."

"You ready to beg me yet?" she breathed in his ear. "I'm waiting."

Lightning-swift, his head turned to find her throat, an electric suction of lips on flesh hard enough to raise the blood against her skin—a brand of possession she'd have to hide. She voiced a cry of protest but couldn't pull away. Panting, she rested her brow against his sweat-slick shoulder.

"I'm going to make you come so hard you pass out," he growled against her skin. "And that's a promise. Now suck my cock."

She reminded herself she was in control—she was—but his barely leashed violence, straining hard at his bonds, left her lightheaded. She trailed her tongue down his smooth chest, over the tight quivering plane of his abdomen, tasted his sweat on her lips. Just above his violently erect cock she lingered, breathing in the scent of incense and arousal that rose from his skin. This was a line they'd never crossed when they were kids.

In fact, it was a line she'd never crossed.

Period.

With anyone.

The head of his cock was slick and drooling with eagerness. She knelt on hands and knees before him, cool air kissing her bare bottom as it peeked beneath her skirt, and heard him curse at the visual.

"Angel, you look unreal," he rasped, jerking hard at his bonds. "Give me your mouth. I'm dying here. *Please.*"

"That's the word I've been waiting for. Keep saying it," she whispered, and wrapped her mouth around his cock.

It was like wrapping her lips around an electric cable. She'd planned to prolong this singular moment, but his hips jerked forward, lodging his length in her mouth in urgent entreaty. His taste zinged against her tongue. His cock filled her mouth to overflowing and nudged the back of her throat. And all she needed to do was hold steady as he lunged savagely at his bonds and thrust into her mouth, rhythmic curses and pleas for *more* and *oh angel* and *please gods please* rising from his straining throat.

She gripped his hips for balance and closed her eyes, fireworks exploding against her lids. Because the same hammer of need that pulverized him was pounding through her and she was going to fly apart if he didn't… *oh gods, oh please…* if he didn't…

The air sizzled with the tingle of psychic energy. Bits of charred rope rained down on her bare shoulders. And suddenly he was free, pushing her back on the bed, fierce and hungry as he crawled between her thighs. And they came together the way they always used to do, except before it was always with clothes on. His desperate thrusts against her own pounding need—

With nothing but trust and a promise between him and the obliteration of all her boundaries.

His slick cock bucked against her soaking wet slit, one twist away from penetration, midnight hair falling over incandescent eyes as his stare locked on hers. Her own urgent cries rose as she grappled to clutch his ass, fingers digging into skin stretched taut over muscle. Hard and fast, he pistoned into her heat, cock grazing her clit. And she exploded like a dying sun, hips riding him in a frantic rhythm as her world went supernova. He voiced a hoarse shout and the hot rush of his release spurted over her thighs and belly.

She must have passed out at the paralyzing peak of pleasure.

Precisely the way he'd promised.

When her vision cleared, he lay collapsed across her, naked and drenched with sweat and semen, frantic heart thundering against her ear, damp hair flung across his face. Her own ragged breaths loud and labored in the darkness.

When she stirred under his weight, he rolled off with a sigh, but wrapped a possessive hand around her wrist.

Keeping her close.

"Drove me insane having you push me away," he mumbled. "No more running."

"I'd like to say… no more leaving," she panted. "But you can't promise me that, can you?"

His silence was all the reply she needed. But she saw it in her lifemate's head. His race still needed him. For the Valyrian Precursor, duty still came before love. The familiar fist of rejection gripped her heart and squeezed.

Heat gathered in her throat and prickled behind her lids. She pushed out a shaky breath and closed her eyes.

His hand slid up her naked thigh, slick with both their juices. "Still technically a virgin, as instructed. Although if we're really trying not to conceive, angel, this isn't the best way to avoid it."

"What do you mean? I'm half Valyrian," she reminded him, eyes still closed. "I'd have to want to conceive."

"I'm your lifemate and I just made you come so hard you passed out," he murmured, nuzzling her shoulder. "Your nubile young body might have gotten a different message than the one your logical samurai head meant to send. Not to mention I just came harder than I've ever come in my *life*—all over you. Without a contraceptive. If we did want to conceive, you and I, it's not impossible this could do the trick."

She opened her eyes. "But I don't want to conceive. Not without a consort."

"You'll have a consort in six days." A frown shadowed his sculpted face. "Not that I'm looking forward to that. But whoever gets you gets me. At least when I'm not on Valyria."

She rolled to face him and propped her head on her fist. "What exactly are you saying?"

"I'm saying," he said darkly, gaze sliding over her body in a look that screamed possession, "Dex isn't the only man on this battleship who's staking his claim. I'm saying I have no intention of letting you go flying off to the Omega Sector in some rust bucket with that pirate to die in his suicidal war. I'm saying you're my lifemate and I should never have walked away from you, damn it! I punked it all up."

He dragged in an unsteady breath. "I'm saying you and I are a package deal."

The utter certainty in his tone made her blood boil. As though she had no say whatsoever in her own future. As though he hadn't already walked away once and wasn't fully capable of doing it again.

As though she could ever trust him.

She shot up to sit and tugged her dress over her breasts. "And *I'm* saying you make way too many assumptions. I have a plan for this Tombola and you have nothing to do with it. Hells, Zorin doesn't even know you—"

"And he's your plan, is he?" Careless of his nudity, he uncoiled to his feet and loomed over her. "You're going to pick some Syndax pirate for a consort? I don't care if he makes you come until you see comets. Or if he has a snowball's chance in a solar flare of defeating Dex in battle. You think his son's going to rule the galaxy?"

Pulling her dress over her hips, she shot him a sharp look. "His *son*? What in the name of the Ninety-Nine Gods are you talking about?"

In a flash of green light through the dirty porthole, their gazes locked. And she had it from his head in a heartbeat.

"There's another prophecy about me and this flipping Tombola?

And my hypothetical son's supposed to rule this whole punked-up galaxy?" Suspicion raked through her, sharp as shattered glass through her lacerated heart. And as painful. "Is that why you showed up on Mogadon?"

Caution flashed across his face. "That's why the Senate of Psychics sent me. But, listen, it's not why *I* came—"

"And when exactly were you planning to tell me about this extremely relevant prophecy? Not until after you had your chance to sire another gifted offspring for Valyria—this time with the Kryll maharani, right, stud pony? That whole 'no penetration' newsflash must've really cramped your style."

"It wasn't like that." He scrubbed a frustrated hand over his face. "Don't look at me like I've betrayed you all over again. Just let me explain—"

He reached for her but she scrambled away, swinging her booted feet forward and jumping to the floor.

"Whatever you're selling, I'm not buying." She snatched up a towel from the washstand and vigorously scrubbed away the slippery residue of their passion. Wishing she could scrub away as easily the memory from her brain. "Is that why you're here now? Because you're on a mission to sire the galaxy's next overlord?"

"I'm here now because you called me." Clearly realizing playtime was over, he pulled on his breeches. "Because you needed me. If I wanted you to conceive, I wouldn't have stopped. I would've done what I've wanted to do forever and come with my cock buried deep inside you."

Still unlaced, he shot her a smoldering look. "And you would have let me."

"Oh, really?" She stopped scrubbing long enough to snort. "How do you figure that?"

"I'm very good at what I do, Kaia."

"You're very arrogant. I'll give you that much." She tossed the towel aside, tugged her dress over her thighs, and glared at him. "Let me be crystal clear. I've just spent the past eight years mourning you. Because I thought you were *dead*! And you let me go right on doing it. I'd have to be a fool to let you back in my heart—and my bed—after that stunt."

"I'm already back in your bed." Grimly he jerked his laces tight. "In case you haven't noticed."

In the midst of swinging her saber over her shoulder, she reversed the blade and pointed it at his chest. "I hope you enjoyed it. Because what we just did won't get a repeat. The next guy I sleep with is going to be my consort."

"You and I aren't finished. Not even close." He dragged his tunic over his head and glowered at her. "Meteors. You're my lifemate! You know that bond's for life. You'll always be in my head. And I'll always be in yours."

"*Always* is a long time." She buckled on her belt, snatched up her discarded mask and headed for the door.

"Where in the seven hells do you think you're going?" Caught in the midst of pulling on his boots, all he could do was glare. "Just planning to sashay past Dex's guards into his quarters at oh-two-hundred and say 'Honey, I'm home'? Looking like you've just had the ride of your life, with my smell and my taste all over you? You've already got him wound tight enough to go atomic. Just once in your reckless daredevil life, be reasonable!"

"Reasonable?" One hand on the door, she swung to face him.

Fully dressed, dark and deadly, psi fire sparking around his clenched fists, he rose and nailed her with a searing look. "You belong with *me*. The sooner they all know I'm part of the deal, the smoother this Tombola's going to go."

"That's not going to happen," she said flatly. "Go back to Valyria. Lifebond or no lifebond, you and I are history."

As she stormed into the dingy corridor and slammed the door between them with a sonic *wham* of fury, she just wished she could make herself believe it.

CHAPTER THIRTEEN
The Combat

The Mogadon centurion had fists the size of sledgehammers. And he swung them with the same clumsy imprecision.

The Valyrian telepath who taunted him in the fighting pit was one fourth his size but considerably faster on his feet. Not to mention clearly prescient. Whenever those hammering blows landed, the young telepath simply wasn't there.

Which was driving Dex's centurion berserk.

In his role as arbiter of the Tombola combat—one of dozens he'd overseen that day—Dex pivoted deftly aside as the centurion steamrolled past. Tidily avoiding a punch that would have taken someone's head off if it ever connected.

Once again, the telepath danced away.

And the centurion missed him by a Mogadon mile.

Thwarted, winded, the brute hunched over and heaved for air, sweat streaming over massive muscles to slick his naked torso. Which left nowhere to hide a blaster, because Tombola combatants went unarmed to their duels on this—Day Two of the auction for Kaia's bed.

These combat trials were optional, but a popular strategy for cash-strapped candidates to advance. If a man won his match, he secured an automatic place among the final two hundred. The maharani herself chose the rest, based on personal preference, to survive this brutal first culling.

While the centurion wheezed, the spectators ringing the sunken pit hooted and jeered. The close air reeked of blood and pheromones.

And the temperature had climbed enough to make him sweat.

Dex took a quick tally of his praetorian guard, stationed strategically among the odorous masses with stun rifles fixed to deter a riot. Deeming their placement and vigilance satisfactory, he allowed himself a cautious nod.

Sated by last night's sexual exploits at the saturnalia he'd arranged for their delectation, this unsavory herd was restless but—for the moment—controlled.

Even if only barely.

And the main reason the herd was restless, Dex noted with a spike of annoyance, was the main reason he'd been restless all bloody day himself.

Perched in the viewing box over the fighting pit, Kaia looked like a million creds in a cybersuit of sleek bronze silk that encased her slender curves but left her golden neck and shoulders bare.

And that subtle sign of favor afforded him a surge of violent satisfaction. Because Tombola gifts had been arriving at his quarters by the crateful all morning. Yet the gift she'd chosen to wear next to all that supple skin was *his*.

The cybersilk suited her perfectly.

Precisely the way he'd known it would.

Never mind the blatant impropriety of the maharani accepting an intimate gift from her Tombola master. Or his own impropriety in gifting it to her as though he were a suitor himself.

Since Zorin's arrival on the scene, Dex was rapidly ceasing to care what constituted appropriate behavior for himself at this Tombola.

But he cared very much what constituted appropriate behavior from everyone else.

Which would clearly preclude whatever provocative stunt Ben Nero was trying to pull directly before the outraged eyes of Kaia's infuriated suitors.

At this very moment, Dex's former best friend was sitting entirely too close to Dex's Tombola ward. Leaning to murmur entirely too intimately in her ear. Reaching to stroke entirely too insolently the soft copper tendrils spilling down her neck from the coil on her head. In short—looking entirely too perfectly like an amorous suitor making his own move for the maharani's bed.

Which was precisely what he *was*, Dex knew. Because of course he'd seen the vid feed from the dance floor of the Blind Tiger.

And the inflammatory kiss those two had shared was so combustible they'd nearly scorched his screen.

Even before Nero swept Kaia into his arms and strode someplace Dex's ubiquitous sensors couldn't follow to do something Dex's ubiquitous sensors couldn't see.

While I sulked all night in my ready room over that bloody Syndax and my bloody father, Nero was on the hunt. Stalking his prey and staking his claim. The two of them were together.

The two of them were together without me.

In consequence, Dex was seething with enough frustration, jealousy and arousal to fuel the starship's propulsion reactor.

Only the fact that Kaia was so blatantly spurning her lifemate's current advances—sitting stiffly erect and staring pointedly away while temper warmed her cheeks and flashed in her orchid eyes—spared a bare shred of Dex's sanity and preserved the entire scene from bedlam.

Even as Ben leaned close, his sculpted face brooding with purpose, to nuzzle her naked shoulder.

Irritably Kaia shrugged him off. But Dex wasn't buying her determined display of annoyance for an eyeblink.

Not since he'd seen that kiss.

Will you belay that, Ben? Dex wished to gods the man wore a comm link. *Before your antics cause a bloody riot. Damnation! You're supposed to be my neutral second. These suitors are already rancid with suspicion. When we boot the first three hundred from this battleship six clicks from now, we'll be exceedingly fortunate to avoid a mutiny.*

Looking startled, Nero's head snapped toward him. Apparently he'd done that unsettling trick of his again—plucked the thought right out of Dex's cranium. He wished like hell the man would stop doing that.

Even if his unspoken umbrage did achieve the desired effect.

This time.

Shooting Dex an irate flash of his insolent eyes, Nero dropped his hand and gave Kaia a modicum of space.

Dex's tension ratcheted back a notch.

Too bad the reprieve couldn't last.

In the fighting pit below, the telepath sneered at the brick-faced centurion. "Are you quite finished flailing at me with your great hairy paws? Because I'd love to present my bid to the maharani before I die of old age."

Oh, blast.

With a bellow of rage, the brute lunged for his tormentor. Laughing, the telepath skipped aside—then caught his foot in the combat-churned soil and went sprawling. The incensed Mogadon dove for his fallen foe. Ham-like hands engulfed his throat to throttle the life from him.

In the stands, Nero leaped to his feet.

"No strangulation," Dex fired off, scrambling to stay with the action. Today's round of contests—unlike the ones that followed—ran to first blood only, never to the death. "Centurion, acknowledge!"

Blind with rage, the centurion ignored him, inexorably crushing the windpipe of his empurpled antagonist.

Which was considerably more disrespect than a First Indomitable on shaky terrain could afford to tolerate before a roomful of his rivals.

All around them, men surged to their feet, roaring for blood. Any tick now, those bruisers in the boxes would be brawling. Above, Nero was swearing and tearing off his gloves.

"Centurion!" Dex barked. That slab of a face swung toward him.

Right into the vicious snap of Dex's right hook.

The shock of impact vibrated up his arm. The crunch of breaking bone sliced through the pandemonium like a machete through meat.

Blood spurting from his shattered nose, the centurion howled and attacked. Dex ducked the hammering counterpunch that would have crushed his skull. And followed up with a savage undercut to the jaw that connected hard enough to snap the guy's teeth.

"Stand down, Centurion!" Dex rapped out. "Report to your *primus* for remedial discipline. You've forfeited your place in this Tombola—"

"You farking forfeited *yours*! You're no leader of mine—you with your Valyrian catamite and your Kryll whore—" Sputtering obscenities through his broken mouth, the centurion palmed something from his trousers.

Still reeling from that ruinous slur, Dex barely glimpsed the flash of deadly steel before that lethal fist shot toward him.

He twisted aside, but his ribs burned under the blade's stinging kiss. A gasp of shock stole his breath. The world slowed to a crawl, an infinity of time stretching between beats of his labored heart.

The roar of the spectators spiraled into shrillness—fueled by those close enough to see the shiv clenched in the oaf's fist. Hot blood rolled down Dex's ribs and darkened his slashed jacket. His battle sense tingled until it sizzled.

Knowing it must now be dawning on a ship full of dangerously overstimulated Mogadon that they might shortly be hailing a new First Indomitable.

Over his own rapidly cooling corpse.

And the thought of what that brute would do to Kaia—what he'd permit those five hundred thwarted suitors to do—was sufficient to chill Dex's blood to liquid nitrogen.

Simply not happening.

Not on my watch.

Slowly his gaze rose to find Kaia. Her face was stricken and bleached with horror, her eyes incandescent and blazing with rage. Quicker than electron backlash, his Tombola ward launched into a tight triple somersault that vaulted her over the viewing box to the lower tier. She landed in a crouch, one level above and thirty cubits away. Screaming her defiance, she freed her saber with a *shing.*

His rebel samurai was hurling herself headlong to his defense. Clearly not knowing or simply not caring that being rescued from combat by a woman might spare his life—at least momentarily—but would signal the end of his command.

Stay there! he fired at her, one hand raised to hold her. Fierce as a tiger, eyes burning electric, those Valyrian torques around her wrists pulsing with platinum fire, she froze where she stood.

Clearly reluctant as all seven hells.

But heeding him.

There's a good girl. Kindly stay out of trouble and let me handle this.

Grinning savagely through shattered teeth, the centurion closed with his knife.

"You sorry son of a bitch," Dex muttered. "You could've had a proper chance in the fighting pit."

His booted foot swung up to connect with the man's brawny wrist. The shiv went sailing through the air. The centurion bellowed and charged him, relying on superior mass and weight to bring Dex down.

With barely a flicker of a tick to react, Dex pivoted tightly to send the knife-edge of his foot punching into the guy's beefy throat.

Cartilage crunched.

After that it was all over except the wheezing as his once-loyal centurion slowly suffocated to death.

Ignoring the sickening flash of white pain that flared with every breath and the alarming fog that blurred his vision, Dex scooped up the bloody shiv. Gripping it with casual menace, he glared at the howling horde.

To pull it off demanded every particle of his physical presence. But even gasping with pain and bleeding like a butchered steer, he hadn't lost the knack.

Slowly the screaming chaos dwindled to a sullen mutter.

"Would anyone else care to question my authority?" He infused his voice with every ion of the icy calm he was famous for. A calm he was far from feeling—already wounded and spectacularly ill-equipped to fend off another challenge.

To his profound relief, no immediate challenge emerged. Which merely meant whoever was trying to kill him lacked the confidence to move against him openly.

Yet.

"May I presume no takers?" Carefully concealing his relief, he thrust the shiv through his belt. "In that case, we'll recess for thirty ticks until the next combat. Prefect, send out the acrobats. And haul this space trash out of here."

Beside him, the breathless telepath huddled on his knees, massaging his bruised throat. Ignoring a vicious stab from his wounded side, Dex pulled the young fool to his feet and administered a brisk shake.

"Next time don't taunt your opponent, lad. Especially when he's five times your size. You'll advance to the final two hundred by default. Felicitations."

Clenching his jaw over a hiss of agony, Dex managed to stride across the fighting pit without wincing and exited through the ready room to escape the mutinous mob.

The curtain had barely fallen behind him when Kaia launched herself into his arms.

"Gods of my father, Dex! He hurt you. I felt it."

He would have protested by reflex that he was entirely fine. But that protest would undoubtedly have interfered with the novel sensation of Kaia—his fiery rebel—all distressed and demure and downright clinging in his arms, supple curves sleek with strength and lilac eyes enormous with concern. Desperate, she searched his face for damage.

Heedless of the surrounding scuffle as two prefects muscled the dead centurion through the curtain and Marcus hovered with a med kit and Nero loomed over him like he was half-tempted to fall into Dex's arms himself, Dex dragged Kaia's slender silk-clad hips hard against his and kissed her.

He kissed her the way he'd been burning to kiss her since seeing that bastard Zorin with his hands all over her. He kissed her to claim her and tell the whole damn world to back the hell off. That she was his.

And to hell with the farking Tombola and to hell with her farking father.

She was *his*.

That soul-deep admission he'd been fighting like the very devil since the moment they'd met filled his chest to bursting with an overwhelming shout of certainty. And even hurting like blazes and bleeding his guts out on the carpet, the potent knowledge of precisely what that admission would mean fueled a violent surge of lust that shot straight to his cock. Making him more than ready to cement his claim the way he'd done two nights ago when he kissed the hell out of her back on Mogadon.

Only this time they weren't stopping.

She was his.

"Gods, Dex," she sighed into his mouth—a shaky whisper of surrender. A surrender she didn't even realize she'd given.

And that soft, sexy sound ignited every Mogadon mating instinct he possessed.

He growled into her mouth and deepened the kiss, tasting honey and hunger in the way she gave him access. The way her hands trembled as she clutched his back. The way her mouth melted under his urgent press.

His palms slid over her sleek hips to ease her against his straining shaft. A locomotive of craving slammed through him like a Mogadon mining train. He savored the sweet softness of her lips, the low moan of her submission, the sudden fire of her need. Every flicker of her response and every atom of her essence told him she was his.

Dimly he was aware of Nero claiming the med kit from a chuckling Marcus, herding out the gaping prefects and their grisly burden. When Dex finally surfaced for air, they were blessedly alone.

Except for Nero.

Who stood three cubits away watching them kiss with an intensity that sent a jolt of high-voltage lust straight through Dex's shaft.

Reminding him with searing immediacy just how mind-blowing it had felt kissing his boyhood best friend. The way he'd dreamed about doing for a lifetime.

And just how hard it had been to stop.

"Damn," Nero said huskily. "Don't let me stop you. Just let me watch."

Kaia stifled a breathless laugh and slipped out of Dex's arms. "Don't tease. He's hurt."

"It's nothing," Dex said automatically.

But now that he wasn't kissing the hell out of Kaia, he couldn't ignore the hot trickle of blood beneath the waistband of his trousers.

"Don't be such a tough guy," Nero muttered, nimbly sifting through the med kit. "Take off your shirt. Unless you want me to do it for you."

That growled threat was enough to make him want to take off a lot more than his shirt. Because he knew neither one of them had forgotten just what Nero had promised they'd do if he ever got his hands on Dex's body.

Even though he'd been promising himself ever since that was never going to happen. Because the next time, he didn't think he was going to stop at a kiss. Especially if Kaia was involved…

"Here. Let me help you." Beautifully flustered and diligently avoiding his gaze, Kaia eased him out of his jacket. He peeled out of his ruined shirt, quietly amazed by the novelty of having anyone at all give one flaming shit about his injuries.

And touched.

Despite himself, he was touched.

The wicked incision slanting over his ribs was a good handspan wide and two fingers deep. His ribs had done their job and kept the blade away from his vital organs. But enough blood still oozed from the ugly slice to make Nero curse.

"That prick is flipping lucky you crushed his throat," Kaia gritted out. "Or I would have done it myself. Only I wouldn't have been nearly as gentle. *Sit*."

Bemused, Dex found himself firmly seated on an ottoman with

Kaia kneeling between his knees, wielding gauze and antiseptic with skill and determination.

"Easy with that," he complained as she cleaned him up and disinfected with grim purpose. "Stings like the devil."

"Try to relax. I know what I'm doing. I'm a Prime Class samurai, remember?" She arched a burgundy brow. "This isn't my first knife fight."

"I'll try to bear that in mind," he murmured. Wondering if she'd still be so beautifully receptive if he kissed her again. And wondering like blazes just how receptive she'd be at all if he weren't injured.

Perhaps I ought to get injured more often.

"You're going to need stitches." The cushion sank as Nero sat behind him, still rummaging in the kit. "This silicon adhesive should hold you together till we get you to sick bay."

Dex gave a noncommittal mutter.

Nero's tone darkened. "Promise me you'll go there."

Faced with Kaia's ferocious scowl, Dex laughed and raised his hands in surrender. "All right, all right! I'll go during the next recess."

With Kaia's exotic jasmine and ozone fragrance swimming through his synapses and Nero's lean feral heat licking against his back, Dex found himself positively starting to enjoy the doctoring process. In fact, he couldn't recall ever enjoying being injured quite so much.

As Kaia and Nero between them taped his wound shut, Dex slid his hands around her slim waist and eased her close.

"The silk," he said, by way of excuse. "It looks stunning on you. Just like I knew it would."

Smoothing silicon over his skin, she glanced up beneath her lashes, a glitter of gold dusting her lids. "I knew it was from you. It's the only thing anyone sent me that I could bear wearing."

And if he'd been entertaining any question at all about the thoroughly inappropriate nature of his attachment to his Tombola ward, the rush of possessive pleasure that seared through him at her admission would have erased all doubt.

"I want to shower you with silks," he whispered. "I want every man on this ship to know you're mine."

"That could prove a bit awkward," Nero said dryly, his clever fingers smoothing over the silicon. "You know, given the four hundred ninety-nine men swimming in testosterone who just bid a fortune for her bed? What're you planning to do—jettison them all out the nearest airlock?"

Dex was framing a curt riposte when Nero jabbed an antimicrobial injection into his exposed deltoid.

"Ouch, damn it!" Dex complained. "Warn a man next time."

"Where's the fun in that?" Nero capped the sharp and tucked it away. "Just be thankful I didn't insist on injecting you somewhere else. Because I was definitely tempted."

"Hold up, Dex." Kaia sat on her heels to study him, an unhappy furrow creasing her brow. "If you feel… the way you say you feel… why in the nine realms have you been avoiding me like a spacepox outbreak? I haven't even seen you since yesterday."

Dex hesitated, not having expected to discuss this particular topic in Nero's presence. Because the Valyrian Precursor was a sexual rival, wasn't he? But it wasn't as if he'd have any luck at all keeping it secret, with Nero casually strolling in and out of his head like he had an engraved invitation.

"I needed to clear my head." Frowning, Dex glanced toward the curtain, wondering just how much longer Marcus would be able to keep them all out. "Now I need to talk to you. About that Prime Class bastard Zorin."

"Then you need to talk to *us*." Nero's breath brushed Dex's naked shoulder and sent an erotic shiver slipping down his spine. "Especially if you're contemplating what I think you're contemplating. Because it's going to change things pretty radically for all three of us."

Bristling with sudden hostility, Kaia stiffened in Dex's arms. "This has nothing to do with you."

"You know that's not true." Nero's deft hands glided over his bare ribs.

Just finishing the job of patching him up, Dex told himself. But he found himself wondering exactly how much he'd protest if Nero slid his arms around his waist and eased those clever fingers over his cock.

Beneath his hands, a frisson of awareness rippled through Kaia's kneeling frame. Her lavender eyes lifted and her lush lips parted. It was the easiest thing in the world to lean in and kiss her.

She moaned into his mouth, capable hands gripping his thighs for balance.

Behind him, Nero whispered, "Gods and demons. The two of you are killing me."

His hands spanned Dex's ribs a breath before his soft lips grazed Dex's shoulder. And the double hammer of raw pleasure that seared through him—Kaia's mouth under his kiss, Nero's lips on his body—wrenched a groan from Dex's throat.

He devoured her eager mouth and dragged her close. Aware with a pleasure so sharp it was painful of Nero, still behind him, hands sliding forward to grip Dex's thighs. Nero nuzzled the side of his neck—the molten slide of a wicked tongue, the graze of teeth sharp enough to menace—and Dex arched into the kiss in a blatant demand for more. His heart pounding so hard it threatened to burst right through his chest.

"Tell me what you want," Nero breathed against his skin. "Tell me, Dex. After ten flipping years, I need to hear it."

"You," he groaned between kisses, loving the way she tasted, the way she yielded. She was his. She was *theirs*. "Both of you. I want—both of you. Just—this once."

Behind his zipper, his cock was throbbing, so painfully hard he knew he'd explode in his trousers if someone didn't—

Panting into Dex's mouth and kneeling between his spread thighs, Kaia closed her hands over Nero's and eased him forward. In a single exhilarating instant, Nero's fingers closed over the straining bulge of Dex's cock. Dex groaned and rolled his hips into that sizzling contact. He pulled Kaia into him, hands urgent as he gripped the sweet curve of her ass.

Nero's hands wrapped around his shaft and kneaded his rigid length like he'd been born and bred to service him. Even through his trousers, every exquisite stroke triggered pulses of paralyzing pleasure.

A pleasure he'd been waiting endless years to feel.

"I want you naked on the floor," Dex rasped, beyond reason or restraint. "Both of you. On your knees. Now. *Right now*."

"Hold on," Nero panted in his ear, still working him, so guttural with passion Dex barely recognized him. "It kills me to say this. But—gods, Dex—not here. Not when we're going to have a swarm of jealous candidates and an army of overzealous prefects crawling all over us. Because after a lifetime of wanting this with both of you, I have zero intention of being rushed."

The electric danger of discovery should have shocked him to his senses. But Dex wasn't sure he wanted to stop—wasn't sure he *could* stop even if his entire praetorian guard marched in here singing a war chant. In fact, he could climax in about two ticks from what Nero was doing to him now.

Right in front of Kaia's wide-eyed, utterly fascinated face. Hearing his breath roughen and quicken until he moaned with every exhale. Seeing his brow furrow and his mouth open and his head fall back in ecstasy. Watching every telltale flicker of response chase across his face. Watching him get off so unmistakably and uncontrollably on the feel of another man's hand wrapped around his cock.

"He wants it, Ben," she said throatily, her eyes never leaving his. "He's really close. He wants you to jerk him off until he spills in his pants—"

With a groan, Dex dragged her close and fused their mouths together, claiming her wet heat with a fiercely dominant kiss. His hands cupped the fullness of her breasts, jutting nipples searing his palms through her cybersuit. Reveling in the desperate way she moaned and arched and pressed into his touch.

Ben quickened his knowing stroke up and down Dex's shaft… up and down… *dear gods, just like that…* so single-mindedly focused on finding the perfect rhythm and pressure, so earnest and eager to please him he was flipping every switch on Dex's Mogadon circuit board. Then one hand eased lower to cup and fondle the tingling tightness of his balls.

Oh Ben. You're so perfect for me. You're both so flipping perfect.

"Tell me if you like what I'm doing, space cadet," Nero whispered, breath ragged in his ear, all silken tongue and feral teeth scraping his skin to make him shudder. "I intend to make you lose your cool and collected Mogadon mind. And know that it's me doing it. Do you like this?"

Dex's balls clamped tight against his body, and a jet of tingling pleasure shot down his cock.

"Gods on the mountain," he gasped. "I can't—can't hold back— oh gods—"

The sudden echo of brusque voices and the businesslike tramp of booted feet dragged Dex violently back to vigilance.

Nero released him and sprang to his feet, breathless and gorgeous and uncharacteristically disheveled. While Kaia slid free and scrambled up, delightfully flushed and flustered and looking like a woman who'd just been kissed senseless.

Both achievements for which Dex took personal credit.

Even while he leaped for his torn jacket and struggled into it. Fiercely willing the massive erection behind his zipper into surly subsidence.

Grimly aware he was kicking out enough mating scent to give anyone with a nose a damn good notion just what they'd been doing in here.

Thank Ceres for whoever's coming and whatever confounded problem they're bringing. Or I wouldn't have stopped until both of them begged me to let them come.

And I can't.

I can't.

Because it would never be just once.

He was standing rigid at the viewport, back turned to the world, when those booted feet tramped into his ready room and snapped to a halt.

Then he heard that wretch's voice. That voice he'd loved as a boy. That voice he hated as a man. That voice whose buried amusement made him grit his teeth in impotent rage.

"Sorry to come barging in, folks. Sure hope I ain't interrupting?"

#

Standing on the threshold of Dex's ready room—which used to be Zorin's ready room back when he ran the show—Zorin figured he could've played stupid and faked ignorance of whatever steamy scene he'd just sashayed into. But that would imply he was either a fool or a coward.

And no Syndax leader stayed leader for long once that got around to the horde.

He raised a casual hand to signal the Syndax guarding his ass on this floating fortress to spread out and secure his flank. Men he knew. Men he trusted. Men who'd sprung him from the Mogadon slammer and followed him into exile.

But he was still Mogadon enough himself not to want them anywhere near Kaia.

He found her without even trying. Lurking in the shadows—clearly her standard tactic. She kept a pretty low profile with all those randy beaus. But Zorin would've found her blindfolded.

This whole shindig had started as a cold-blooded strategy to secure himself a Kryll alliance and deprive young Draven of his formidable Kryll ally.

Not to mention siring the galaxy's next grand poohbah. Just in case there was any merit to that Valyrian prophecy his spies had sniffed out.

Now, he was all too aware, it was also about the girl.

Now that he'd seen her in action, somersaulting two tiers down into a mosh pit of bloodthirsty suitors, ready to slice somebody's head off with that cyber saber just to protect someone she cared about? She'd just confirmed every instinct he had.

That girl would make one hell of a consort. The Syndax horde would respect her. He could trust her to have his back. And she'd make one hell of a mother to his children.

Her lavender eyes slid over him in that wide-eyed, openmouthed appraisal that turned his crank every time she did it. Like the sight of his freakishly big body in his battle-scarred starmetal and space boots made her mouth water. Neptune's knickers, an old space pirate like him could get used to being looked at like that.

Especially by a girl who looked the way she did.

Did she even know she was doing it?

Carefully she checked out his tattooed, dreadlocked, leather-clad pirates, and he watched that clever mind catalog all she saw. He liked the lively flash of curiosity behind all that exotic beauty. Liked the forthright questions she was obviously burning to ask, silent but eloquent in her quizzical frown.

Leather creaked and chains clinked as his boys took her in, same way she was scoping them out. This was their first chance to get a good gander at her—the future queen of the Syndax horde. He figured they'd need a few breaths just to pick their jaws up off the floor.

Ben Nero slid casually between them, putting Kaia at his back and breaking their collective stare.

Zorin's question was still hanging in the air.

"You want an honest answer?" Nero said. "Then yeah, big guy, your timing could've been a little bit better."

One corner of Zorin's mouth lifted in a grin. He couldn't help it.

He liked the kid. "Thanks for giving me the straight-up, gorgeous. That's the way I like it. Saves time for all of us, don't it?"

The telepath was a good six cubits tall, graceful as a woman in the fur-lined cloak and medieval splendor of his feudal planet. He'd tower over most men—but Zorin wasn't most men. He topped the telepath by a lot.

As he prowled past, Zorin gave in to impulse and tousled the guy's sleek black hair. The way he did his junior prefects when they'd done something smart to earn his praise.

"Careful," Nero murmured—a low growl he wasn't expecting. "I don't mind being touched. But I like to touch back."

Not much caught him off guard these days. Zorin wouldn't live long if it did. But the flash of heat in those smoking purple eyes hit him low in the groin like a secret caress. A complication he definitely wasn't looking for. This whole situation was plenty volatile enough without Zorin packing a boner for Dex's wannabe boyfriend.

Zorin passed it off with a chuckle that gave away nothing and kept on moving.

Hells, at his age? He was flattered. Even if he'd stopped messing around with boys years ago. Told himself he'd outgrown it, with a hard assist from Max Draven's interdict—right around the time he started mentoring his best friend's son. He'd put up walls ten parsecs high where Dex Draven was concerned.

For both their sakes.

Now he angled for the man himself. All grown up and plenty old enough to be deadly. His slim erect silhouette stood rigid at the viewport, hands clasped behind his back, the light of a distant sun gleaming in his burnished hair.

Dex addressed him without turning, every word glacial, chiseled and chipped from ice. "I presume there's an exceptional reason you're polluting my presence without an express invitation? Some reason beyond ogling my Tombola ward?"

Silently Zorin filled in the words he didn't say. *And some reason beyond hitting on the guy you got the hots for yourself, huh, Dex?*

Ah, to be young. The three of them were all so young—Dex and Kaia and Nero—all damaged and adrift and so gods-damned gorgeous they'd break even his battered old heart. All trying so hard to figure out some way to love each other.

But these three were a neutron bomb without a safety. This thing would blow up in all their faces.

And he planned to be there when it blew. She'd need someone to help her pick up the pieces.

"Sure," Zorin said amiably, answering the question. "You took me off the combat roster. I'm here to get that fixed."

He kept his pace easy, appreciating the nerve it took for Dex—who'd taken a pretty good hit from that shiv, but was doing a solid job hiding it—to keep his back to the guy he viewed as his ultimate nemesis.

Not to mention the four Syndax he'd brought with him. All armed to the teeth.

When he was six cubits away, Dex turned his head slightly and spoke over his averted shoulder.

"You signed up to fight three men at once. Three of the fiercest fighters in this Tombola. And as strongly tempted as I am to permit it and rid the galaxy permanently of your parasitical presence, the Apocrypha rules expressly forbid it."

"You're the head honcho of this hootenanny. That means you make the rules." Zorin leaned casually against the viewport, but kept a respectful distance between them. No need to go jerking the guy's chain.

Just breathing the same air was checking that box.

Dex stared straight through the viewport. Over the bracing musk of mating scent, the chemical bite of antiseptic tinged the air. And the man's chiseled profile was drawn tight with hidden pain. "I'll allow you to fight one man. One man of my choosing. Not three."

"Come on, kid," Zorin said patiently. "You know I'll go through anyone you got like a neutron torpedo. You've seen me in single combat. Why not make it a fair fight?"

"Oh, now you're going to fight fair, are you?" Dex's tone was biting. "That's more honor than you ever granted my father. Or me, for that matter."

Zorin held on to his temper. "We already talked about your dad. And the reason I lit out of here rather than fighting you had nothing to do with your honor. It had to do with mine."

"Yours?" Dex pivoted to confront him, cobalt eyes blazing with contempt. "How do you figure?"

"I figure your dad was a public menace. When his mind went, I put him down like a rabid wolf. And I don't regret it. But you…" Zorin hesitated. "Aw, come on. You really need me to spell it out?"

After the way we left things eight years ago? The night I finally kissed the heck out of you and got shot all to shit for my pains?

Every Draven syllable emerged with an icy edge. "Indulge me."

Zorin heaved a sigh. "You were my student, okay? It wouldn't have been a fair fight. It woulda been slaughter. And that's the gods' honest. I'd already messed you up enough. I didn't wanna kill you, kid."

He still didn't.

War or no war.

But he wasn't sure his former student was gonna give him any goddamn choice.

"I'm properly addressed as *commander*," Dex said tightly. "And letting me live then was a mistake. As is lying to me now. Aren't you going to tell me you loved me like the son you never had?"

The buried pain in his voice lashed Zorin like a whip. In truth, his feelings for young Draven, barely old enough to be legal at the time, had been anything but paternal. And the fact that Max would've ripped his balls off for seducing his son—*before* he crucified him—had way less to do with Zorin's monumental restraint than his own unyielding code of honor.

He didn't put the moves on his students.

Period.

But he didn't see any point going into all that now.

"Put me back on the combat roster," he said levelly. "Me against any three you want. If I lose, I'm out. You're rid of me, I'm off your ship, and the *Relentless* is off your ass." He rocked back on his heels and hooked his hands in his utility belt. "If I win? I go straight to the head of the line."

Dex studied him through narrowed eyes. The younger guy wasn't wearing a shirt under his open jacket, and the white flash of silicon tape stood out against an expanse of sun-bronzed skin and rock-hard muscle that an old warhorse like Zorin had no business even noticing on a kid in his twenties.

But if Draven didn't want to leave a trail of hard-ons and heartbreak from here to the Gamma Sector, he could damn well button up and spray something on him to suppress all those pheromones.

Zorin cleared his throat and got his eyes up where they belonged. "That's a fair shake and you know it, *Commander*. We got a deal?"

Unexpectedly Kaia emerged from the shadows, moving like liquid gold in all that sleek bronze silk. She prowled to a neutral point between them, a proper five cubits off.

Plenty close enough to distract the dickens out of him with that head-spinning hit of ozone and jasmine.

"Hold on a sec." She planted a hand on her hip. And he wondered if the concern that thickened her husky voice could possibly be for him. "I don't think this is a good idea. Most of the suitors who signed up for combat are Mogadon. Your two armies are at war. And the rules demand a halt at first blood—but accidents do happen. Look what just happened to you, Dex, for flip's sake!"

"I'm fine," Dex said brusquely, shifting on his feet. Clearly fighting every instinct in his DNA to get his hands on her body and stake his claim and keep Zorin the hell away from her. "And I don't anticipate any further breaches of discipline quite so soon after I dealt with the last one."

"It isn't safe," she pressed, her shimmering eyes holding Zorin's. "Nothing about this entire Tombola is safe. It hasn't been… a typical auction."

"That's cuz you're not a typical girl, sweetheart." Zorin gave her a one-sided grin. "This is one hell of a hootenanny, ain't it? You worried for those Mogadon or for me?"

"You, of course." Hearing Nero's chuckle as he drifted up behind her, she colored up pink in a way that charmed the socks off him. "I mean, all of you. Obviously. A man just died out there ten ticks ago."

He wanted like hell to touch her. Because her honest concern for his safety was just about more than his old ticker could take. But he knew Dex would never stand for it.

And now Ben Nero was right behind her, smoky eyes locked on Zorin, one hand toying with the soft copper curls that spilled down her neck.

Just because he was her lifemate and he wanted Zorin to know he could.

That's right, big guy, Nero's distinctive tenor whispered in his head. *She was in my bed last night and she'll be there again tonight. Anyone who gets her also gets me. Think you could handle both of us?*

He had to chuckle at the guy's bravura. *Let's tackle one battle at a time, okay, gorgeous?*

"Don't laugh. I mean it, Zorin," Kaia pressed, eyes anxious as she searched his face. "You don't have to do this. I'll advance your name anyway. You're the only Syndax candidate."

"As if that's a point in his favor," Dex sneered.

That's not why you'd do it, sweetheart. You'd do it cuz you're into me. And if I'm lucky enough to outlast this endurathon for your bed, I'm gonna do it on the strength of my own merits.

But he only said gently, "If I run into something I can't handle, samurai, you'll just have to protect me. Unlike young Draven here, I don't have to prove my manhood to the masses. And I'm not too proud to accept a woman's help."

Her lips parted and pleased color flooded her tawny skin.

Damn, but he wanted to kiss her.

Instead he got back to business and shifted his focus to Dex.

"So do we have a deal, kid?"

Dex unlocked his jaw and bit out, "Very well, Syndax. We have a *deal*."

But if Zorin was hoping for a handshake, he wasn't getting one. Pointedly dismissing him, Dex pivoted away.

"I'd say I sincerely hope they kill you, pirate. But I'd vastly prefer to reserve that pleasure for myself."

CHAPTER FOURTEEN
The Syndax

"Gods and angels of the nine realms." Back in the viewing box for the day's final combat, Kaia gripped her chair until her fingers throbbed. "Those are Kryllian bloodletters. *Shit*."

In the fighting pit below, three robed shadows spread out to claim the battlespace. Silent and sinuous as serpents. From the quadrant where he stood alone before a thousand hostile eyes and three trained killers, Zorin waited easily with booted feet spread, big hands loose and empty at his sides.

And just watched them come.

From his seat at her side, Nero eyed her white-knuckled grip and the flush of fury climbing in her face.

Not that he needs visual cues to know I'm seething.

"No, I don't," he agreed, a bare murmur under the ominous hush that had fallen like a hammer over the sweating masses. "But what exactly are Kryllian bloodletters? And why do they make you so furious?"

"They're assassins." She pushed the words past the dry knot in her throat. "Hired killers. Trained from boyhood to fight as a single seamless unit. Kryllian merchants use them in the desert colonies to guard their spice convoys. Those three are brothers. They bid for me together."

She pulled in a shaking breath and tried without success to loosen her clenched fists. "And they're *not* the ones I'm furious with."

Nero's sharp gaze shot to the slender uniformed figure with burnished hair and flashing epaulets who stood erect on the arbiter's platform over the fighting pit.

The man who'd matched Zorin with these three killers for the day's most hotly anticipated bout.

"Ah," he said succinctly. "So Dex is the target of your formidable wrath. I confess I'm still not clear why. You know he wants Zorin out of the bidding. And he wants the *Relentless* and her nukes out of firing range—truce or no truce. From that perspective, Silent, Sly and Slithering down there look like an inspired choice."

"I'm furious because he knows I rejected their bid!" she fired back. "Three Kryllian brothers? Are you kidding me? I'd never get rid of the chains. That's why I ruled them out. And I made my feelings on the subject crystal flipping clear."

"And now Dex is giving them another chance. But they won't advance. Not when they have to get through Zorin to do it."

"You don't know what they are," she whispered, chafing her arms against the deep-space chill as the killers closed on the space pirate's solitary, strangely heroic figure. "They don't know how to wound. They don't know how to maim. They only know how to kill."

"Chin up." Nero's deft touch brushed her unhappy jaw. "You want him for a consort, don't you? Maybe you should try trusting him."

If the Kryll were a flight of arrows, an invisible archer had just released their bow. With a silent rush, the kill squad sliced toward Zorin in a javelin of deadly whirling grace. Three dervishes perfectly matched in menace, pale robes flying around spinning shapes. When they were nearly within reach, the leader flung something to the ground.

A chemical bomblet exploded with a sharp *crack* that made Kaia flinch. A cloud of ocher smoke swirled up.

Concealing the Kryll and their prey.

Suspended in that taut, uncanny silence, Kaia leaned forward, seething with tension. Acrid smoke wafted over the lower tier. Rustles and coughs swept the uneasy audience.

"What is that?" Nero rasped, one sleeve over his nose.

"It's a mild irritant. Too mild to disqualify," she said bitterly, eyeing Dex's contained vigilance—too skilled a fighter himself to jump blind into that trap. "It burns the eyes and throat. Makes the target easy prey. Bloodletters cultivate immunity so they're unaffected—"

The meaty thud of flesh on flesh punctured the spellbound silence. Echoed by a single agonized groan.

Along with everyone else, Kaia strained to see.

"Blast! Can you see anything?"

Before Nero could respond, a shadow moved in the smoke. A tick later Zorin emerged, rangy and swift as a wolf in his battle-scarred armor. A clear energon visor encased his head—a portable device that provided a time-limited supply of oxygen during short spacewalks. She used them herself running deep-space maintenance on the *Angel*.

The breath rushed out of her lungs in a shudder of relief. He looked unhurt.

For now.

Slowly the smoke thinned and eddied away. Revealing the bloodletters still on their feet, one hunched and moving stiffly.

An approving murmur rippled through the ranks. By surviving that deadly rush, Zorin had impressed the madding crowd. The chink of creds changing hands rattled against the rafters. Men placing bets on how much longer he'd last.

Dex's curt edict crackled through the charged atmosphere like lightning. "Poisoned weapons are strictly prohibited by the combat rules in the Tombola contract. Another stunt like that one, Kryll, and I'll rule for the Syndax by default. Consider yourselves cautioned."

Feeling the way he did about Zorin, Kaia knew what it cost Dex to say so. A flicker of appreciation for his integrity curled through her. Honestly, the man was an enigma. How anyone of integrity could sanction a biowar against the entire Syndax horde…

With the smoke dispersed, Zorin tapped his titanium collar, and the force field dissolved. Already one of the bloodletters was whirling in, booted feet scything through the air in an attack that would break bone when it landed.

Heart sledgehammering with adrenaline, Kaia leaped to her feet. Knowing such a blatant betrayal of concern was reckless, when she'd barely shown a flicker of interest for anyone else's fate.

But simply not caring.

She wanted to be down there with Zorin. Evening the odds. Watching his back. Fighting at his side.

In fact, the realization of just how much she wanted that popped in her brain like a lightbulb of revelation.

Patiently the pirate waited and watched. A breath before impact, Zorin exploded into action.

A dodge—a heave—a brief violent tussle that lodged Kaia's heart in her throat like a stone. Then the Kryll went sailing through the air. He collided with his brother with a sharp cry. The two crashed against the rim of the fighting pit in a tangle of limbs and fabric.

Instantly the brothers were scrambling up. But one was shaking his head. Swiftly a patch of crimson darkened the battle-scarf tied around his head.

"Head wound," Nero muttered. "He felt that. Hells—*I* felt that."

"You." Dex jumped lightly to the fighting pit—making Kaia fear for his newly sewn stitches—and pointed to the bleeding man. "Out."

The Kryll looked mutinous, but Dex was unyielding. "Out of the fighting pit. And find a medic for that head."

Scowling and unsteady, the Kryll wove toward the ready room.

Nero eased Kaia back to her chair. Barely knowing what she did, she laced her fingers tightly through his.

The remaining brothers converged, closing in for the kill. No flashy displays now that their foe had proven immune to their psychological impact.

Just focused and deadly purpose.

Zorin parried a flurry of blows and crescent kicks far too fast to follow, effortless as a wolf batting away a pair of playful pups. He was too big, too armored, too strong, too fast. Too everything. Even for a pair of trained killers who'd fought as a unit for years. All too clearly, their strategy now was to wear him down—older than they were by decades, encumbered in boots and armor.

But they'd reckoned without the superb physical conditioning of an ex-First Indomitable.

Pivoting away from their gambits to crowd him, pin him, negate his formidable reach, Zorin fended them off. Until the briefest window opened in the Kryll defense.

Then one capable Syndax fist shot out like a battering ram.

The nearest brother flew back ten cubits. He landed hard on his caboose and just stayed down, blood spurting from his shattered nose.

"You. Out. Medic." Dex's clipped command left zero space for emotion.

But Kaia didn't doubt he was feeling it.

She was feeling it herself, the buoyant swell of elation that left her giddy. Zorin was going to win—against no fewer than three Kryllian bloodletters! He was going to catapult to the head of the queue. Once he did, she'd make damn sure he stayed there. And the Patriarch, fanatically committed to the sacred virtue of neutrality, would favor a Syndax suitor.

Wouldn't he?

The last Kryll circled like a sand hyena, wary now he'd seen his brothers' fate. Knowing what he faced.

A flipping force of nature.

But still confident he'd prevail. Even a half-Kryll hybrid like Kaia had enough telepathy to know. Sly and Silent might be space dust.

But Slithering had an actual plan.

Zorin stood solid as a mountain, mighty chest barely moving as he pulled in air. Watching him wait, Kaia's gaze ricocheted between him and Dex. Suddenly she understood where the current First Indomitable had learned that perfectly contained patience.

And her certain knowledge of the unbridgeable abyss that yawned between master and student made her heart bleed. That shattered trust between them had been Max Draven's final casualty.

Faced with the last Kryll standing, a lesser man would've crowed or taunted. Zorin only lifted one big palm and curled his fingers in a casual come-hither.

Just enough of a prod to spur the Kryll to spring his trap.

Sneering beneath his battle-scarf, the Kryll slid forward, one sleeve sweeping down in a parabola of deadly motion. The dark cloud of a microfiber steel net whirled through the air to settle soundlessly over Zorin's massive frame.

A man could escape a steel net in one of two ways. He could pick his way free of the unbreakable mesh with time. Or he could cut his way free with a blowtorch.

Zorin, at the moment, had neither.

Meanwhile, the Kryll was lining up the kill shot. Freeing from his robes a flipping *nerve gun*.

Kaia hadn't even seen one in years. Nerve guns were outlawed and illegal across the galaxy—due to the irreversible damage they inflicted on their victims.

Permanent paralysis.

She surged to her feet, dragging a startled Nero with her. Dex was charging into the fray, shouting rules and prohibitions no one in the room was heeding. Because this combat was no longer a Tombola bout.

It was a hit job.

The only reason that a Kryll would be using a disqualifying nerve gun was because someone had paid him to do it.

All around her, men were on their feet roaring. Zorin's tattooed Syndax drawing blasters and converging on the pit.

All moving *way* too slow.

Kaia screamed with rage and reached for her saber. Nero flung his arms around her to hold her, shouting words in her ear that made no sense.

The Kryll leveled his weapon from six cubits away.

Way too close to miss.

THE ASTRAL HEAT ADVENTURE CONTINUES WITH RENEGADE ANGEL: AN ASTRAL HEAT ROMANCE # 2

Fully written, edited, and releasing on December 1, 2021

Preorder your copy here.
https://books2read.com/RenegadeAngel

For a sneak peek at the first chapter available immediately—and to find out what happens to Zorin!—sign up for my newsletter here.
https://dl.bookfunnel.com/4bvs7j26aq

Want to share your thoughts on *Interstellar Angel*? You don't have to write a lot. Even a few words helps! Reviews persuade readers like you to give writers like me a chance. To post a review with your favorite retailer, here are the links:

https://books2read.com/InterstellarAngel

Prefer to review on Goodreads? You can do that in a flash here:
https://bit.ly/3fRrxjZ

OTHER STEAMY ROMANCE READS BY LAURA NAVARRE:

Fantasy Historical Romance: The *Magick* Trilogy
Magick by Moonrise
https://books2read.com/MagickByMoonrise/
Midsummer Magick
https://books2read.com/MidsummerMagick
Mistress by Magick
https://books2read.com/MistressByMagick/

Steamy Historical Romance Standalones
By Royal Command
https: //books2read.com/ByRoyalCommand

ACKNOWLEDGMENTS

They say writing and publishing a book takes a village. When you're a debut reverse harem sci-fi romance author with three back-to-back releases, it takes a starbase. I could never have written the *Astral Heat Romance* series without the encouragement and insight of my cosmic mate and hubby Steven—my first writing mentor, alpha reader, business partner and CEO at Ascendant Press. And I can't rave enough about my editor, Deb Nemeth, who first acquired me for a traditional press way back when I was starting out, and works with me again now. She makes my prose sparkle and my stories sing. Also high on my eternal-gratitude list are my writing guru Angela James, my awesome cover artist Kim Killion, my diligent copy editor Elizabeth Flynn, my miracle-working formatter and uploader and hand-holder Judi Fennell, my friend and indie inspiration Dana Delamar, my marketer Heather Roberts at Elle Woods PR, and every single one of my wonderful ARC reviewers and readers! I appreciate you all to the moon and back.

ABOUT THE AUTHOR

A long time ago in a galaxy far away, Laura Navarre was an award-winning dark historical romance author for Harlequin, while her diabolical twin Nikki Navarre wrote sexy spy romance. In a daring bid to escape a global pandemic, armed only with an MFA in Writing Popular Fiction, Laura voyaged through a wormhole to an alternate universe where she crafts turbocharged, epic, hyper-erotic reverse harem sci-fi romance starring three super-sexy heroes, one seriously kickass heroine and plenty of sleek, sizzling outer space action.

Laura's intergalactic adventures are trackable by humans and aliens alike on social media here:

Facebook: www.facebook.com/LauraNavarreInterstellarRomance
Twitter: www.twitter.com/LauraNavarre
Goodreads: www.goodreads.com/LauraNavarre
TikTok: https://www.tiktok.com/@LauraNavarreAuthor
BookBub: https://www.bookbub.com/authors/Laura-Navarre
Website: www.LauraNavarreSciFi.com